# THE
# WINTER
# GUEST

## W. C. RYAN

ZAFFRE

First published in the UK in 2022 by
ZAFFRE
An imprint of Bonnier Books UK
4th Floor, Victoria House, Bloomsbury Square, London, WC1B 4DA
Owned by Bonnier Books
Sveavägen 56, Stockholm, Sweden

A CIP catalogue record for this book is
available from the British Library.

Hardback ISBN: 978–1–83877–150–8
Trade paperback ISBN: 978–1–83877–151–5

*Also available as an ebook and an audiobook*

1 3 5 7 9 10 8 6 4 2

Typeset by IDSUK (Data Connection) Ltd
Printed and bound in Great Britain by Clays Ltd, Elcograf S.p.A.

Zaffre is an imprint of Bonnier Books UK
www.bonnierbooks.co.uk

*For Alicia*

# CHAPTER 1

Kilcolgan House stands at the end of the long drive, caught by a moment of moonlight. Its granite walls, slick with the earlier rain, shine silver; its roof glows; its many large windows are like mirrors to the sky. The bad weather has passed for the moment and only the breath of a breeze flutters the long grass in the home meadow. From the strand, through the trees, the roll of the waves can be heard. Here, at the house, the only sound is the steady drip of leaking gutters.

It is a large house, built to reflect the significance of the family who built it. It stands on a rise that overlooks the sea and the surrounding country. When the original Prendevilles – hard-knuckled invaders in the service of a Tudor monarch – took the land, the first house they built was a bastion to defend against the people from whom the land was taken. It had thick walls and high, small windows, and a courtyard into which livestock could be brought in times of trouble. The bastion still stands within the dwelling that took its place, built onto and around and through. The older structure within accounts for the strange shapes of certain rooms and some, at least, of the draughts and creaks and other phenomena that the Prendevilles and their few remaining retainers barely notice. What might seem odd to a stranger is, to them, quite usual. They are accustomed to the ways of the house; they know its whims. Prendevilles have become part of the fabric of the house; the dead living on in the stories held within its walls.

The house, despite its grandeur, has seen better days. The moon is kind to it, but its slates are no longer regular; moss fills each crack and gap in the stonework and, in the daylight, there is an air of abandonment about the place. The future of the house is no longer certain. If the Prendevilles are aware of this, they show no sign of it, continuing on in long-accustomed inertia, while the house slowly disintegrates around them.

Within the house, most are asleep. All except for Bridget, a housemaid, who sits in the entrance hall, wrapped in the butler's greatcoat, alongside the glowing embers that are all that is left of a peat fire that burns there throughout the day. She stares into it, mesmerised, and then, before long, she too is asleep.

Outside, a sea mist creeps up over the long beach, then, slowly, makes its way across the rocks, the road, the demesne wall. It hides the men who walk within it – men carrying rifles in their hands and blankets slung across their chests. They wear long coats, collars pulled up against the cold, and flat caps that would obscure their eyes, were there light enough to see them. For two years now the men, and others like them, have been fighting for the independence of their country. It has been a long and bloody war and the men on the coast road are tired of it, but still they walk towards Kilcolgan. The fog does not slow them. They know where they are going. They climb the wall where it has tumbled inwards and then they are among the trees, as is the mist. They slip through the bushes and low-hanging branches until they find the drive that leads to

2

the big house, where the commander orders two of the men to the small cottage standing beside the gate. Its inhabitants know better than to resist; they allow themselves to be bound and gagged, then are lowered carefully to the floor, where they lie, listening as the men make their preparations in the dark. They hear the sound of a tree trunk being dragged across the avenue and the commander's quiet orders as he positions the men of the flying column.

Soon all is quiet and the men wait in the bushes with the mist gathering around them. Their fingers are stiff around the guns they hold, but they are used to the cold. They breathe on their hands to put some heat into them and think, perhaps, of warm beds they have known in the past. They are patient.

Then, in a pause between the breaking waves, they hear the drone of a motor car approaching from the west, the direction they have been told to expect it from. The fog thins for a moment and they can see the white glow of approaching headlights. They lean forwards, lifting their weapons in preparation, smelling the oil and metal of the rifles as they bring them close to their cheeks. The car is getting closer now, and its engine seems to vibrate through their entire bodies, shattering the stillness that came before. The gates have been left open for it and there is only the slightest reduction in speed before the twin beams that are the car's headlights, blurred by the fog, swing in. The engine is now louder still, perhaps amplified or distorted by the fog, and it feels as though it is coming straight at them. Someone fires a shot, just at the moment that the driver sees the log that has been dragged across the driveway, and the car swerves into the wall of the gate lodge. There is a screeching and tearing of metal, and then nothing except for the low coughing rumble from the engine, which still turns over.

The men wait in the dark, listening for an order, the only sound a scrape of metal as the car sags. One of the headlights has survived, lighting the gate lodge and revealing the car's long, black shape. After a moment, a man stands up in the open car, a pistol in his hand. The firing starts again, each shot like a hammer on the nail of a coffin.

Afterwards, the commander walks over to the motor car, his pistol at the ready. The men follow, rifles shivering in their hands; they are not certain if it is from cold or the excitement of it all. A bullet has taken away much of the face of the man behind the wheel, but they recognise him from the bottle green of his uniform and the crowns on his epaulette. Beside him lies a young man wearing a black bow tie, with a pistol in his hand. They do not know him, but they decide he is no innocent. The woman in the back seat is a different matter; she has not been hit by any of their bullets and is alive, but unconscious. They find a blanket for her in the car's boot and make her comfortable, but they do not stay to tend to her. The police from the town will be here soon, and the work they came to do is done.

The men leave, walking quickly away through the trees. They will walk until the morning and then rest up in a house that is expecting them. The Prendeville woman is a bad bit of business, but they hope she will survive. How could they have known she would be in the car? She, of all people, should have known better.

They leave behind the occupants of the car, their shapes indistinct in the mist that still moves slowly across the tableau, bringing with it the damp smell of the sea to blend with the stench of cordite and blood.

Harry Cartwright, formerly of the British Army, lies awkwardly over the back of the passenger seat, his head and hair hanging down behind it. His fingers still grasp for the revolver he took from Inspector Teevan's holster to defend himself, and which was taken from his dead hand by one of the ambushers. There is not much blood, at least not that can be seen at first. Cartwright's face is largely unmarked except for a tiny hole above the hairline where a small-calibre bullet caught him just after he stood up in his seat and found himself looking down to where another bullet had hit him in the chest.

The body of District Inspector James Teevan is slumped behind the steering wheel, a victim of that single first shot. The men of the flying column were pleased to have killed him, holding him responsible for recent reprisals carried out by a company of the Auxiliary Division of the RIC based in the town. The Auxies, as they are known, are mostly British ex-officers, veterans at a loose end after the brutality of the Western Front, and not really under any man's command, except perhaps for Major Abercrombie. It was Abercrombie who led the Auxies who burned out nine cottages on the other side of the hills three days before. Abercrombie took the three local men from the burning buildings, who showed up dead the morning after. The burning of the dwellings and the killing of the men were a message to the rebels, and this was their reply. It is a long-running correspondence between the two sides. The correspondence will continue tomorrow and in the weeks that follow, back and forth. It does not matter much to either side that the victims of their reprisals are often undeserving.

The final occupant lies in the back seat, her arm across her forehead as though to shield herself from the little light there is, the blanket wrapped round her. Maud Prendeville's face – as much of it as can be seen – is still. The men, knowing her and her family, have made her comfortable. The Honourable Maud Prendeville, after all, is a hero of the struggle for independence who fought beside Pearse and Connolly in the Easter Rising. She is the last person the men of the flying column would have wanted to hurt.

Inside the gate lodge, Patrick Walsh, gatekeeper and gardener, lies alongside his wife upon the flagstone floor of their small kitchen, hands and feet bound. He has heard the men discuss Maud Prendeville. Now he works with his wife to release the cords that tie his hands, anxious to help the daughter of his employer, whom he has known since she was a child. They curse each other as they fumble with the knots, but the task is difficult and the progress is slow and the minutes are ticking by.

Through the trees, although it cannot be seen from the gate, lamplight colours the windows of Kilcolgan House yellow, one after another. Other members of the Prendeville family are gathering in the cold entrance hall in dressing gowns, alerted by the gunfire, their faces anxious in the candlelight. Maud's sister, Charlotte, asks if someone has already dropped their house guest, Harry Cartwright, back from the card evening, and looks grave when the answer comes that he has not. Bridget, the servant girl, is sent to fetch Billy from his room but she does not find him there, although he will soon arrive from the direction of the stables. In a few minutes his father, Lord Kilcolgan, Charlotte, Billy and Sean Driscoll, the housekeeper's son, will make their way down to the gate. For the moment, however, they hesitate, perhaps because while they remain uncertain about what has happened, there is still hope.

If, at their moment of indecision, someone were standing beside the wreck of Teevan's car, they would see a figure approaching through the trees. The mist and the dark would make it hard for them to tell if the figure is male or female, young or old, or anything much about them, except that they seem to know their way. They take their time, yes, but they move with purpose and seem to know how remote the place is and that the gunfire can only have been heard by the Prendevilles up at the house, if it has been heard at all. Pat Walsh and his wife can be discounted, they decide. They are certain they will have been tied up by the ambushers – it is the usual way these things are handled.

The Prendevilles are not an immediate risk. The house is a walk along the drive and the family will not rush into the dark to confront men with guns. Who would? They will call the RIC station in the town, of course, but the call will have to go through the exchange, which takes time. While the station possesses a number of Crossley Tenders that could make the journey in a quarter of an hour if they drove at full speed, the constables will have to be woken and organised. When they do come, they will come carefully, conscious of the risk of a second ambush. In summary, the chances of interruption are slight.

Inside the cottage, Pat Walsh grunts as his hand at last comes free. Then he hears the sound of the approaching footsteps, barely scraping the gravel, and he knows it is not the police or the family from the house. Walsh rubs at his wrists and whispers to his wife, who whispers back. Then they are silent.

As the figure comes closer to the car, the remaining headlight gives out, leaving behind a profound darkness before the soft yellow beam of a trench torch illuminates the car, then the victims and finally the windows of the gate lodge. Nothing stirs in the silence.

Cartwright is checked for signs of life, although the examination is perfunctory. It is a shame about Cartwright; he had no part in this business. No time at all is spent on Teevan and there is no regret at his passing. And then the figure leans over Maud Prendeville – surprised to find her here but accepting her presence. When Maud's

7

wrist is lifted to check her pulse, the young woman's eyes flicker for a moment but she does not wake.

Eventually, after some time spent contemplating the prostrate Miss Prendeville, the figure seems to come to a decision and turns their attention back to Teevan. The inspector is searched efficiently and thoroughly but not, apparently, with any success. Cartwright is then also searched, and it is noticeable that there is no squeamishness; this is a person used to blood and death. It is also clear they intend their search to be undetected. The figure wears thin kidskin gloves, so that no awkward trace is left on a surface. Each button that is undone is done up again. When the inspector's coat is opened to check his inner pockets, it is replaced just so.

Once Cartwright and Teevan have been checked, and then checked again, the figure turns their attention to the car, opening the glove compartment and the side pockets and looking under the seats. A document case is found in the boot and it is gone through quickly. Nothing. And then the figure turns their attention to Maud Prendeville.

Maud is wearing a long black velvet travelling coat, and clutched in her left hand is a small evening bag. The coat has pockets, but the bag seems more likely. It requires some careful effort to detach the bag from Maud's grip, but then it is open and there is the item which the figure has been searching for. They had not expected to find it in her possession, but perhaps they should have. The handbag is returned to the young woman, empty now. Then the figure hesitates, looking over their shoulder, peering into the misty darkness, crouching down and turning off their torch as they do so.

It is more of a feeling than anything. They have heard nothing definite. There is hardly any breeze, certainly not enough to shift the leaves or move a branch – the sea mist barely moves at all.

And yet there is a sense of someone out there – or perhaps something – and an unexpected scent that is both sweet and corrupt. For a moment, the figure thinks it sees the pale shape of a woman moving through the mist, but when they look again there is nothing. They shiver involuntarily, all the same. There have heard the stories about the big house and the coast road and the Prendevilles. This evening is not the first tragedy to come to pass in this place, and the Prendevilles have been an unlucky family through the centuries. Some say cursed. But that is all nonsense and time is passing. The torch is turned on one last time to make certain all is left as it should be. The figure takes the opportunity to light a cigarette and turns back to the business in hand.

When they do so, the yellow beam of light finds Maud Prendeville's wide gaze staring upwards at them, her mouth a round O of surprise. Is there recognition? Perhaps the figure thinks so. Because they take a small pistol from their pocket, lean forwards so that it is only a matter of inches from Maud Prendeville's appalled gaze, and fire. Once is sufficient. The dilemma is no longer a dilemma.

The figure turns, without any detectable emotion, and walks back the way they came. They do not hear the sobbing from Patrick Walsh's kitchen, and it is just as well.

If the dead at the gate lodge could speak, they might tell of their hopes for a future that will not come to pass. They might talk of their loves, for they did love and were loved in turn. Those that love them will mourn them, and those that did not, will not. In time, they will pass from memory and be forgotten.

But in this place, each mist that comes in from the sea, each breeze that stirs the heather, will carry the whisper of them always.

Even if the living do not hear it.

# CHAPTER 2

When Tom Harkin leaves the pub, it is nearly midnight – and it is too late. Much too late. He can't remember a thicker fog. He can taste it on his tongue like wet charcoal. On top of which the Corporation, in protest at the British curfew, turns off the electricity at half past eleven these days. He looks down at the yellow semicircle of light from the doorway in which his polished black boots stand, tendrils of mist from the river swirling slowly around them, and he thinks about the warmth he is leaving and the darkness of the journey ahead. He pulls up the collar of his coat and tightens his belt, but already the cold has crept inside to his skin.

'Good luck,' Malone says, blurred, even though only a few feet separate them.

Then the door is shut and the light gone, and Harkin sighs because, on top of everything else, he is wearing the wrong boots. He takes three steps. *Click, clack, click.* He will have to walk on his toes. Like a ballerina. And it is four miles to Ballsbridge, in the fog, to where his other pair, the brown ones with the rubber heels, await him. If he gets there.

As soon as he steps off the pavement, he can see nothing – he must feel his way along the street, towards the river, listening for other footsteps and half-wishing he'd taken the revolver Malone had offered him, before he remembers the weight of a gun in his hand and he shivers.

This war against British rule is on a different scale from the war he fought in France. The battles now are between handfuls of men, but the killing is still the same. He knows there are sentries and patrols and checkpoints between him and his home, and every policeman and soldier will have their finger on the trigger of a gun. He has a pass that allows him to be out during the curfew hours, thanks to a highly placed official in the government admin- istration based at Dublin Castle. If he is able to show his pass, he'll be fine. But will they even ask, what with the fog and not knowing if the footsteps in the dark might not belong to a man with another gun? He isn't sure, if he were in their shoes, if he would be able to stand there, waiting, and not fire – just to make whoever it is go back the way they came. He thinks about that fellow they shot off his bicycle the other night, on his way back home from a late shift at the Guinness brewery.

That fellow's pass was good too.

The mist clings to his face and clothes in a cold, damp sheen, and the cobblestones are slippery underfoot. The temptation is to walk quickly, to warm himself up, but if he takes his time, he can listen and make less noise. The city is quiet, but not silent. The sound of a foghorn, muffled and lonely, comes along the river from the port and he can hear conversations in the houses he passes, and once a gramophone.

He considers his options – Sackville Street is to be avoided. There are sentries outside the GPO and O'Connell Bridge is always guarded. Capel Street is a possibility, but then he hears the distinctive rattle and wheeze of a Crossley Tender from that direction and adjusts his course to avoid it, making his way down a narrower street that runs parallel. The Crossley comes to a halt somewhere and he can hear shouting – English voices – but it isn't for him. He steps into a doorway all the same, finding the breath in his chest hard to come by, and waits until the Crossley moves off. He follows the noise of it as it goes towards the river. He thinks they must have been Auxies; their accents were those of the officer class rather than the other ranks that make up the Black and Tans, the other temporary RIC recruited from Britain. Then he can't hear the tender anymore and he is unsure if it has travelled out of earshot or perhaps come to another halt. He knows how fog can alter sound, and he wants to be certain it is safe before he goes forwards.

He curses Malone. Three hours late for the meeting, and there had been nothing he could do except wait for him. The list that he brought with him, now in the breast pocket of Harkin's jacket, is as good as a death sentence if an Auxie patrol searches him. The thought of it makes the adrenaline course through his body. Somewhere above him a baby begins to cry and he listens as the mother soothes the child back to sleep. He hears the bells from Christ Church ring for midnight. When they finish, and he has heard nothing more of the Auxies, he forces himself out of the doorway, keeping to the same slow, steady pace, preparing himself to answer the challenge if it comes, listening for anything that might signal danger.

He needs to get across the river. O'Connell Bridge, to his left, will be too dangerous, and the possible presence of the Crossley rules out trying Grattan Bridge, which spans the river to his right.

He feels boxed in, with only the Ha'penny Bridge, the narrow pedestrian arch between the alternative crossings, as a possibility. It's not the worst option, however. There is a better chance it will be unguarded than the others. He reaches the end of the street, and he knows from the dank, fetid smell that the river is just ahead of him. He listens for a moment, uncertain where the bridge is from where he is standing. He knows the city well, but he has lost his bearings somewhere along the way and he stands there, panic building, unable to decide whether to go forward until he finds the embankment wall or stay where he is until he is sure it is safe.

He is still frozen in indecision when he hears a low voice, to his left. An English voice. He can't make out the words, but he can hear someone responding and then the scrape of a match. He holds his breath and listens to the metallic sound of a car door opening and then closing. The Auxies. He wants to go back the way he came, but his feet seem to be stuck to the pavement. He knows this kind of fear from France and he knows he will get past it in a few moments. Not entirely, of course – fear doesn't just switch itself off – but enough to be able to move and think. He forces his lungs to take in some air and then slowly exhales, listening to the Auxies murmuring to each other.

Then he hears the sound of a rifle bolt being pulled back.

He is still standing there, locked into the box of his own terror, when he feels, to his surprise, a soft hand take his elbow. It pushes him gently forwards and he does not resist. He knows, somehow, that he is being helped. When he hears the Crossley's engine start up, seemingly only a few yards away, he allows himself to be directed, more quickly now, until he can make out the shape of the narrow entrance to the cast-iron bridge only a few steps ahead of him. There is no guard on it that he can see. To his left, the headlamps of the

14

Crossley are turned on. He walks forwards, hearing the hollow noise of his feet on the bridge, hoping the sound will be inaudible to the Auxies over the engine. He looks back to see the twin beams of light on Ormond Quay, blurred by the fog but not more than fifty yards from the bridge's entrance. His helper pushes him forwards once again and he takes the hint, encouraged by a shout from the direction of the Crossley, and walks across the bridge as quickly and quietly as he can.

When he turns to thank his saviour, there is no one there, only the faintest scent of a woman's perfume.

He remembers the perfume. Even though he has not smelled it for several years.

# CHAPTER 3

*M*ud and water. As far as the eye can see. A dark, fetid brown, with the only variation the grey-yellow faces of the dead, the mud-smeared pallor of the living and, overhead, the iron sky. The water has the thickness and colour of mud and the mud has the consistency of water. It makes no difference. You can drown in either. The rain is a constant rattle on his helmet, from which it drips down onto his sodden trench coat. He is shivering with the cold, the wet and, of course, the fear. His orders are to hold this pockmarked string of shell holes, regularly added to by the German artillery. It is, apparently, the remnants of their second trench, although there isn't much left of it. A torn sandbag here, a duckboard there and, across from him, the muddy grey cloth of a dead German corporal, his head half-buried, his left arm elsewhere. The trench has been filled and flattened so that it's more of a dip in the ground than a fortification. Sometimes they are not even sure they are in the trench. It disappears completely in places. His company are like archaeologists discovering its remnants, digging it out as deep as they can before it fills with more of the mud. The Germans know where it is, though. Their guns are zeroed in on it and they send over a shell every five minutes, right on top of them. The stretcher bearers take the wounded back. The dead they leave where they fall. The mud buries them soon enough.

*He looks at his wristwatch but his hand is shaking so much he can't make out the time at first, and then he has it. Half past twelve. Lunchtime in Dublin. His mother will be sitting opposite his father at the dining room table, and the thought is so out of place here that he tries to put it from his mind.*

*It's an hour since he went along the trench. Time to go again. He feels fear draining the energy from his limbs and breathes in deeply, filling his nose and mouth with the stench of earth and rot. A job to do is all it is. One knee in front of the other, one hundred yards that way, then one hundred back. It is an achievable task. He swallows, his mouth dry. Then, without a conscious decision, he is moving.*

*All the other officers are dead or wounded, and he's at the point where he thinks they are the lucky ones. He knows this short journey is futile, that it will not make a blind bit of difference, but it is his duty to his men. The mud sucks at him, and he knows he must keep moving. If he stops, the mud will try to take him and, if no one is close and he has not enough strength, it may succeed. He nods to each man he passes, asks him how he does and they lie to each other that all is well, and then he moves on. He counts twenty still alive, three less than the last time, which is better than he had expected. He does not know how any of them have survived this long. It seems an impossibility. He stops when he reaches the end of the trench. The Glosters are meant to be on the left but they have become detached. They could have fallen back, for all he knows.*

*He does not know what they can do if the Germans come at them. The mud has made their rifles useless except as clubs or, with bayonets fixed, spears. At least, he supposes, it will be the same for the Germans. He hears another shell coming in, and buries his face in the mud. It explodes not far behind the trench, showering him with more mud and the scraps of the things it holds – metal, wood, cloth and flesh. The mud-caked private he has been talking to begins to sob. He tries to smile reassuringly, but he can't. He feels the same terror. If he could only stop thinking and feeling and seeing, just for a little while, then maybe he could hold his mind together. But there is no pause to the horror.*

*He makes his way back, passing the survivors, barely enough for a platoon, let alone a company. They gaze back at him. They see him looking at his watch and how his hand shakes. He passes Sergeant Driscoll's corpse, plastered in mud from head to toe, slumped against what passes for a parapet, when the man's pale blue eyes open and stare at him, very much alive. Twenty-one. He nods to Driscoll, suppressing his surprise, thinking that the difference between being dead and alive in this place is nothing more than a flash of blue in a mud-encrusted face. He avoids looking at the others now, not wanting to see the paper-thin skin drawn tight over their bones. He hears another shell coming — high explosive, he can tell from the roaring and the whistle — and he doesn't move or even try to cover himself. There is, he suddenly realises, no point. And then he feels the blast and he is up, weightless for a moment, turning over in the air, glimpsing the wide expanse of mud in all directions, and then he is coming down.*

*The mud is like a wet pillow when he lands.*

*When he opens his eyes — and it could be hours or moments later; he has no idea — his mind is blank. He looks around for a point of reference, feeling his whole body ache with the effort, even though only his head moves. All he can see is mud.*

*And he is alone.*

# CHAPTER 4

'Captain Harkin?'

The boy is young, no more than fifteen, and has a telegram in his hand. Harkin has no idea how he finds himself here, standing in the hallway of the small house in Ballsbridge he inherited from his brother, still with the taste of French mud in his mouth. The transition from nightmare to reality is jarring. But here he is, and here is the boy with his telegram and the same washed-out blue eyes as Sergeant Driscoll from the trench.

'That's me,' he says, his voice hoarser and higher than he would like. 'Mr Harkin though. I'm no longer a captain, these days.'

Each word is an effort. He feels not quite present, as yet. He holds out his hand for the telegram, notices it is shaking, and thinks better of it, placing it instead behind his back and out of view. The boy frowns, those pale eyes taking in the state of him. Harkin looks down in his turn and sees his bare blue-veined feet white on the mosaic-tiled floor, toenails longer and yellower than they should be. At least he is wearing a dressing gown. The boy, it has to be said, is well turned out in his Post Office blue uniform with its red trim. He wears his pillbox hat at an angle Harkin suspects was much considered. Harkin traces a thumb down his unshaven cheek.

'What time is it?' he asks, deciding he might as well know.

'Eleven in the morning, sir.'

The 'sir' is uncertain.

'I am unwell,' Harkin says, by way of explanation. 'I've no idea where the maid is. Gallivanting, most probably.'

'You are Captain Thomas Harkin, though, sir?' The boy asks, and Harkin feels his anger bubbling up.

'Mister Thomas Francis Mary Harkin, formerly captain in the Royal Dublin Fusiliers, currently of this abode. Are you going to give me the telegram or not?'

The 'Mary' has always annoyed him. He doesn't much like the 'Francis' either. The perils of being the child of a religious mother. The boy looks startled and Harkin feels a nagging guilt.

'Is there something owed?' Harkin says, in a gentler tone.

'No, sir.' The boy is politer now. The message is handed over. 'But I'm to wait for a response.'

Of course he is. The envelope is thin in his hand but as soon as Harkin touches the paper, he knows nothing good is inside. The telegram boy knows it as well. The telegraph office reads all the telegrams, and tells the messengers when they contain bad news so they are prepared. This, as it happens, is something Harkin is all in favour of. The surreptitious reading of telegrams by patriotic Irishmen is of enormous use to him in his work. Harkin slides a finger inside the flap and tears it open, aware of the boy's expectation. He opens up the folded sheet and there's the message. Twelve words, two of them a tease, the rest a shock.

DEAR MARY. MAUD KILLED IRA AMBUSH. FUNERAL IMMINENT KILCOLGAN. PLEASE COME. BILLY.

He feels nothing at first. Harkin has, after all, four years in the trenches behind him and something of an immunity to death. His memories of Maud Prendeville are from long ago but they surface now. The warmth of her in his arms, her mouth against his. The smell of her perfume . . . and then he finds the world tilts slowly on its axis as the memory of the perfume from last night fills his nostrils. He reaches out a hand to steady himself against the wall. Maud Prendeville wore the same one. A cologne of some description. He used to know the name, but he can't recall it now. He gasps and sees sympathy in the boy's eyes.

'Have you a pencil?' he asks the boy, when he feels himself a little recovered from the shock. The boy opens the square leather holster on his belt and produces a pencil and a small notepad which he opens in anticipation.

'Are you ready?' Harkin can hear the strain in his voice.

The boy nods.

'Will attend. Tom.'

If he could underline the 'Tom' he would. 'Mary' is a joke that wore thin some time back. He finds thruppence for the boy in his overcoat, still damp from the fog last night, and sends him on his way.

When he has closed the door, he stands in the hallway for a minute and thinks back to the events of the night before. It must be his imagination. He knows his dreams have become more real in recent months. It is not possible that the woman in the mist could have been Maud. The thought reassures him, but a doubt remains.

He walks into the darkness of the sitting room, lit only by the slivers of dusty light that edge in through the drawn curtains. Unsettled, he puts the telegram back into its envelope and places it on the mantelpiece. It is only when there is a slight cough from behind him that he realises he is not alone. Harkin swallows, his mouth suddenly dry. He looks about him for a weapon and his eye falls on the glimmer of the long brass poker among the fire irons to his left. He marks its position and turns to see who has broken into his house. A large man in a grey three-piece suit with a carnation in the buttonhole is sitting calmly, a cup and saucer in one of his large hands. For a moment he thinks it is Martin, his dead brother, sitting in his favourite armchair, and he feels fear's grip on the back of his neck. But then the big man looks up at him, his expression a passable imitation of innocence, which is an achievement on a face that looks as though it's been carved out of rock with a heavy hammer.

'I let myself in. I was worn out from knocking.' The man gestures towards Harkin with his cup. 'I made myself some tea, I didn't think you'd mind. There's more in the pot – will I get you a cup?'

Harkin feels the tension drain out of him with the shuddering breath he releases.

'Vincent?' he says, by way of greeting, and puts a question into the name, as though Vincent Bourke has been up to no good. Which, he thinks, is almost certainly true. 'I thought you were . . . someone else. Was the door not locked?'

The big man's mouth widens into a grin.

'It was. I like to keep in practice.'

Harkin says nothing, wondering if he should get a new lock put on the door and knowing it wouldn't make much difference.

'I wish you wouldn't do that. If a door is locked, it's polite to wait until the owner opens it.'

'But if I can open it myself, why wait?' Bourke examines him for a moment and his smile slips. 'I'll get you your tea,' he says. 'You'll feel better for it.'

24

While Bourke departs in the direction of the kitchen, Harkin opens the curtains and lets in the winter sunlight. The air is chill and he remembers that Kathleen, the maid, is visiting her mother. He looks around the room, unchanged since before the war, when he and Martin would sit here and talk about politics and motor cars and whatever else came to mind. He remembers, suddenly, Maud and Martin at the piano, their faces glowing in the candle-light. Only him left alive from that evening. He rubs a hand across his face, feeling the sting of tears forming in his eyes.

Bourke returns, handing him the promised cup of tea, with a shortbread biscuit leaning into the saucer. He watches Harkin take a sip.

'I heard Malone was late last night,' he says, eventually.

Harkin nods.

'Was it the fog?'

Harkin shrugs, thinking back to the evening before, remembering once again the pressure of that inexplicable hand on his shoulder down by the river and the smell of Maud's perfume. He suppresses the shiver that comes with it.

It can only have been his mind playing tricks on him.

'He said there was a raid on Bachelors Walk that nearly picked him up and he had to go to ground. After that he took a round-about route to make sure he wasn't followed. He said there were peelers all over town and he was lucky to get there at all. I didn't hang around to question him. The curfew had already started.'

The big man considers this, and gives a non-committal nod.

'Did he bring the list?'

Harkin goes to the hallway and takes the envelope from the pocket of his overcoat. The envelope contains a summary of the enlistment information of 163 Cadets of the Auxiliary Division of the Royal Irish Constabulary, including their home addresses in England. The Auxies like to burn the houses of members of the IRA. The list opens up the possibility of paying them back in kind. Bourke opens the envelope and scans the contents, whistling.

'I wouldn't like to have carried this across town past curfew. A good thing you did, though. The pub was raided after you left and Malone taken. Better for all of us, especially him, he didn't have the list.'

Harkin considers the implications of this news. Malone, he realises, knows where he lives. Knows his real name.

'He's solid, isn't he?' Harkin says, as much to reassure himself as anything. Then reconsiders. 'Isn't he?'

'Solid enough. They'll give him a going-over, of course. Might be best if you lie low for a while. Maybe get out of Dublin.' He pauses, and that look of contrived innocence returns. 'The boss has a suggestion, as it happens.'

Suddenly he knows, though he doesn't know how, that this proposal will be something to do with Maud.

'Go on.'

'You knew Maud Prendeville before the war, right? And the family? Quite well, he thinks.'

'I knew her well enough,' he says. 'That telegram was from her brother.'

'Well, isn't that a coincidence? The boss had a telephone call from Sir John Prendeville this morning, himself. Sir John's a little ticked off at the minute, what with the IRA having killed his niece in an ambush.'

Harkin shakes his head slowly.

'So the telegram said. But it's not possible, surely? Maud was . . . well . . . Maud Prendeville.'

26

'Indeed. The boss isn't happy about it either. A flying column killing a hero of the Easter Rising in a crossfire? It's a gift to the Brits.'

'Do we know anything about the circumstances?'

'Not much. The column are adamant Maud Prendeville was alive when they left, although unconscious. They say they heard a single gunshot five minutes later. In other words, they say someone else plugged her. But then, they would.'

Harkin looks at the piano and the spot where Maud had placed her hand that evening, remembering the soft smile she'd given him.

'So where do I come into this?'

'You know Sir John, don't you?'

'I know him well,' Harkin says. 'I was his private secretary before the war, when he was still a Home Rule MP.' He pauses, examining Bourke. 'I take it the boss also knows I was engaged to Maud?'

Bourke nods.

'The boss mentioned it. He sends his sympathy. And his apologies.'

'Apologies?'

'The boss wants you to go down and talk to him. There needs to be an investigation and you're the perfect man to do it, he says. As of this morning, the insurance has a substantial policy on Miss Prendeville's life in Sir John's name. The paperwork will come over later on.'

Harkin nods. On paper at least, he is employed as a claims assessor for the All-Ireland Insurance Company. It's a real company with real insurance business, but it's also a front for the General Headquarters intelligence operation, of which Harkin is a senior member.

'I see. I'm to assess the claim, as it were?'

'Exactly. If it really was someone else, deal with them and get the hell out of there.'

'And if it was the flying column?'

Bourke looks uncomfortable.

'The boss chose you for this job because he knows you've a sensible head on you. It won't be easy. The column are very active down there, and we want them to carry on being active. On the other hand . . .' Bourke pauses, as though remembering the boss's exact words. 'He said to remind you we're very short on guns.'

Harkin smiles at Bourke's look of puzzlement. What Bourke doesn't know, because he isn't one of the handful of people in Ireland who do, is that Sir John Prendeville has been instrumental in arranging the shipment of 200 Thompson sub-machine guns from New York for the IRA. A shipment that is due to be arriving in less than two weeks' time.

'He says he's sorry to have to ask you,' Bourke says. 'But you know the family, you knew Maud, and it's a good idea if you're out of town for a few days.'

Harkin nods, remembering Malone's arrest.

'And if he talks?'

'We're battening down the hatches, and you being out of the way is a part of that.'

# CHAPTER 5

Harkin stretches himself out when the elderly lady, and the staring, glass-eyed fox stole she wears around her neck, leaves the train. He's relieved to have the compartment to himself. It has been one thing being scrutinised by the old woman, but having the dead fox eyeing him up as well has been disconcerting. He takes out his cigarette case, almost as battered by the war as he is, and settles himself more comfortably into his seat.

The cigarette case has seen better days – each dent telling the story of a trench or a battle or a near miss. None of them are good stories. It was, coincidentally, a gift from Maud and he's stuck with it for some reason. There is an inscription on the inside that he makes a point of not reading. He knows what it says and he feels the sadness tugging at him like a rip tide. He stares out the window at the passing fields, wet and dark in the early light. His fingers aren't steady – they haven't been for weeks now – but he manages to light up without too much trouble and exhales a ring of cigarette smoke which hovers in the yellow light of the carriage for a moment before dispersing. The villages and towns, the stone walls, the haggards, barns and low-slung cottages, all seem to sag into greater degrees of dilapidation the further the train rolls west and the more light there is. It looks as though a war has passed through the countryside; that impression is not incorrect, although it is a war of hedgerows and alleyways. The war has been going on for two years now, and it has been hard for a people who were already used to hard times. There are a lot of hungry, desperate people in the country these days but it won't be long, he thinks, until the war is won.

Matters are coming to a head, whether the British authorities know it or not.

The weather continues to disappoint as the train continues through the rolling landscape. Whips of rain lash the window like a punishment and the steam from the engine is thrown up and down by the wind, so that one moment he can see rain-misted hills in the near distance and then he and the train are hurtling alone through a white cloud. It doesn't matter. He is not really interested in the scenery. Instead he allows his mind to wander, and finds his thoughts returning to Maud.

He knows more about her death now – from the report of the unit responsible for the ambush and the RIC reports which one of their sources has passed on. There is more detail in the RIC reports but the two accounts are consistent. They both agree that Maud was in the car when it was ambushed and that she died as a result of a single gunshot. The RIC's report adds the detail that the gunshot entered her forehead just above her left eye, with powder residue indicating it was from close range. The RIC's conclusion is that all deaths were caused by the IRA. They seem to have no interest in considering why Maud might have been shot in the head from close range by other republicans, nor have they taken into account that the killer must have been looking right into Maud's face when they did it. Harkin knows a little bit about killing and this strikes him as unusual. In his experience, if men have a choice, they'll avoid looking directly into the eyes of a person they are to kill. The blindfolds that the condemned are given at executions are as much for the firing squad as for those about to be shot. Even in the trenches, in the middle of a desperate battle, if enemy soldiers attempting to surrender had to be killed, it was done from behind. Whoever fired that weapon must either have hated Maud, or be a cold-blooded killer, and he doesn't know how anyone could have hated Maud.

The last time he saw Maud must have been six years ago. Her face seems to slide away when he tries to recall it, but her death has brought up a wave of memories of their time together. It helps that there was a good photograph of her in the paper, one from before the war – her face turned slightly away from the camera to show her profile. Now he can pin his memories to the photograph: dancing at a ball in Dublin; her visiting him in the university rooms he shared with her brother; a picnic on the strand at Kilcolgan. He remembers Maud leaning into his shoulder as they looked out to sea, the sun warm on their skin. Afterwards they walked back along the drive that led to the house and he remembers the black windows gazing down at them, the spirits of the place behind each one. Harkin looks at the rain that is now streaming back along the window, blown by the train's speed into long lines that run across the glass. He doesn't know how the Prendevilles stick it in that dark mansion, perched on the edge of the world, its granite walls fighting a perpetual battle against Atlantic storm and rain. Maud had been living there for the last four years, since she was injured in the Rising and withdrew from the struggle for independence, and from one Tom Harkin – a man who loved her.

To his surprise, a tear begins to trace a path down his cheek.

Each mile the train journey brings him closer to the house, the more unreal the whole situation feels. Now the rain has given way to a low morning mist that lies thick across the fields and it feels as though the present world is blurring around him. The house and Maud, in contrast, becoming clearer in his mind's eye.

He must have drifted off then, because when he wakes up it is in the darkness of a tunnel, with smoke and rock flickering past the window, half-visible in the light from the train's corridor. There are two men sitting across from him. One has taken the seat by the window and the other sits beside the door. They are wearing long greatcoats and when Harkin's eyes adjust to what little light there is, he sees the coats are khaki brown, torn and crusted with mud. They wear no caps or helmets; instead their faces are covered with the white bandages of gas attack victims, soaked with blood where the eyes and mouth should be. He swallows hard, feeling the fear squeezing his chest.

For a long moment, he stares at them. He knows they are not there – that if he reaches out to them there will be nothing but air – but that doesn't mean they are not real – to him, at least. They fill his gaze as the sweet smell of rotting flesh fills his nostrils. He wants to look away but he can't. He wonders if they can see him. What can they think of him, a survivor, when they are dust in some nameless grave?

He closes his eyes and when he opens them the train is back among the open fields and the men have gone. He sees his reflection in the glass of the compartment door, black eyes and white face and the scar of a mouth. He looks half-dead himself.

He manages to light a cigarette, his hand shaking once again, and is aware that the train is slowing for the next station. He sees a platoon of Auxiliaries waiting on the platform, armed to the teeth, slung with bandoliers of ammunition like Mexican bandits in a moving picture. Even in his current state, Harkin is alert to the danger they represent. He watches as they swagger up and down the platform, their hands on the butts of their holstered revolvers, bothering the citizenry on the platform before they eventually board, when they start on the passengers. He is in a first-class compartment, and therefore hopes he is of no interest to them. Someone wealthy enough to afford a first-class ticket is likely to be a loyal citizen, keen to keep on as they have been going on, which is why he travels this way. If they do look in at him, he hopes they'll see nothing more than a man on his way to a funeral, in a well-cut woollen suit and stiff collar. And if they are still curious – well, he has the truth to protect him. Three years in France. Royal Dublin Fusiliers. Captain. Military Cross. He might even know one of them from over there. Crucially, they will not know about his current incarnation as an IRA intelligence officer.

Unless, of course, Malone has blabbed.

The thought of Malone causes an unseasonal sweat to break out along his spine and he closes his eyes to whisper a short prayer and remind himself that, with luck, the arrest will have been for nothing more than late-night drinking.

When he hears the sound of the compartment door sliding back, he finds himself looking up into the grey eyes of a middle-aged man in a dark green tunic, worn over khaki jodhpurs. His tam-o'-shanter cap is worn at a rakish angle and Harkin notices that the button on his holster revolver, reversed for an easy draw, has been undone to make that easy draw still easier. He wishes he hadn't.

33

'Papers,' the Auxie says, in a Yorkshire accent.

Harkin reaches into his inside pocket and hands them over. The Auxie looks at them intently and Harkin waits for the acknowledgement of their shared military history, but none comes.

'Harkin, is it?'

Harkin feels his mouth go dry but answers as nonchalantly as possible.

'Yes.'

'Where are you travelling?'

Harkin tells him his destination.

'You live there, do you?'

'No, I live in Dublin. I'm travelling for a funeral.'

The Auxie looks up.

'Whose funeral?'

Harkin considers telling him to mind his own business, but he can hear shouting from further along the train and something tells him that the Auxies are not in a quibbling frame of mind.

'She was in the paper. Lord Kilcolgan's daughter—'

He is about to go on, but the Auxie interrupts him.

'I know who she was.' He looks back at Harkin's papers, squinting. 'Were you a friend of hers or her family?'

There's an edge to the question; Maud's republican activities are, after all, well known. There's no need, he decides, to mention he is her former fiancé.

'I served with her brother in the war. In Flanders and elsewhere.' He nods towards the strip of medals on the Auxie's chest. 'You?'

The Auxie doesn't respond at first, looking down for an instant as though he'd forgotten they were there.

'The same,' he says, examining Harkin coldly. 'Do you mind me asking you a question?'

'Of course not.'

'Why am I checking papers and getting shot at by your coun-trymen while you're sitting on your arse in first class?'

Harkin opens his mouth to say something and then closes it. He doubts there is an answer to that question that won't come back and bite him.

The Auxie smiles a grim smile.

'Nothing to say to that, eh? I thought not. You lot are all the same. I've got a tip for you, though, old comrade. Keep your head down where you're going. Because we're going there, too, and we've got a score to settle.'

He throws the papers in Harkin's lap and slides the door shut with a bang.

Harkin breathes out a long, shallow breath and concentrates on breathing in another. Outside the carriage, the rain has turned to mist that is closing in around the train even as he watches, darkening the green of the grass to black, and everything else to a hazy, drifting grey.

It feels as though he is entering another world.

# CHAPTER 6

The train slows until, with a final screech of the brakes, it comes to a shuddering halt. He remembers the station, although it is hard enough to see even the opposite platform with the mist that passes the window in a shifting pattern of shadow and swirl. They have reached the end of the line – a two-platformed terminus where it will be difficult to avoid the Auxiliaries, so he sits and waits.

It isn't hard to follow their progress. Their detraining is loud and boisterous, the sound muffled and distorted by the mist, their calls and laughter like the foghorns of passing ships. They are curiously undisciplined for a body of men who are largely former officers. When the last of them leaves, it is as though the station itself sighs with relief.

Harkin waits for another minute, stands and pulls down his suitcase from the luggage rack, then puts on his trench coat, buttoning it up to the neck. His hands are still unsteady but there's nothing to be done about that. He pulls the belt tight around him, hoping it will hold him together.

The fog extends even under the shelter of the station's cast-iron roof, forming halos around the gas lanterns that hang at regular intervals. The platform is empty except for the two dark shadows approaching from the far end of the train. They take their time. Somewhere, the driver is checking the train's wheels; the clang of his hammer is a steady rhythm. When the figures emerge from the mist, Harkin can see it is the stationmaster and a guard, looking for stragglers like himself. The stationmaster doffs his cap and Harkin tips his own homburg in response. He wonders if it's the homburg that inspires the deference, or the carriage. He forces a smile, then turns to walk to the exit, casting an eye over the posters for dog food, cigarettes and wanted IRA men, and takes a deep breath. He still has that sense of not quite being present – the encounter with the Auxie has shaken him. He finds himself looking at the ground to place each step, his balance uncertain. When the voice comes, it startles him.

'Captain Harkin, sir? Can I take your bag?'

Harkin looks up. The man standing in front of him is wearing a tweed suit and military boots. He bears a strong similarity to someone he knew in Flanders.

'Sergeant Driscoll?' Harkin asks, hearing the fright in his voice. He remembers the trench in Flanders just before he and the others were blown to pieces. He wonders for a moment if he is having another one of his visions. 'But you're dead.'

Driscoll looks down at himself, patting his chest and waist.

'Still here, I think.'

Harkin's relief is so pronounced, he feels tears well up. He looks away to hide them.

'I thought everyone in that trench had died. I'm pleased to be wrong.'

Driscoll smiles as though Harkin has made a passing remark about the weather.

38

'I wasn't sure if you'd remember me.'

Harkin takes a moment to gather himself.

'I remember you well enough. Sergeant . . . John . . . Driscoll.' Harkin is conscious of how hesitant he sounds. 'They told me in the field hospital that the relief found only me alive.'

Somehow his suitcase is now in Driscoll's hand and he wishes it weren't. Its drag on his arm was a tangible thing, and he has the sense that he is not quite tethered to reality without it. On top of which, Driscoll walks with a pronounced limp. Driscoll shrugs.

'No, me and a few others made it out. It was us carried you back, not the relief. We wouldn't have left you there.'

'Thank you.'

Harkin finds that a nervous laughter is bubbling up inside him. He pushes it back down. Driscoll's smile is polite, but there is something behind it. As though Harkin is missing something still. He wonders what state he was in when they carried him out. With luck he was unconscious.

'Did many make it out?' he asks.

'A few. More than you might have thought. We were back in the trenches within a month. I caught a bullet in my hip soon after that and when I recovered, I was assigned to the quartermaster and light duties. I wasn't sad to see the back of the trenches.'

Harkin nods and a silence falls.

'How was the journey down?' Driscoll asks.

There's a slight tease to the way the fellow says it and it gives Harkin the jolt he needs. Driscoll is also the name of the man he is meant to be making contact with – the intelligence officer for the local Volunteer battalion. And Sean is, of course, the Irish for John.

'You're the Sean Driscoll I'm meant to be looking out for?'

'The same.' The man gives him a slanted smile, his pale blue eyes almost kindly. 'I was always Sean, but the recruiting sergeant wrote down John and I was stuck with it for four years. I work at Kilcolgan. Master Billy asked me to come and fetch you.'

The connection is clear to Harkin now. Somehow no one had thought to mention in the report or his orders that the local intelligence officer happened to work for the Prendevilles, or he might have made it back in Dublin.

'Well, then. We can talk on the way.'

# CHAPTER 7

Driscoll has a horse and carriage waiting outside – the yellow glow of the station's lights gilding the black horse's wet back. Harkin can taste the sea when he breathes in, the salt mixed with the smell of kelp. He remembers the street just past the railings, and the town, but all that can be seen of it now are vague outlines in the grey gloom. Harkin watches as Driscoll ties his suitcase to the luggage rack and then swings himself up awkwardly into the carriage.

If anything, the fog becomes thicker as they make their way slowly through the town – the horse's hooves sounding like a muffled echo of themselves. The few shops and pubs glow like islands in the mist, while somewhere a church bell rings, its mournful sound seeming to come from behind them one moment, and from up ahead the next. A donkey cart loaded down with milk churns looms towards them from the other side of the street. The flat-capped farmer holding the traces looks in their direction with such a blank expression that Harkin is not even sure that he has seen them.

Perhaps the horse knows the way, because its pace is steady. Time, by contrast, seems to slow. When the gaps between the buildings on either side begin to widen and then begin to be replaced by hedges and low walls, Harkin has no idea how long they have been travelling or how far they have come. He is only conscious that the sway and roll of the buggy is lulling him into something like a waking sleep.

'There's a checkpoint up ahead.'

Driscoll barely whispers the words but Harkin feels the tiredness slide away from him in an instant. A barrier has been placed across the road, behind which stand the shadows of greatcoated men, armed with rifles, and the shape of an armoured car. Driscoll pulls slowly on the traces and the horse comes to a halt some ten feet short of the men, still little more than silhouettes. There is a long, silent pause which gives Harkin the opportunity to remember Volunteers he has known who were stopped at checkpoints much like this – then found later in an alley or at the side of some boreen. He reminds himself that he is a former British officer, with nothing to fear.

Unless, of course, Malone has talked.

A large policeman in an oilskin cloak with thick white sergeant's stripes on his cuffs approaches. His eyes are hard to make out under the brim of his peaked cap, and Harkin finds himself instead trying to deduce his intentions from the hang of his enormous walrus moustache.

'Good morning to you, Sergeant Kelly.'

The sergeant nods by way of response to Driscoll's greeting, pushing back his helmet to examine Harkin. His eyes, now that Harkin can see them, are intelligent and not unfriendly.

'Who is your passenger, Sean?'

'Captain Harkin. He served with young Mr Prendeville in the war. He's down from Dublin for the funeral.'

The sergeant regards Harkin calmly.

'Did you come down on the train, Captain Harkin?'

Harkin is surprised they have not been waved straight through. Harkin uses his officer voice – the clipped, neutral tone expected in the army – to answer.

'I did, although it's Mr Harkin, these days. Is there anything I can help you with, Sergeant?'

The sergeant's helmet is spotted with rain and his face damp, although he seems oblivious to it. His impassive features make Harkin feel uneasy. The usual reaction of the regular police to the discovery that he is a former officer is a degree of deference.

'Did you meet anyone on the train down, Mr Harkin?'

Harkin examines the sergeant's face for any evidence of particular intent behind the question, but there seems to be nothing untoward.

'No one, apart from an old lady who got off in Mullingar. A platoon of Auxiliary cadets got on a few stops later but that was about it.'

'They'll be here for District Inspector Teevan's funeral, I'm afraid to say. Will you be coming to that, yourself, Mr Harkin? To District Inspector Teevan's funeral, that is?'

The sergeant's question is unexpected, but the very blandness of its delivery suggests there is a purpose behind it.

'I'm afraid I didn't know Inspector Teevan . . .' he begins, and when he pauses, uncertain how to proceed, the sergeant interrupts him.

'He was a good man. An Irishman, like all of us. I doubt there will be more than a handful come to see him put in the ground, except those of us who served alongside him. Sean here, for one, isn't likely to pay him the respect he's due. Are you, now, Sean?'

Harkin is aware, without looking at him, of Driscoll's discomfort.

'You know I have the Prendevilles to attend to and poor Mr Cartwright's body has to be returned to his family. Inspector Teevan was not the only loss.'

'That's true enough. But even if Miss Prendeville hadn't died, we wouldn't likely have seen you at Jim Teevan's funeral. Now would we, Sean?'

The sergeant's voice is low and Harkin doubts that the men on the checkpoint behind him can overhear the conversation. It might well be that the sergeant doesn't want them to listen in, and Harkin is struck again by the lack of hostility. He is unsure what to make of it or, indeed, how to react. Should he try to bluster his way out of the situation? In the end he takes his lead from Driscoll, who says nothing.

'Well, I won't ask you for your papers, Mr Harkin. I'm sure they're very impressive. I'll know where to find you if I need you.' He turns to Driscoll, his voice lowering still further. 'I wouldn't be surprised if there isn't trouble in the town over the next few days, Sean. I'd stay out of it, if I were you.' He looks intently at Driscoll for a moment, as if to see if he is taking heed. Then he nods. 'Give my regards to your mother.'

The sergeant stands aside and calls out for the barrier to be lifted. As they pass, the policemen seem cold and dispirited – as if Teevan's death has taken the fight out of them. When they are clear of the checkpoint, Driscoll turns to Harkin and nods over his shoulder.

'My mother's first cousin. He's not active against us, if you know what I mean. He does what he's ordered to, but nothing more than that. That's the case with most of the old RIC around here. The Auxies and the Black and Tans are a different story.'

'And Teevan?'

Driscoll considers this for a moment.

'It wasn't him the column were after,' he says, shrugging as if to say that there were no tears shed all the same.

'Who were they after?'

'Major Abercrombie. He commands the Auxiliary company in the town. He's earned a bullet twenty times over. It was him was meant to be in the car.'

# CHAPTER 8

They follow the road west and the fog gradually dissipates, leaving Harkin with a view to his right of stone-strewn hills with more gorse than grass, and to the left, through the scattered trees, the occasional flash of white waves along a grey shore, not more than a hundred yards away. The wind is picking up and the sky is low above them, filled with bruised clouds that promise to wipe away the last of the mist.

They travel in silence until they see the blackened timbers and thatch of a still-smouldering cottage built hard up against the road, its whitewashed walls streaked with soot. A small crowd stand around it, sombre and silent as they pass. A woman is crying loudly from within the building, and he can see that a few recovered possessions are piled on a small cart. Some of the men in the crowd nod to Driscoll while others look at Harkin with a cold hostility, one turning away with a comment that is met with a murmur of approval. He can see the bitterness in their dark eyes and gaunt, smudged features, and anger comes from them like the rustle of leaves in a forest. He sits and looks down at the long black coats and flat caps and he knows he looks like the enemy to them, sitting beside Driscoll in his homburg and trench coat.

'What happened?' he asks, when they have passed.

'One of the lads in the column lived there. The woman crying in the house is his mother.'

'And the son?'

'Abercrombie and his men took him last night. He was found at the crossroads this morning.' Driscoll's tone makes it clear the Volunteer was found dead. 'Those Auxies on the train will be out tonight as well. A district inspector is worth a half a hundred houses, and woe betide anyone of ours they come across till things calm down.'

The road winds alongside the rocky shore and, after another mile or two, they find themselves following, on the one side, a long strand striped with lines of seaweed and, on the other, Kilcolgan's high demesne wall. Driscoll nods his head in the direction of a gap where the stonework, undermined by the roots of a tree, has collapsed out onto the verge.

'You haven't been here since before the war, have you?'

'No.'

'Kilcolgan has changed since then,' Driscoll says. 'The last few years have been hard on the place. There's no money left to keep it up. Just by way of warning.'

Harkin recognises the tall pillars standing either side of the gates, now covered with thick ivy that the carved eagles which top them, wings bunched for flight, will never break free of. Driscoll allows the horse to come to a slow, swaying halt, pulls the brake back and looks over at him. Without a word, they climb down and Harkin follows the limping Driscoll in through the gate.

There was a photograph in the paper of Teevan's bullet-riddled car leaning into the gate lodge wall, but it's gone now. All that remains are the white scars where bullets struck the stone, a boarded-up window and a dark stain where the engine's oil leaked out. The drive leads on through the trees towards the big house, visible through the winter-stripped branches. Its familiar windows stare down at Harkin, mirroring the sea and the shore.

'Tell me what happened.'

Driscoll walks away from the gate lodge, towards a log that has been pushed to the side of the drive, up against the laurel bushes that line it.

'They blocked the drive with this.'

Harkin nods, before walking a short distance into the woods. Empty brass cartridges lie scattered among the rotting leaves and moss.

'The RIC didn't collect these? When they were investigating?'

Driscoll laughs.

'Investigating? As far as they're concerned the case is closed. They took the bodies and the car away and took a few photographs, but past that they didn't bother much. They know it was us set the ambush and what more do they need to bother with?'

Harkin knows Driscoll is right. In the parts of the country where the Volunteers are active, the RIC are no longer acting as a police force in the way they used to. He turns to look back at their surroundings.

'Tell me how it happened?'

'Commandant Egan and the column arrived about an hour beforehand. They secured the gate lodge and took up positions, as well as barricading the road. When the car came in, Teevan must have seen the barrier, because he swerved and hit the wall. There was some return fire but they hadn't a hope. A neat job if Miss Prendeville hadn't been in the car.'

49

Harkin looks around and can see how the ambush played out, where the gunmen were positioned, and can almost hear the fusillade of bullets. He can also imagine Maud's terror, surrounded by the flash of muzzle fire – the Volunteers close to the car as they would be in a night ambush. He feels a familiar nausea as he imagines the stench of cordite and blood. He walks a few steps away from Driscoll, towards the house, giving himself time to recover.

'But she survived the attack?' he says, over his shoulder.

Driscoll nods.

'So I'm told. Teevan and Cartwright were dead, or as good as. Maud may have been knocked out when the car hit the wall but she was still breathing and there was no visible wound. They made her as comfortable as they could and left her, knowing we'd come down from the house soon enough. A few minutes after they left there was a single shot. I heard it as well.'

'And it was that shot that killed her?'

'So it seems.'

'You said "so I'm told"?'

Driscoll nods, his expression darkening.

'I wasn't here when it happened. I was at my mother's house.' Driscoll nods towards Kilcolgan. 'It's behind the house, past the walled garden. The first I knew of the ambush was the gunfire. If I had known about it, I'd have asked them to get out of it. There's ten places better they could have done it along the coast road without bringing me into it.'

'Your mother's house?'

'She's Lord Kilcolgan's housekeeper. I grew up here. I help out around the place. It suits me. It also allows me to go about the country when I need to for brigade business.'

'So you're the intelligence officer but you didn't know what was going to happen? How did Egan know the car would be visiting Kilcolgan?'

Driscoll takes a deep breath, frowning; as though marshalling his thoughts is an effort.

'I'm not the only intelligence officer in the brigade. The column had its own intelligence officer, Matt Breen. The other intelligence officers and myself pass on information to them, but the column makes its own decisions as to what targets to attack and when. They don't consult with anyone. It wouldn't be practical and it's more secure that way. I didn't even know they were anywhere close. I thought Egan was in the hills to the east. Forty miles away.'

'But it was your information they acted on?'

'No. Now, I knew Harry Cartwright and Maud were going to play cards at Sir John's that evening. I also knew Maud was meant to be staying the night and coming back in the morning. Cartwright was getting the early train to Dublin, so he would come back that evening if someone would give him a lift, but I didn't even know Teevan and Abercrombie would be at Sir John's, let alone that one of them would be driving. But the column knew. Even if I had known about it, it's not something I'd have passed on to them. I'd never have put the Prendevilles at risk. Never. On top of which, it's not good for my health to have the column shooting up Auxies on my doorstep, drawing attention to me. Last, and not least, the Auxies are currently based in the old poorhouse in the town and they don't much like it. There have been several offers to rent Kilcolgan from his Lordship as an alternative. His Lordship would have taken the money long ago, only for Maud being opposed, and an ambush at his front gate might well be the thing that would have pushed him into doing it.'

'And will he take the money now?'

Driscoll shrugs.

'Who knows?'

Harkin thinks back to the conversation with Kelly at the checkpoint. If Kelly knows about Driscoll, as he seems to, then others might as well. He presumes Driscoll is aware of the danger he's in and he wonders why he hasn't gone to ground, at least for a week or two.

'So who did tell the column about Abercrombie?'

'Breen had an informant who passes us messages to him through a priest in the town.'

'Who is this informant?'

Driscoll puts a hand to his chin, running a thumb along its length.

'I don't know. Breen kept his identity to himself. If you ask me, it's likely it's an RIC man. The information we get from him includes details of troop and police movements in this part of the county, as well as warning of the big sweeps. It's helped Egan stay out of the way a fair few times. My guess is he'd have to be a sergeant, at least, to have the information he gives as early as he passes it on – but the truth is it could be anyone. There's never been a question of money or anything, as far as I know. Whoever it is, they seem to be straight and they must have been informed of Abercrombie's movements.'

Harkin thinks back to the checkpoint and the sergeant's warning.

'Might it be Kelly?'

Driscoll shrugs once again.

'I think Kelly would have come to me rather than Breen. Because of the connection.'

Harkin gathers his thoughts. If the column's recollection is correct – that Maud was killed by someone else shortly after the ambush – then it seems likely that whoever killed her must have either been part of the ambush or have known it would take place. There is a third possibility, of course. That it was someone from the house itself.

'I think we need to find out from Matt Breen who his source was, for a start.'

Driscoll rubs his chin, a gesture that is becoming familiar to Harkin as a precursor to bad news.

'That may be difficult,' he says. 'That was Matt's house we passed.'

Harkin remembers the woman's crying and the hostility of the crowd.

'You didn't think to mention that when we passed?'

'Would his name have meant anything to you?'

Which is probably a fair point, Harkin concedes.

'Was he tortured?'

Driscoll nods.

'I saw the body.'

'And you're not worried he'll have talked? That the same thing will happen to you?'

Driscoll meets his gaze for a moment, then looks away. It seems it's not a subject he wants to discuss.

'I'm needed here,' Driscoll says. Then, after the briefest of pauses. 'If you want to find out who the source is, it'll have to be through Father Dillon. He's the parish priest at St Ann's. It's a small church in the town, a little out of the way. I'll try and talk to him this afternoon – I have to meet the two o'clock train anyway.'

Harkin looks around him. The only sounds are the cry of a gull from the shore and the crunch of the gravel underfoot as he shifts his weight. There is an atmosphere about the place that he doesn't like. As though something bad has happened here, which of course it has, but something else as well. He glances up at the house and its empty windows, black against the grey granite.

'I'll need to talk to him as well.'

Driscoll nods.

'I'll see what I can do.'

'This card evening they were at? Who else was there?'

'Moira Wilson, she has a fishing lodge between here and Ballynan – that's where Sir John Prendeville lives. The Eustaces, who live further along the road.' Driscoll indicates further to the west. 'Dr Hegarty from the town, Teevan and Abercrombie from the barracks, Maud and Cartwright, and, of course, Sir John himself.'

'Why didn't Abercrombie drive them back, as was originally planned?'

'He was called away. He and Teevan drove separately, so I suppose Teevan felt obliged.'

'Any idea why Maud changed her mind about staying?'

'You'll have to ask Sir John.' Driscoll takes a deep breath and exhales. 'Do you mind my asking what the point of all this is? The column didn't kill her, but your investigating her death isn't going to change anyone's opinion one way or another.'

Harkin holds his gaze, then gives him a half shrug.

'Maud Prendeville was one of the last to leave the burning GPO in 1916 and one of the last to surrender after the Rising. Her being killed by her own comrades is not the way we'd like to have her remembered. If there is any chance we can find proof that will stand up to scrutiny, then we need to find it.'

'And what about the fact she was travelling in a car with an RIC district inspector. She was in the wrong place at the wrong time. She'd have told you the same herself. Our lads didn't kill her, but they easily might have.'

Harkin smiles patiently.

'As I said, if they didn't kill her, then I need to find out who did.'

Driscoll looks sceptical.

'What are you going to do? Go round asking questions? The police won't like that much.'

'Sir John took out a life assurance policy on Maud's life some years ago. I work for the insurance company who issued the policy. I have all the paperwork. They may not like it, but they can't stop me.'

Driscoll looks at him in astonishment. Harkin shrugs.

'It's a real company. It's all above board.' He nods over to the gate lodge. 'What about these people? I'd like to talk to them for a start.'

'Patrick Walsh and his wife. They were tied up, they saw nothing.'

'They might have heard something, though.'

Driscoll nods, although his lack of enthusiasm is clear.

'They're staying with his brother the other side of town for a few days. I'll see what can be done.'

'And I'll need to meet with Commandant Egan as soon as is possible.'

'I'll pass a message on.'

Harkin takes a few more steps along the drive towards the house. The coat feels heavy on his shoulders. He is tired. He wonders, for a moment, what he is doing here, of all places.

'So after you heard the gunfire?' Harkin says, summoning up the energy to continue. 'What happened then?'

'I went to the house so no one could point a finger at me. Then Billy, myself, Charlotte and Lord Kilcolgan went down to the gate.'

'And you heard no more gunfire?'

'Apart from the single shot. A few minutes after the ambush itself.'

'You'd reached the others when you heard it?'

'I was just walking in the door.'

'How long did it take to get there?'

Driscoll looks sheepish.

'I had to get dressed. And my mother didn't want me going out. It took a little while.'

'How long exactly?'

'Maybe five minutes. I don't have a watch.'

'The others were there, though? When you arrived? Lord Kilcolgan and Billy and Charlotte? What about the servants?'

'There aren't many. My mother, who was in the cottage. Murphy the butler, but he's not much use these days, and then Bridget the maid.'

Harkin takes one final look around.

'Anything else you'd like to tell me?'

Driscoll rubs his jaw once more. Harkin waits. For some reason Driscoll appears to be embarrassed.

'There's one thing,' Driscoll says, his eyes shifting away from Harkin's. 'Billy saw the White Lady. Just before the ambush. A ghost.'

Harkin can feel his eyebrow rising and Driscoll, glancing back at him, sees his bemusement.

'Look, I know what you're thinking, but the story is that before a Prendeville dies, the White Lady appears. So they say, anyway.'

'And the White Lady is . . .?'

'You'd better ask the Prendevilles.'

As they walk back to the carriage, Harkin sees a scrap of white in the undergrowth to the side of the path. He leans down and finds a half-smoked cigarette butt, damp from the rain, although the label is still legible. There is a small shield embossed in gold on the paper, and then the words *Péra – New Bond Street*. Frowning, he reaches into his pocket for his handkerchief, folds the cigarette butt up into it, and follows Driscoll to the carriage.

# CHAPTER 9

The hall door is opened by an elderly servant in a butler's coat that seems too big for him, as though he has shrunk in on himself. Harkin remembers Murphy, but this is a diminished version compared with the one he recalls. The butler glances quickly past Harkin, his watery gaze scanning the immediate surroundings of the house, a nervous tongue flicking over his purple lips.

'Murphy, it's good to see you again.'

'And yourself, Mr Harkin,' Murphy says, looking out past him once again. 'You didn't walk here from Dublin, did you?'

The butler seems frail to the point of decrepitude but he spins Harkin around with ease, before pulling off his coat with a practised tug that sends shrapnel grating inside Harkin's shoulder.

'Driscoll picked me up from the station.'

'Of course he did. Of course he did.'

Harkin looks about him. The long central hall relies on whatever light comes through the windows at the front of the house and those that circle the high roof above. The day, unfortunately, is overcast and when he looks up Harkin can see how the glass in the windows has been clouded by years of grime. The resulting gloom shadows the interior of the house, reducing the furniture to dark shapes. The walls are lined with dead animals, clustered in groups. As his eyes adjust, he sees a tiger, a lion and a small herd of decapitated antelope. The little light there is illuminates bared teeth and staring glass eyes.

'Had you any trouble on the road?' Murphy asks, leading him into the house.

'No. Apart from the fog.'

As he follows Murphy, he pass more animals: stags, a quantity of villainous-looking foxes, a badger and, for some reason, a border terrier. He can see cobwebs stretched between antlers and bare patches where fur has been taken by moths. The slain creatures look down on him – reproachful, melancholy, or, in the foxes' case, furious.

'Thank God for that. What with Egan's bandits seen this morning coming down from the mountains only five miles from here.'

Harkin is brought back to the conversation with a jolt. He wonders if the information about the column is correct.

'So close?'

'He has the whole country in a state of terror,' Murphy says, in a doleful tone.

There is movement on the staircase at the end of the long gallery and two huge wolfhounds come loping out of the gloom, tongues lolling and grey coats matted, their paws padding on the marble tiles. They approach Harkin with curiosity, the smaller of them sniffing at his crotch. They smell of wet wool and forest floor.

'Get out of that, Fiachra,' Murphy says, half-approvingly. 'Leave Mr Harkin alone, like a good beast.' He makes no effort to remove the dog, however, so Harkin pushes it away himself.

'He likes you,' a voice says.

When Harkin looks up he could swear he sees Maud Prendeville coming down the staircase, caught in a rare shaft of light. She has the pallor of a spirit, but then her heels begin to click as she approaches him across the marble chessboard floor, so he presumes she must be real.

'You look as though you've seen a ghost,' she says, squinting at him with amusement.

She is not Maud, he can see that now – although she has the same clear green eyes. He remembers, in the nick of time, Maud's younger sister.

'You must be Charlotte.'

He gives Fiachra a sharper shove, which the dog seems not to mind, sauntering off towards the peat fire that glows in the large fireplace and arranging himself in front of it like some canine pasha.

Charlotte takes his hand and he is grateful for the solidity the touch offers him. She would have been about fifteen the last time he saw her, which would make her twenty-three now.

'Did you have a pleasant journey down, Mr Harkin?'

He remembers his manners, at last.

'I am very sorry about Maud, Miss Prendeville. A terrible business.'

She gives him a half smile.

'Thank you.'

She examines him, as though seeing him afresh. When she speaks again, her tone is grave.

'I prefer Charles,' she says.

'Charles?'

'To Charlotte. Should we ever move past the formalities, Charlie is also acceptable.'

# CHAPTER 10

The dining room is, like the rest of the house, dark; its three large windows look out towards a black, squall-torn sea and a troubled sky that is blacker still. Harkin finds himself sitting at one end of a long table that has been set for five, although two of the places remain empty. The silver cutlery gleams dully in the flickering light of a single candle. Marble columns line the walls and another smouldering peat fire, bigger than the one in the entrance hall, pops and wheezes behind him. Portraits of Prendeville ancestors line the yellow silk wallpaper. Long-nosed, haughty men, and pale women each as elegant as the fashion of the time allows her. Lord Kilcolgan sits, slouched beneath their gaze at the top of the table: a silvering thicket of hair, half-closed eyes, another of those long noses, and a moustache that obscures his mouth and much of his chin. Charlotte sits opposite Harkin. The candle flickers in time with the rain that lashes the windows.

'We have a generator, you know,' Lord Kilcolgan mutters as Murphy places a bowl in front of him, the soup sloshing as it lands with a bump. 'For electric lights and so on. But they won't send a fellow from London to fix it. Say it's not worth risking a life with the situation being what it is. So we're reduced to candles.'

Harkin looks up at the layer of dust that covers the bulbs in the chandelier hanging over the table, and tries to remember if they were lit the last time he was here. He thinks not. Perhaps his expression reveals his thoughts because he sees Charlie glance at him quickly before looking away.

'Father,' she says.

'I know,' Kilcolgan says, nodding in Harkin's direction. There may be a smile underneath the moustache but Harkin cannot see it. 'I have become something of a bore about the electricity. Without the lights the house is too dark, you see. Too many shadows.'

The conversation lapses. Harkin finds his attention drawn, not for the first time, to the empty places. Charlie sees the movement of his eyes.

'I'm sure they'll be here soon. Murphy, is there any sign of Billy?'

Murphy shrugs and seems to think this is a sufficient response. Then he seems to remember there is a stranger present and summons an ingratiating smile for Harkin.

'I told him he was mad to go out, but he wouldn't listen,' he says. Then adds, as an afterthought, 'Miss Charlotte.'

'What soup is this, Murphy?' Lord Kilcolgan asks, examining it.

Murphy looks down at the bowl he is carrying and frowns.

'I'll ask herself,' he says.

He puts the last bowl in front of Harkin, and then disappears through the side door from where he can be heard descending the servants' staircase. In his absence, it seems to Harkin that the shadows in the room grow closer. The soup is the same grey as the exterior of the house.

'Mushroom,' Charlie says. 'It could be something else, of course, but I believe it should be mushroom. Today is Tuesday.'

Harkin lowers his head to hide his smile. He can hear steps climbing the stairs from the kitchen. He feels laughter building inside him and he knows it is of the nervous variety. He reminds himself that there is grief in the house.

An attractive woman in her late thirties, wearing a black dress with a high collar, and with her hair tied back, steps into the room and stands facing the table. She is silent, but her demeanour seems to be one of tested patience. Lord Kilcolgan looks a little unsettled by her arrival.

'We didn't mean to disturb you, Mrs Driscoll.'

'I exist to be disturbed, my lord. Did you have a question about the food?'

'Only that we were wondering what the soup was?'

'Can you not tell?'

'Is it perhaps mushroom?'

Mrs Driscoll's severe expression is hard to read, but on balance Harkin thinks she is not pleased by the question.

'Does it taste of mushroom?'

'It does,' Lord Kilcolgan says tentatively.

'Well then. Will you be wanting anything else?'

'That will be all for the present, thank you.'

The family exchange glances when she leaves and would perhaps have discussed the conversation, but Murphy returns, wheezing, from his journey to the kitchen. He makes a slow, careful expedition around the table, picks up a fork from the empty place setting for a reason that isn't quite clear, then disappears into the bowels of the house once again. Charlie gives her father a meaningful look.

'Yes, but what would he do with himself?' Lord Kilcolgan says. 'And we are used to him.'

'Hasn't he a daughter in Dublin?'

'Despises her. And she's not very fond of him. There's nothing to be done. Anyway, Mrs Driscoll wouldn't hear of it. There would be war if we were even to suggest it.'

Charlotte turns to him, her green eyes shadowed.

'Mr Harkin, you must see how reduced Murphy is. From when you last saw him.'

He pauses, considering his response. Then smiles.

'He does seem a little smaller.' He glances up and sees Charlie's grave expression and wonders if they have not noticed. 'And older, but isn't that often the way of things?'

'Quite so,' Kilcolgan says, after a long pause, then closes his eyes and lifts a spoon to his mouth. The soup leaves a creamy tideline on his moustache.

There is a clatter of boots running along the central hall and then heavy steps pounding up the central staircase. Something is knocked over along the way and clatters to the floor. The steps pay it no heed.

'That'll be Billy,' Lord Kilcolgan says, and there is a flicker of disapproval in his expression. 'He'll be soaked to the skin. Change of clothes, I shouldn't wonder.'

Sure enough, not more than a minute passes before the man himself appears, finishing the knot of his tie as he enters, his hair and face still wet from the rain outside, his cheeks rosy with the cold. He is wearing a dry tweed jacket.

'Don't get up, Mary,' he says to Harkin with a nod. 'I shall slip in, almost unnoticed.' He glances towards his father, who mutters something under his breath. 'Well, perhaps not entirely unnoticed.'

Harkin returns his friend's smile but it's immediately clear to him all is not well. The jollity seems forced and underneath the tousled blond hair, Billy's eyes are dark. His mouth curls, first up, then down, and Harkin wonders if Billy is even aware of it. If he didn't know better, he'd think Billy was on the verge of tears.

'It's good to see you,' Harkin says, and tries to send Billy some comfort through the warmth in the words.

'Mary?' Charlie asks.

'Yes, very unusual name,' Billy says, his brittle jollity back in play. 'Do you think there is some soup left in the tureen? I think I'll make poor Murphy's life a little easier and help myself.'

He stands and walks over to the serving table, lifts the cover from the tureen and inhales.

'Mushroom?' he asks and, when there is no answer from the table, he begins to help himself. Harkin can hear the rattle of the serving spoon against the china. It seems Harkin is not the only one with jittery fingers.

'Mary is my second name,' he says, feeling he should say something to distract the others from Billy's shakes. 'My mother is religious.'

'His other name is Francis,' Billy says. 'That's a girl's name, too.'

'Francis with an *i*,' Harkin adds. 'After Saint Francis. Who was not, so far as history records, a girl. That would be my confirmation name.'

There is yet another awkward silence in which Harkin contemplates the unusual situation of being the only Catholic present. It isn't as though there is a shortage of them in the country.

'Are you religious, Mr Harkin?' Charlie asks with a too bright smile.

He wonders if she is mocking him. He considers his answer and sees, in his mind's eye, an expanse of mud and water and broken things. Broken men as well. The image is so real that he feels sweat prickling his forehead and neck, and the mushroom soup rising up in his throat. He swallows it back down.

'No.'

He sees that Billy's face has lost all of its colour, despite the yellow light from the candles. A gust of wind rattles the windows and scatters rain against the glass. It reminds Harkin of machine-gun fire. He wonders if Billy had the same reaction to the question.

'Billy tells me you work for an insurance company,' Lord Kilcolgan says, when the quiet becomes oppressive.

Harkin thinks this is an odd choice of topic to get the conversation going again, given where it must inevitably lead. Still, it will be good to get it out of the way.

'The All-Ireland Insurance Company. We're a relatively new business, Irish-owned for Irish customers.'

'I see,' Lord Kilcolgan says, and Harkin can hear the question in the response. He can imagine Kilcolgan muttering something about Sinn Feiners if he were not present.

'And Maud was insured with them?' Charlie says, and he can see something like suspicion in her gaze. 'It seems a strange coincidence.'

'Not really. Your uncle was one of the original investors. I believe he took out various insurance policies when the enterprise began to trade, in order to give the company a start on the business side. These included life assurance policies on his close family members, as well as other risks, which he has maintained.'

'What?' Billy says, his interest piqued to the extent that he suddenly shrugs off his dark mood. 'All of us?'

'Not you, Billy,' Harkin says. 'You were uninsurable at the time.'

'Fair point,' Billy says. 'The war and all that.'

Harkin watches as his friend's gaze loses focus. He knows where it has returned to.

'In any event, as Billy may have mentioned, I have been asked to conduct a brief investigation into Maud's death, for the underwriters.'

Billy continues to examine his soup, not meeting anyone's eye, but Harkin can see he has the others' attention.

'And Sir John thought it would make sense for me to undertake the investigation immediately, given I would be here for the funeral.' They appear uncertain so he adds, 'An investigation is standard in this situation.'

'What situation?' Charlie asks, her words carrying a detectable chill.

'A violent death.' He regrets, too late, the bluntness of the words. 'The underwriters, you see,' he adds, as though absolving himself and the All-Ireland Insurance Company.

Lord Kilcolgan may not even have heard, for all the reaction he gives.

'And how did you end up working for this insurance company?' Charlie asks, in an offhand way that does not deceive him.

'Your uncle recommended me to them when I left the army. I was looking for a position and Sir John was kind enough to offer an introduction. You will recall I was his private secretary at one time, so he felt he could recommend me.'

His answer flows easily enough off the tongue. He has spent some time anticipating the questions he might be asked, and preparing his responses. Lord Kilcolgan has leaned back into his chair, his eyes shut, and he appears to be asleep, but then there is a quiver of the soup-lined moustache and a growl emanates from underneath it.

'Is there some question as to who is responsible for Maud's death, Mr Harkin? I wasn't aware of any.'

'The IRA has issued a statement—'

Harkin is cut short by a bark of laughter from Kilcolgan. It is not happy laughter. There is contempt in it.

'So you intend to uncover the real perpetrator. Is that it, Mr Harkin? You don't believe the rebels are to blame?'

Harkin chooses his words carefully.

'The report does not solely address culpability. My instructions are to review the circumstances. As you know, I cared a great deal for Maud. I will not shirk from assigning responsibility where it belongs, if I come to a firm conclusion.'

Lord Kilcolgan looks out of the window at the dark clouds, the wind and the rain. In the shadowed room, his features are indistinct.

'And if you discover someone else killed her, Mr Harkin? Then what?'

# CHAPTER 11

The rain has blown through by the time lunch ends, and a watery and patchy sunlight glints off the wet grass of the home meadow. Harkin makes no resistance when Billy takes his elbow and guides him down to the strand, even though another bank of dark cloud is already coming in from the west. The rain has softened the bite of the cold seaweed-scented air but he can still feel it scraping the Dublin soot from his lungs, particle by particle.

They take their time. They walk in silence and Harkin is grateful for the quiet. They walk into the wind at first, and it flings sand and salt at them while waves roll up the beach with a steady, relentless rhythm. The tide is going out and they follow the looping, froth-marked line of the waves' utmost reach and, when they reach the rocks and look back, theirs are the only footprints that mark the sea-smoothed surface. Indeed, were it not for the granite bulk of the house on its rise, they might be the only people left in the world, for there is no sign of anyone else.

'She never fully recovered,' Billy says in a low voice.

Harkin isn't sure whether Billy is speaking to him or to himself. He waits for a moment, to be sure one way or the other.

'It wasn't only the injury,' Billy continues. 'The fighting was very hard during the Rising, with shelling and machine-gun fire and many dead. We both know how these things can knock a person off their stride.'

'We do,' Harkin says, thinking back to the gassed soldiers on the train.

'She told me she wasn't herself when she sent you the letter calling off the engagement. It was something she regretted. There was nothing to be done about it, so I didn't tell you, and I don't think she regretted the decision – only the means of delivery.'

Harkin remembers that when Maud's letter came, they had been fighting on the Somme, and he'd been so certain he was going to die that it had been something of a relief. Maud and Ireland had seemed to exist only in another world, to which he had thought there was little prospect of returning. He had loved her, certainly, but by then the war had its teeth in him. It is only now, over two years since the end of it, that he feels something like himself again – even if the nightmares and day visions still surface from time to time.

'What happened to her?' Harkin asks, curious now. 'I know she stayed through the fighting, looking after the wounded and loading rifles, and when they broke holes through the walls to escape, she went with them.'

Billy pauses, taking his time.

'She was shot in the shoulder. Father was able to keep her out of jail and get her back here quietly, but it wasn't only a physical wound. I suppose she'd had an idea of a revolution being like the storming of the Bastille – all flags and cheering. Instead it was like any other war, and it shook her. When she wrote the letter to you, she was at the lowest point. She didn't feel she could carry on with the rebels either. She thought she'd failed them somehow. And with Arthur and myself in France, along with you, she felt she was pulled in two directions.'

Harkin remembers a notice in the *Irish Times*.

*Major the Honourable Arthur Prendeville, Irish Guards. Passed away from his wounds at Kilcolgan House on 12th December, 1919.*

Poor Arthur; it had taken him a little over a year to succumb to a wound received six days before the armistice. Of all the pointless deaths, the ones from the last days of the war, when everyone knew it was over, were the hardest. Harkin has to look away from his friend. The rawness in Billy's face is nothing to do with the exfoliating wind.

'I heard she wasn't well afterwards,' Harkin says, as gently as he can when half-shouting over the waves and the wind. He has heard some hints of her condition but nothing more. Within the movement, she is still held up as an example to be followed. 'Did it persist after those first few months?'

'It did. But here's the thing. She was better the last year or so. Certainly since Arthur died. It was harder while he was still alive. We all knew he wouldn't last long. But once he passed on, it was a relief for all of us. She started to ask about you, from time to time.'

'About me?'

'Just to know how you were – that sort of thing.'

'And that was a recent change?' he asks, unable to disguise his curiosity.

'She hardly could have. You were . . .' He seems to choose his words carefully. '. . . An awkward memory.'

'Do you think she met someone, perhaps? Someone else who cared for her?'

Billy shrugs.

'I wouldn't know. I know she stopped being such a recluse. She went up to Dublin from time to time. She went to Paris with a school friend. Maybe Charlie would know more.'

'But it's possible?'

'You think someone committed *un crime passionnel*? In Kilcolgan?' Billy snorts.

'It does seem quiet,' Harkin says. Billy smiles in response.

'The social highlight of our month was an invitation to play cards at my uncle's house.' Billy nods along the coast towards the West. 'Except I haven't the head for cards these days and Uncle John and I don't get on. Just as well, given the outcome.'

'Is he the same?'

'Uncle John? A little quieter but still as sanctimonious as ever. Tells me I have responsibilities and so on. I knew if I went along that night he'd only get me in a corner and tell me what a disappointment I am.'

They stand for a while, hands deep in their pockets. Harkin can barely feel the tip of his nose and suspects it may be dripping.

'Why do you stay here?'

'Money. We haven't any. We have the house and what's left of the land, but no one can pay rent these days. I don't have a choice.'

'You could get a job?'

'In London, perhaps, or Dublin, but I wanted to be here after the war. Just to walk around and ride a horse and enjoy not being shot at.' Billy glances over at Harkin, smiling. 'Then, of course, people started shooting each other here as well. You're right though. I should get out of here. Stand on my own two feet.'

'What about Sir John?'

'Oh, Uncle John has money, of course. He got everything when his rich American wife passed away. But he keeps it to himself. Father has to go begging to him for a few bob to keep the roof on top of the walls.'

'Driscoll tells me the Auxiliaries want to rent it for the duration of the Troubles.'

Billy looks over at the house.

'If it weren't for Maud, I think the IRA would have burned the place down by now.'

Which is true, Harkin reflects. Now that she's dead, they may still do.

'Can you tell me about the evening of the ambush?'

Billy pushes his hair back, and Harkin can see the strain and sadness.

'There isn't much to tell. Maud went to the card evening with Harry Cartwright around half past six – Uncle John picked them up. Maud was going to stay over. She must have changed her mind. Probably because Abercrombie was there. She wouldn't have been comfortable with him being under the same roof.'

'And yet she ended up coming home with Inspector Teevan.'

Billy shakes his head.

'I'm not saying she would have gone out of her way to take a lift from Teevan, but she knew him from long ago. He's from nearby and was always a decent sort. Abercrombie is a very different beast. I avoid him myself but Maud despised him and everything he stands for.'

Harkin considers the arrangement for the evening, given how close the two houses are.

'Would that have been unusual? For her to stay over?'

Billy shrugs.

'Not down here. The roads aren't as safe as they might be at night. The local Volunteers have a tendency to dig them up and block them to disrupt the police and military. Then there's the Auxies, who are a law unto themselves. Where possible, people travel during the day.'

'And her and Sir John? Did they get on?'

'Thick as thieves. Always have been, but more so recently.'

'And you?'

'Maud and I?' He looks confused. 'She was my sister.'

There's not much Harkin can say in response to that, other than to nod in agreement.

'I meant you and Sir John.'

Billy laughs, although it comes out more like a croak.

'We're going through a rocky patch. It's hard not to remember his goading us all into joining the fight. Arthur and I would have joined up anyway, but there was something not quite right about his enthusiasm for other men fighting a war he chose not to. It's not as though he was so very old. Willie Redmond was fifty-five when he joined up. John was forty-one. And then there's the knighthood they gave him for his patriotic efforts, which he had the gall to accept. So, no, we are not great friends. We tolerate each other at best.'

Harkin nods his agreement. Whatever about Arthur and Billy, he doubts he would have gone into the army were it not for Sir John's persuading him and others like him that it was a sure way of achieving Home Rule for Ireland and effective independence.

'What about Harry Cartwright?'

'A chap I went to school with. He thought he'd see the insurrection at first hand. He was a lovely fellow. Couldn't believe his luck at making it through the war. He often spoke of his good fortune.'

They smile. It's not that they care nothing for Billy's dead friend; it's just that they are a little numbed to the futility of young men's lives being cut short.

'Was he friendly with Maud?'

'No. If she *was* seeing someone, it wasn't him. He wasn't her sort. He was like a puppy. Always delighted with everything. She liked him well enough, but no.'

'So she left Sir John's house – for whatever reason . . . and then?'

Billy shakes his head sadly, as though he can shake her bad decision away.

'The first I knew about it was the shooting. I thought there must have been an ambush on the road and worried that poor Harry might have got caught up in it.'

'A lot of shooting?'

'Enough to get the job done. Rifle fire mainly. Forty or fifty shots? I had a look around in the morning before the police took the car away. Mainly .303s but some Mausers and pistol casings.'

'Were you asleep?'

Billy avoids his gaze.

'Not exactly. I was out for a walk.' He looks away, avoiding Harkin's gaze. 'I don't always sleep well these days. I like to go down to the stables at night. To listen to the horses. I like to listen to them sleeping. Don't ask me why.'

'I won't,' Harkin says, thinking of the times before the Troubles began, when he would wander the streets of Dublin until the sun came up.

'So what did you do?'

'I told myself I should stay where I was and leave whatever was happening to the police.'

'But you didn't do that in the end.'

'No. I remembered Harry was meant to be being dropped back, so I went back to the house, loaded up the shotguns, and then we walked down to find out what had happened. Four of us. Me, Sean Driscoll, Father and Charlie. We didn't take the guns in the end. Sean thought better of it. Father, too, I think. We were better off going down unarmed.'

'What about this final shot, after the others?'

Harkin glances across as he speaks and is surprised to see a sudden shift in his friend's expression. It might be that he is taking a moment to think back to the events of the fatal evening, or it might be something else.

'Yes, that's right. A few minutes after.'

'And everyone was with you in the house?'

'I was just walking up to the house when I heard it. Sean wasn't long after me.'

'How long after you?'

'A minute or two. No more than that.'

Harkin says nothing, remembering how Driscoll had said he had been right behind Billy and wondering if the discrepancy might be significant. He might need to have another word with Driscoll.

'What did the shot sound like?'

'You mean what weapon? Definitely a pistol, but not a big one like a Webley. If you are asking was it the one that killed Maud, then I would say it was. That's not to say it wasn't the IRA who fired it.'

Harkin thinks about Maud, lying in the back of Teevan's car, her killer looking down at her. He feels anger writhing in his stomach. That someone would kill her in cold blood. He waits a moment before composing himself.

'Driscoll said something unusual happened. The night of the ambush.' Billy's expression is that of an animal, perhaps a rabbit, caught in the open by complete surprise. 'The White Lady, I think he said.'

'The White Lady,' Billy repeats, and there is something like relief in his expression. 'That's all nonsense. A family superstition. I did see something but I was imagining it. Driscoll was with me and he saw nothing.'

'I thought he was behind you?'

Billy glances at him quickly.

'Earlier. I went out to the stables and he was passing. We walked for a while. There's not many around from the war, Tom. And Driscoll is solid, unlike me.'

'What did you see?'

'Something in the trees. It was most likely a deer, but at the time I wasn't sure. The story is that there is a smell that comes with her of rotting flowers, and I did smell something for a moment but it could have been anything. When Maud died I suppose I jumped to a conclusion.'

Harkin wonders why Billy isn't telling him the truth, but he nods his acceptance anyway. He pulls out his watch and looks at the time, taking a deep breath. He has someone else he needs to see.

# CHAPTER 12

The library at Ballynan House, where a maid has seated Harkin to wait for Sir John, is impressive; the walls are filled with bookshelves that reach up to within a few feet of the high, moulded ceiling. It smells of leather and paper and has the kind of stillness that rooms like this, insulated by millions of printed words, often seem to have. The only noise is the ticking of a clock that sits on the wide partner's desk that fills one half of the room. It is also warm with large cast-iron radiators giving off a kind of heat Harkin doubts is ever felt in Kilcolgan even in the summer. The frigid landscape which the two long sash windows look out on to seems a million miles away. It is a room that is designed to tell you something about its owner, he decides, and makes himself comfortable. He has little doubt that he will be kept waiting. It has always been Sir John's way.

When his host does finally enter, ten minutes later, Harkin is reminded how handsome the man is. He has chiselled cheekbones and honey-brown eyes that match the tweed suit he is wearing. He must be in his late forties now, but he looks younger and, somehow, even in the middle of winter, Sir John seems to be a little tanned. Perhaps it is something to do with the radiators.

Sir John smiles, although there is little happiness in it.

'It's good to see you, Tom. It's been far too long. I only wish it were under happier circumstances.'

'I was sorry to hear about Maud,' Harkin says, and Sir John gives a short jab of his head in acknowledgement, half-closing his eyes. His mouth compacts into a thin line, barely visible. When he speaks, his words are muffled so that Harkin has to lean forwards to hear them.

'An awful thing.'

Sir John seems to gather himself then, and directs Harkin back to the chair he has just risen from, before sitting down himself in the armchair that faces it. He crosses one leg over the other and folds his hands on his lap, looking at Harkin as though, for a moment, he has forgotten why he is there.

'Would you like to smoke?' he asks abruptly, as though he had drifted off somewhere else. He reaches into his jacket pocket to produce a blue enamelled cigarette case with gold hinges. A rich man's trinket.

'I'm all right,' Harkin says. 'But thank you.'

Although when the smell of the cigarette fills his nostrils, he feels a craving.

'How are things over at the house?'

'As you might expect. I told them I was here to investigate Maud's death for the insurance company.'

'How did that go down?'

'As you might expect,' Harkin says, flatly.

Sir John nods.

'I was surprised when I heard they were sending you, of all people. But I can see the advantages. You knew Maud, after all, and we know you.'

'I suppose that was the boss's thinking.'

'Did Driscoll pick you up at the station? Your superior tells me he is a Volunteer officer.'

'He did.'

'His involvement came as a surprise,' Sir John says. 'I would have thought, having served in France, he would have had his fill of fighting.' Then he seems to remember that Harkin, too, is now a Volunteer officer. 'Of course, both of you are to be commended for your commitment to the cause.' His smile seems strained. 'Did you come across him in France?'

Harkin thinks back to the trench.

'We were blown up by the same shell.'

Sir John's eyes seems to sharpen and Harkin wonders what the reaction signifies. Perhaps he thinks Harkin is making a joke in poor taste. Harkin decides it's best to change the subject.

'His mother works for the family?'

'She's the housekeeper.'

'And his father?'

'He died shortly after Driscoll was born,' Sir John says. And then, in answer to Harkin's unanswered question, 'Her parents worked for the family and she grew up in the house. She took a job in Dublin and married there, but when her husband died, she came back. She hasn't left since. Driscoll grew up here. He's always been very close to Billy, they were bosom friends when they were children. In fact, I think that's why Driscoll went to France – because Billy was going.'

Harkin remembers them being friendlier than was usual between an officer and someone from the ranks. It makes Driscoll's assertion that he wouldn't place any of the Prendevilles in harm's way more convincing. Or perhaps not.

'What is it he does for the family?'

'Anything that needs doing. Between his mother and himself, they keep the place just about standing. My brother takes little interest these days . . . since Arthur's death. You'll have seen yourself what a state the place is in,' he says, after a pause. 'They do what they can.'

Harkin can't help but look around him at the splendid room in which they are sitting. Sir John's American wife died in a hunting accident not long after the marriage, leaving him rich and with plenty of time to meddle in Home Rule and, now, rebellion. Sir John must see some of this in Harkin's expression, because he shrugs, unembarrassed.

'I help when my brother permits me, but a place like Kilcolgan needs an income and active management. It has neither.'

'What about Billy?'

'Billy? Just another mouth to feed. He seems oblivious to his responsibilities. He seems oblivious to everything.'

It isn't his business, but Harkin wonders, if anyone owes anyone anything, if it isn't Sir John Prendeville, the prominent nationalist who'd thought that Home Rule could be bought by young Irishmen shedding blood in the defence of the empire and who'd sent Billy and his brother off to war, who is in debt. The same Sir John Prendeville who is about to provide 200 Thompson guns to the IRA, so that young men can kill and be killed all over again in furtherance of a cause that Sir John believes to be just.

'What is it you want me to do?' Harkin asks. 'About Maud.'

There is no thought behind the words, but he can hear a trace of irritation in his voice and reminds himself that he is here to ensure Sir John's guns are delivered, and how important that is.

Sir John's expression hardens.

'Maud was murdered by the IRA. I would like someone to be held responsible for that.'

'Am I right in thinking you expect some sort of punishment to be administered?'

'Isn't that why you're here? I should be able to ask for that, surely.'

'And if it wasn't a Volunteer?'

Sir John gives a snort of disbelief.

'Then you had better find out who it was. Although the idea that someone just happened to wander along to the site of the ambush and kill Maud coincidentally seems most unlikely.'

'The column had no motive to kill her either, and say they were not responsible.'

Harkin watches Sir John's jaw twitch as he struggles to contain his anger.

'If nothing else, they were responsible for a reckless attack that left her dead.'

Harkin nods slowly.

'I'll investigate. You have to understand there are questions that have to be asked before I take a man's life. That is, just so we're clear, what you're asking me to do, isn't it? An eye for an eye?'

Sir John looks uncomfortable and the anger seems to seep out of him.

'If it does come to that,' Harkin continues, his voice carefully neutral, 'will you want to be present? To see the job done?'

Sir John frowns.

'You are, I presume, making some sort of a point.'

'I only want you to be aware of what you're asking me to do. In any event, at present I'm only certain that Teevan's motor car was ambushed and that Maud died in it. I'm not certain the two events are connected, strange as that may seem. If the column killed her, they wouldn't have to make up a story. She was, I'm sorry to say, in the wrong place at the wrong time.'

Sir John begins to speak but Harkin holds up his hand to stop him. The conversation is draining what little energy he has left, but he makes the effort to keep calm. Harkin has to suppress the urge to remind Sir John that his Thompson machine guns, with their rapid fire and .45 calibre slugs, will likely increase the number of unintended civilian casualties still further. He smiles and attempts to put an apology into it.

'I will find out who killed Maud and I'll deal with it. The life assurance policy, which I understand you're aware of, is an advantage, so I can ask questions openly. I have a few for you, as it happens.'

Sir John, to his surprise, gives him a grave nod.

'Of course.'

'Was Maud seeing someone? Romantically?'

Sir John's eyes seem to bulge and Harkin decides it was probably a question he should have worked up to. Sir John restrains himself, however, and answers calmly.

'I'm not privy to my niece's romantic inclinations. However, no. I am unaware of any such relationship.'

'Who was she friendly with, or unfriendly with?'

Sir John sighs.

'We are a very small community down here. There are some tradespeople in the town but we do not see them socially. Dr Hegarty passes muster, and his daughter, Mrs Wilson. Her husband, Robert, was killed at Cambrai and she runs the fishing lodge between here and Kilcolgan. She has some respectable long-standing guests who we also see from time to time. And then there are the Eustaces, and some of the army officers at the barracks. A lot of the people we would have considered friends have sold up or gone away until things calm down.'

'What about Teevan and Abercrombie? They were here that night.'
Sir John shrugs.

'I have to keep up an appearance of loyalty to the Crown. And they play bridge reasonably well.'

'How did she get on with them?'

'She didn't like Abercrombie but she tolerated Teevan. The inspector was well respected around here before the Troubles and she knew him from then. Abercrombie is a different kettle of fish.'

'But she came to play cards with them?'

Sir John looks uncomfortable.

'She did not know Abercrombie would be present. She came to keep Cartwright company as much as anything.'

'Would Billy not have been better? Cartwright was his friend, wasn't he?'

Sir John shrugs.

'Billy does not much care for me at present. Or cards.'

'Was there anything unusual about the last few weeks? Any disagreements or people staying at the house? Anything at all?'

'Not really. A cousin of ours on my mother's side, from Hampshire, came to stay a few times, but you would have met him at lunch.'

Harkin remembers the empty place at the table.

'Perhaps he was delayed. Tell me about him.'

'Hugo Vane. He's over here buying horses for the army. We don't have many guests these days, what with the roads being unsafe, so he's been very welcome.'

'Is he a civilian contractor or military?'

'He was a major in the Glosters during the war. I'm not sure how he ended up on the procurement side of things, but I believe he retains his rank.'

Now that Harkin thinks of it, Vane's name rings a bell. As does his occupation. He's sure one of the spies Vincent Bourke and his colleagues dealt with recently was supposed to be buying horses. Perhaps it would be sensible to pass a message back to headquarters to enquire after this Major Vane.

'Tell me about your card evening.'

'It was a small gathering. Cartwright, Dr Hegarty from the town, Moira Wilson, who as I mentioned is his daughter – she and Maud were friendly in Dublin, the Eustaces, Inspector Teevan and Major Abercrombie, Maud and myself. Some of Mrs Wilson's ladies – her permanent guests – were meant to attend but didn't feel up to it in the end. They are quite elderly.'

Harkin looks at the older man in surprise, making the connection.

'Mrs Wilson is Moira Hegarty?'

'She was. Of course, you would have known her in Dublin as well. She was at university at the same time as you.'

Harkin shakes his head in bemusement. He does indeed remember Moira Hegarty. He remembers her very well indeed.

'I thought she went to London.'

'She did. It's where she met Robert Wilson. They came back before the war and built the fishing lodge.'

Harkin takes a moment to collect himself, then brings the conversation back to the card evening.

'As I understand it, Maud was meant to stay the night with you. Why did she change her plans?'

Harkin watches as Sir John takes in a deep, ragged breath.

'I don't know exactly. It seemed to be a spur of the moment decision, quite late in the evening. Abercrombie had left earlier – there was some business needing attending to in the town, he said. He had intended to run Cartwright home and, in his absence, Teevan said he would take him instead. Maud decided to go with them. She seemed out of sorts so I didn't try to persuade her to stay. She could be stubborn in her ways. It's only a short distance, as you'll have seen on the way here. I should have insisted she stayed. The roads aren't safe at night. It's why everyone else stayed over.'

Harkin sees his regret and wonders if it is the source of Sir John's desire for justice – that he blames himself.

'What time did they leave?'

'Abercrombie left just after ten. Maud stayed till just before midnight. Teevan drove her and Mrs Wilson home, as well as Cartwright. The others stayed over.'

'Moira Wilson?'

'She was on the way. You'll have passed her establishment beside the bridge.'

Harkin remembers the house, with its long lawn leading down to the road. He thinks it is just as well for Mrs Wilson that her house is this side of Kilcolgan, and not further along. As for Maud's journey? A few minutes in a car. Time enough to get from this world to the next.

'No arguments? Nothing untoward? What about her and Abercrombie?'

'No. We dined and then played cards. However, you are right to say she didn't like the major. I think the fact that Teevan was driving is what might have persuaded her to take the risk. I doubt she would ever willingly have got in the car with Abercrombie, no matter what the circumstances.'

Harkin digests this, thinking it through.

'I'll talk to Mrs Wilson and her father, of course. I'll also want to speak to the Eustaces. And Major Abercrombie.'

At the mention of his intentions with regard to Abercrombie, Sir John's skin seems to visibly tighten. He shakes his head.

'I would advise you to stay clear of Abercrombie, Tom. The man is unpredictable.'

Harkin shrugs.

'I'm a respectable insurance claims assessor. I don't see how he can reasonably object. He may have information about the police investigation he would like to give me.'

Sir John holds up his hand.

'As for a police investigation? I'm not sure there has been much of one. They are satisfied that Egan's column are responsible. The facts speak for themselves. We're old friends, Tom, you and I, so I beg you to proceed with caution when it comes to Major Abercrombie.'

There's an obvious sincerity to the request, so Harkin nods his agreement, although he wonders at Sir John's concern, given he feels comfortable playing cards with the man. He suspects he knows the reason. Harkin, despite being an ex-army officer, is still from a Catholic and middle-class family. As far as Abercrombie is concerned, Harkin will be seen as a potential enemy. Sir John, despite his Home Rule credentials, is part of the Protestant ascendancy and therefore trustworthy. It is thinking like this, in an overwhelmingly Catholic country, that will lead to defeat for Abercrombie and his ilk, sooner or later.

'You will presumably be talking to the local Volunteers?' Sir John asks, interrupting Harkin's chain of thought.

'I should think so.'

Sir John rubs at the seam of his trouser leg and speaks without making eye contact.

'Needless to say, they mustn't be told about the guns, or my role in their procurement. Particularly not Driscoll.'

'I will be discretion itself,' Harkin says, thinking that another reason Sir John might not want his involvement known is if Harkin exacts some kind of punishment for Maud's death. He pauses, remembering that there is a more pressing concern. 'Speaking of the shipment, does anyone else know about it? Locally.'

Sir John looks at him sharply.

'Maud's murder has nothing to do with the shipment,' he says. 'Nothing whatsoever.'

Harkin allows a moment to pass in silence before he responds.

'Except that my presence here is, to an extent, because of the guns.'

Sir John says nothing for a long moment but Harkin holds his gaze, keeping his face impassive. Eventually, Sir John nods.

'The number of people involved is very limited, particularly in Ireland.'

At Harkin's prompting, Sir John lists the men and women who are aware of the shipment. Two are in America, one in Paris, and a handful in Ireland. Sir John has organised things well, except that one of the two women who was aware of the shipment was Maud Prendeville.

'I beg your pardon.' Harkin is surprised that his voice sounds as normal as it does. 'Maud was involved?'

'Yes.' Sir John sounds as though he is confirming an obvious fact, one that Harkin should have been aware of already. 'She assisted me on some aspects.'

This is news to Harkin. He knows that the shipment required negotiations and payment in Paris but presumed that Sir John had taken care of this. Now he remembers Billy's mention of Maud travelling there with a school friend.

'Billy said she visited Paris. Was that connected to the shipment?'

Sir John looks deeply uncomfortable.

'Once or twice. I was not always able to go when a matter had to be discussed.'

'You didn't think this was worth mentioning earlier?'

Sir John appears to be lost for words for a moment.

'Your superior knew of it. If he chose not to mention it to you, I don't see why I should have.'

Harkin thinks on this for a moment and wonders about the mysterious Major Vane and his recent visits. There is still something about the name that nags at him.

'How many times has Major Vane come down?'

'Three.'

Harkin considers this, thinking aloud.

'It is quite a distance to here from Dublin, and a dangerous journey for a British officer, what with an active column in the area, not to mention attacks on trains. He may be family but he isn't close family, is he? Do you think he might have been after something else?'

The air seems to go out of Sir John.

'He seemed to be after Maud, if anything.'

# CHAPTER 13

Moira Wilson's guest house is recently built, although as Harkin approaches he notices that the paint is beginning to peel from the window frames. Harkin hesitates for a moment, then knocks on the door. When it is opened, it is by a woman in a thick tweed jacket, carrying a blood-splattered knife. A clear blue eye examines him through a monocle with a quizzical air. She is as tall as he is, her black hair tied back. The monocle follows his gaze downwards to the knife. She frowns. It only emphasises how clear and smooth her skin is.

'A fish,' she says. 'It needed gutting and there's only me and Mary. You look well.'

'As do you.'

She looks behind him, as though expecting someone else.

'I suppose that's the thing with funerals.'

'What is?'

'You see people you haven't seen for a very long time.'

He finds himself smiling, despite the context.

'It must be nine years.'

She considers this, examining him.

'It feels like more. Are you staying at Kilcolgan?'

'I am.'

'Just as well,' she says, looking him up and down with the monocle. 'I very seldom take male guests who arrive with no luggage. I have standards, you see.'

'Where would we be without standards?'

'Indeed. I am glad we are agreed on that,' she says, lifting the knife and staring at it, as though she had forgotten she was holding it. 'Excuse me, I appear to be holding a blood-soaked weapon. I shall return directly.'

She steps back inside the hallway; there is a clang of metal against metal and she returns, her hands empty. She wipes them on her apron, then checks them for blood. Apparently satisfied, she extends her hand, a challenge in her gaze. He takes it.

'I am glad you are not bothered by the blood, of which there is barely any. Although there might be a slight whiff of fish.' She lifts her hand to her nose. 'Actually, not so slight.'

Harkin doesn't know what to say to that, so instead he follows her into a wide hallway, all oak and dark green wallpaper. The wallpaper looks expensive. A large stuffed bear stands just inside the door, wearing a bowler hat at a jaunty angle and with an umbrella hanging from an upraised paw. Harkin looks round for somewhere to hang his own hat and, in the absence of an alternative, places it on the bear's free paw.

'Is that the right place?'

'I should think so,' she says, reaching out to touch the bear's arm. 'This is Bertie. He guards the house.'

She pats the bear affectionately.

'We're normally closed in January,' she says, anticipating the question. 'We have some permanent guests, but there is little call for sightseeing at this time of year and until the situation changes,

94

not at any time of year. I miss the fishermen. I have to catch the fish myself these days. In any event, you may have to forgive a certain amount of informality.'

'Mrs Wilson?' an elderly voice calls out from somewhere upstairs.

She leans towards Harkin and says in a stage whisper, 'Some of my old ladies are under the mistaken impression they are still living in India, with me embodying each and every one of their army of servants. It is a wonder to me that India has not also rebelled if its inhabitants are constantly chivvied along in the way I am. You'll have a cup of tea? In the drawing room. In, say, five minutes' time?'

'Please don't inconvenience yourself on my behalf. I only dropped in to say hello.'

She looks at him gravely, then opens the door to what appears to be her drawing room.

'Five minutes. And then you will have my undivided attention.'

She smiles one last time and then turns to shout up the stairs.

'I'm coming, Lady Blaney. Directly.'

Harkin walks to one of the drawing room's large windows and looks out at a flat rock a short distance off the beach, revealed by the receding tide. As he watches, a seal rolls its bulk up onto the surface. It looks as though it plans to sleep, and it seems to him a very good idea. He sits down in the nearest chair and closes his eyes.

When he opens them again, it is because of the sound of a tea tray being unloaded onto a low table. He finds himself looking from behind at a young woman in a maid's uniform. When she turns suddenly to face him, it is with a scowl.

'I thought you were asleep,' she says, accusingly.

'I only had my eyes closed.'

She raises her eyebrows at this, and he wonders if she thinks he has been looking at her in a salacious manner. He feels his cheeks redden.

'You must be Mary,' he says, keen to break the silence.

She looks at him suspiciously and hands him a cup.

'There's your tea. Mrs Wilson will be down in a minute.'

Harkin watches her leave the room. She watches him in turn, positioning the tray to cover her lower body. He finds the encounter, short though it has been, disconcerting.

He looks around him. Two long chesterfields take up a large part of the room, while a folded-up card table leans against a tall bookcase, its felt surface marked in places by careless ash. There are magazines in a canterbury rack beside the nearer of the sofas, but none of them look recent. Someone has left some half-finished knitting on one of the several armchairs. It seems comfortable, if a little run-down. He can understand why the elderly ladies like the place.

Harkin looks up as the door opens and finds Moira gazing at him.

'I understand from Sir John you have some questions for me.'

'Did he call?'

'Shortly before you arrived,' she says. 'He said you would drop in on your way back to Kilcolgan. I see Mary has brought some tea. That's good. One can never be entirely certain what she will do.'

'She seems a sensible girl.'

She looks at Harkin in surprise, before taking a seat and lifting the lid of the teapot to look inside.

'Do you think so? I often wonder. She's half wild beneath that demure surface. She might do anything at any moment.'

He smiles. She hasn't changed much at all.

96

'I thought you were in London.'

'I was for a while.'

'Maud never told me you came back. Billy never mentioned you. I had no idea.'

She smiles.

'Would you have come to see me?'

Harkin thinks about the practicality of visiting with Maud living less than a mile away.

'I might have written. We have always been good friends.'

She considers this statement and he detects a hint of mischief to her smile.

'I seem to have always known where you were. I knew about the engagement, of course. Then I knew about the end of the engagement. Perhaps I should have written. But then, I was married, and I'm told it's not done to write to old flames when you are married. I'm not sure Robert would have minded. He was very calm.'

Harkin looks at her in surprise. They had been close, part of the same group of friends at university but perhaps there was something more between them. He decides to change the subject.

'Your monocle . . .' he begins, before finding that he is stranded at the beginning of a sentence it would be foolish to continue with.

'My monocle?' she repeats.

'I meant,' he begins again, 'that it's unusual.' Then he shuts his mouth and concentrates on keeping it shut.

She leans towards him.

'Shall I tell you a secret?'

He feels a slight heat on his cheeks and it bothers him more than it should.

'If you would like to.'

'My left eye is indeed a little weaker than the other, but the monocle is not entirely necessary. I just like the look of it.'

'I see,' he says.

She taps it with a long fingernail.

'It makes me feel a little like a pirate. I know pirates wear eye-patches, but all the same . . . Go on then, ask me your questions.'

Harkin takes a deep breath, gathering his thoughts.

'I'd like your recollections of the evening before Maud died.'

'Are they relevant?'

Harkin shrugs.

'I won't know if it's relevant or not until I hear it, I suppose.'

'Fair enough.'

Moira goes over the guest list, what they ate for supper, who played with who at cards and all the other little details of a social gathering. Her account tallies with that of Sir John.

'Of course, if I had known Abercrombie was to be there for the evening, I wouldn't have gone and I doubt Maud would have either. I don't know what John was thinking. It's not only the Auxies who burn people out, and where would my Memsahibs go if this place went up in flames?'

He wants to disagree with her on this point – insist that the IRA would never burn out a house populated entirely by women – but he knows he cannot. The retaliations on both sides are steadily escalating.

'Did you know Inspector Teevan would be there?'

'Jim Teevan is a different story. He was from the other side of the mountain. He knows everyone around here. He knew he would have to live here after all this is done. Abercrombie sees us as a hostile population that has to be subjugated.'

'Abercrombie left early, though?'

'There was a telephone call from the barracks. It was just as well. Maud wasn't often angry, but she was angry that night. And not just with Abercrombie – with John Prendeville as well. Although she hid that better.'

This is news to Harkin. He leans forwards.

'How do you know this?'

Moira Wilson frowns. The thin lines barely ruffle her high forehead, as though the skin clings tight to the bone underneath.

'I was outside in the courtyard just before supper.' She looks down at her hands. 'You will recall that I like to smoke the occasional cheroot.'

Harkin reaches into his pocket for his cigarette case, and holds it open towards her. She peers inside it for a moment, then reaches out to take one.

'If anyone comes, you will take this from me.'

'I was planning to have one myself.'

'I don't see why that would change things. I quite often smoke two cheroots at the same time.'

Moira Wilson exhales a plume of smoke when he lights the cigarette for her.

'An unfortunate habit, but we all have our weaknesses. Anyway, I was standing there against the wall to stay out of the rain and not be seen when I heard them arguing in John's study. Maud and Sir John.'

'What about?'

'She was telling him she felt he had betrayed her, that he had put her in an impossible situation. I presumed she was talking about Abercrombie being there. Maud didn't approve of Abercrombie's activities, of course.'

It's Harkin's turn to frown.

'That's all you heard? Nothing else?'

Moira Wilson looks slightly embarrassed.

'I moved away. It was a private conversation.'

Harkin tries to make sense of Maud and Sir John arguing, particularly in the light of Sir John saying he'd no idea what Maud had been upset about.

'Were they both angry, or only Maud?'

'Yes, both of them, although perhaps Maud was the angrier. I had the sense neither of them wanted to be overheard. You know the way people like the Prendevilles argue in public, almost out of the corners of their mouths. It was a bit like that.'

'Did she say anything about it to you afterwards?'

'Nothing. But we were never really alone. We sat down to supper and then we played cards, and then Teevan drove us home. I was dropped off first, and you know what happened to the others. She was not in good form, however. She was barely civil and she wasn't the only one, either.'

'Who else?'

She sighs.

'I think it's fair to say Jim Teevan despised Abercrombie, and the major wasn't too fond of him either. They were sniping at each other all evening. They'd had some sort of meeting and it did not go well.'

'Teevan and Abercrombie?'

'Isn't that what I said?'

'What sort of meeting?'

'I don't know. They came out of it when I showed up, the pair of them with faces like thunder.'

'Do you know what had them at odds?'

'I'd be guessing, but I know Teevan thought Abercrombie's methods were short-sighted.'

Harkin nods at this. Most of the Auxiliaries have no ties to Ireland and see the war in purely military terms, with no thought to the long-term effects of their actions. His next question is more delicate, but he can think of no delicate way to approach it.

'Was Maud seeing someone, do you think?'

She considers the suggestion, one of her long fingers tapping gently on her teacup as she does so.

'She might have been, but there aren't many possibilities. All of the young men of her kind were either killed off in the war or are sensibly staying elsewhere for the duration of the Troubles.'

'Her kind?'

'Oh, you know. The landed gentry and the like. She might have been a rebel but she wasn't going to run off with a farmer's son.'

'She ran off with me,' Harkin says.

'She didn't exactly run off with you and you were not any old farmer's son. Do you need me to list all your many accomplishments, your academic brilliance and your comeliness? I have them at my fingertips. Mind you, I'm certain Lord Kilcolgan was delighted she jilted you.'

'I don't doubt it,' he says, smiling. Then he runs over her words again in his mind and finds his cheeks are once again warm. 'She was friendly with you as well, though. She wasn't a snob.'

She inclines her head to look at him with a speculative expression.

'Because I'm only the local doctor's daughter?'

'That's not what I meant.'

She smiles.

'I married Robert, which helped – and you're right, she wasn't like some of the others. Nor was Robert. It helped that he was an atheist, of course. Atheists are allowed to marry the likes of us, you see, which was a great relief to both of us. Otherwise we might have had to live in sin. Not that everyone was pleased for us.

101

Robert's mother didn't speak to him for a year and a half, and my own mother upped and died.' She pauses for a moment. 'She was quite ill already, to be fair, but I couldn't have married someone more unsuitable. An atheist? Ideally she'd have had me marry a priest, but there are practical problems with that.'

He remembers the portrait of a soldier in a captain's uniform in the hall. He decides he must look at the man more closely.

'It must have been difficult,' he begins.

'Before or after he died?'

'Both, although I meant losing him.'

Her half-smile is as brittle as dried paper.

'This used to be a good little business, you know,' she says, changing the subject. 'Nice people came here. I liked them. Now it's just me and the ladies.'

Moira Wilson seems lost in thought, and Harkin doesn't want to interrupt her. After a moment or two, her eyes fix on his and he's aware he has her full attention once again.

'There was a cousin of hers came from time to time, but apart from that, the pool was very shallow.'

'Hugo Vane?' Harkin asks, still curious about this persistent cousin.

'The very man.'

'Do you think there could have been anything between them?'

She ponders for a moment.

'It's a possibility.'

# CHAPTER 14

Harkin takes his time walking back to Kilcolgan, remembering that Driscoll has told him that the house will be full of friends and family for the funeral the following afternoon. The sky is already darkening over the hills to the east when he turns in and passes the spot where Maud and the others died. He stops and listens to the wind in the trees and the sound of his own breathing. There is an atmosphere about the place, an echo of the event itself or something close to it. He wonders if it is only his imagination that he feels Maud's presence close by and the thought reminds him of the incident beside the Ha'penny Bridge. If it really did happen at the time of Maud's death, it poses questions he is not sure he wants to ask or, indeed, to have answered.

Harkin looks along the drive towards the house, its lower windows glowing in the gloom, and thinks he sees movement. He watches and waits and, after a little while, a figure can be seen approaching. A man, as tall as he is, walking slowly as though reluctant to reach his destination.

'Do you mind if I join you?' he says, when he comes closer.

The voice has the polite indifference that suggests an Englishman of the better sort. A good-looking fellow with a straight nose and a military moustache. Harkin doesn't answer, only nods his consent, and they stand for a while, looking at the slick of oil and the chipped granite.

'She didn't deserve this,' the man says. 'None of them did.'

Harkin considers Teevan and the little that he knows about him and can't find it in his heart to disagree. There will always be good men on both sides of a war. He sighs and knows the man will take it as his agreement.

'You must be Harkin,' the man says, turning to look at him.

'And you must be Vane,' Harkin says.

'Shall we walk back to the house?'

It is dark underneath the overhanging trees, and the sound of their footsteps seems amplified in the enclosed space.

'You were delayed this morning?' Harkin asks, when it seems as though the silence between them is becoming awkward.

'Yes, I needed to see a man in Dublin quite urgently. Otherwise we might have ended up travelling down together.'

There is a little more light when they leave the shade of the trees and Harkin glances across at Vane quickly, wondering if there is some significance to his mentioning this meeting. As he does so, Vane leans towards him, as though checking something himself.

'You seem familiar, if you don't mind my saying,' he says.

Harkin keeps his face impassive, reaching inside his pocket for his cigarettes.

'Do I?' He makes a pretence of examining Vane in his turn. 'I don't think we've met but it's certainly possible.'

'You were with the Royal Dublin Fusiliers, weren't you? First battalion?'

'For a while,' Harkin says, alarm clenching at his stomach. 'You?'

'Glosters. Perhaps we met over there? We were alongside your first battalion once or twice. Passchendaele, certainly. Were you around for that?'

There's an intonation to the question that reminds him of when the Germans would send over a single shell for range and distance. This fellow, Harkin could swear, *knows* he was in Passchendaele. He reminds himself that it's likely he has the information from Billy, but Harkin decides to proceed cautiously all the same.

'I don't remember much from Passchendaele. I was knocked about a bit. Concussion.'

'I'm sorry to hear that. I wish I remembered nothing about Passchendaele. Still, that which does not kill you and all that.'

'If you say so,' Harkin replies, and then, hoping to change the direction of the conversation, opens his cigarette case, takes one for himself and offers the case to Vane.

'I don't mind if I do,' Vane says.

'What brings you to Ireland?'

They are close to the house now and Vane halts and, after a brief search, finds a lighter in a pocket. The flame, over which they both lean, reveals an intentness in the major's expression which increases Harkin's discomfort.

'Horses,' Vane says with a smile. 'For the army.'

'I thought the Glosters were an infantry regiment.'

Vane's smile broadens, as if congratulating Harkin.

'Like you, I have other strings to my bow.'

'Like me?'

'Insurance, isn't it? Amongst other things as well, I'm sure.'

Harkin concentrates on his cigarette, doing his best to keep his concern under control.

'Yes.'

'Well then, if you're working in insurance, why shouldn't I be buying horses?'

'No reason at all. Although, I've left the army.'

'Yes, indeed you have. We mustn't forget that. Anyway, these days the army is always seconding chaps here and there.' Vane exhales a cloud of smoke. 'Lord Kilcolgan tells me you doubt the IRA is responsible for Maud's death. That you're down here investigating on behalf of your employers. Did Sir John really have a life assurance policy on Maud? It seems rather odd.'

'I'm not really supposed to discuss our clients' insurance arrangements with unconnected persons.'

Vane chuckles, and the sound of it causes a cold sweat to prickle the nape of Harkin's neck.

'Quite so. Are you permitted to discuss your reasoning for doubting the IRA killed Maud?'

'I don't see why not.'

Harkin chooses his words carefully when he explains about the single shot and the IRA's disavowal of the act. The glowing tip of Vane's cigarette reveals the major's concentration on his words.

'I suppose it's a slim possibility,' Vane says, when he finishes, 'but perhaps a little far-fetched?'

'It just seems an odd inconsistency.'

'Their denying it?'

'Yes. Why bother? She was, after all, travelling with an RIC district inspector.'

The major considers this.

'Will you be asking them?'

'Me? Ask the IRA?' Harkin says, attempting to sound sceptical.

Vane circles his cigarette. Indicating their surroundings.

'I don't know Ireland very well, Harkin, but I should think they might want to tell you their version of the story, if they did in

106

fact leave her alive. They're unlikely to talk to the authorities but they might talk to you. Don't you think?'

'I suppose they might,' Harkin says, non-committally.

'That's what I would do,' Vane says, then adds, examining Harkin, 'I suspect you are well ahead of me there, though. A clever fellow like you.'

There is a short silence which Vane breaks by looking at his wristwatch with the surprise of a man who has forgotten he owned one. He drops his half-smoked cigarette to the ground and stamps it out with his shoe.

'Is that the time? We should dress for dinner.'

'I'll just finish this and I'll be in,' Harkin says.

Vane smiles and makes his way into the house, leaving Harkin with his cigarette.

He stands there, smoking, and thinking back over the conversation. It could be his imagination, but it felt as though Vane was toying with him. If Vane is involved in intelligence, and Harkin has a strong suspicion that he might be, then Dublin should be able to identify him. In the meantime, there are plenty of rocks in this part of the country. If the worst comes to the worst, he will find a rock and hide himself under it. The door to the house opens and Billy comes out.

'Vane said you were out here. Did you bring evening wear from Dublin?'

Harkin gives him a dazed look.

'Not to worry,' Billy says, coming closer and taking his elbow. 'I'll fix you up. You're about Arthur's size.'

# CHAPTER 15

An hour later, Harkin finds himself standing in the long hall that forms the spine of the house, a glass of madeira in his hand, wearing a dead man's clothes and being interrogated by an elderly man of impressive height and even more impressive whiskers. General Somerville is holding a tumbler full of whiskey and, to judge from his red face and slight sway, it's neither his first of the evening, nor a beverage he's unfamiliar with.

'Harkin, you say?' The general looks at him suspiciously. 'No, don't know the name. How do we know you? Who are your people?'

Harkin looks around him at the faded elegance of the mainly elderly gathering and wonders, not for the first time, what he is doing here. He can see Vane on the other side of the room, and notices that the major looks over from time to time, as though checking in case Harkin might run off.

'I went to Trinity with Billy and then I served with him during the war.' The general looks dubious, and Harkin finds he resents the man's questioning him as though he were some wayward trooper up in front of him on a charge. He allows some of the resentment to seep into his reply. 'My father was a solicitor. My mother is a widow. My brother one of the glorious fallen.'

The general's eyes widen, then his downturned lips break into a smile.

'I have you. Maud's chap.' He turns to call across the room in a loud grating voice to an equally tall matron with a pince-nez and a feather boa. 'Clem? He's Maud's fellow. The one she threw over. His father is a solicitor.'

There is a momentary lull in the conversation and twenty or so pairs of eyes turn to face Harkin. Out of the corner of his eye he can see Billy break off his conversation and then he is beside Harkin and taking his elbow.

'General, may I take Captain Harkin away from you?'

'Captain, is it?' the general says, approvingly. 'Of course, of course.'

The general makes his way across the room to pass on this final nugget of information.

'You look a little shook,' Billy says in a quieter voice, even though a sheen of sweat is making his own forehead shine in the candlelight.

'Just tired, that's all.' The evening coat Harkin is wearing smells of mothballs and, as the room warms up, its previous owner.

'You've made quite the impression on Hugo Vane.'

'Have I?' Harkin says, his stomach twisting.

'He's been singing your praises to Father. I told him he must have the wrong fellow.'

'He's an interesting man. Have you mentioned me to him before? Just as a matter of interest.'

'No, not at all. Why do you ask?'

'No particular reason. He said he was in the trenches alongside ours at Langemarck. I was wondering if perhaps you'd been talking over old times.'

Harkin can see a shadow pass behind Billy's eyes for a moment, before he shakes his head, as if to rid himself of the memory of Passchendaele as well as the question.

110

'God, no. I never even want to think about that place, let alone talk about it.'

'Not even to Maud?'

'Maud? Maud had her own problems. I wouldn't have burdened her with mine on top.'

Billy's answer does raise the question of who or what is Vane's source. It's a question that gives Harkin pause for thought.

'Where did all the servants come from?' he asks, nodding at the staff who move through the crowd with a calm efficiency well beyond the elderly Murphy, although under the watchful eye of Mrs Driscoll, who observes them from the second step of the staircase, giving direction when needed.

'Uncle John. The wine as well. He says he wants to see Maud off in style. Drink up. He'll no doubt take back any bottle that isn't empty tomorrow.'

There must be a hundred candles in the room, giving off a scent of beeswax that mixes with the smell of the logs in the fireplace to almost overpower the damp, decay and wet dog that he remembers from earlier. The candles' yellow glow does not quite reach up to the gallery landing on to which the doors to the bedrooms open. He sees a face looking down on them for a moment and thinks it might be Bridget, the maid, but she leans back when she sees him, disappearing into the darkness.

The guests themselves are in good spirits, despite the occasion, and the candlelight is forgiving. Up close it is possible to see that their dress is often from ten or twenty years earlier – a little worn and in need of alteration, the white waistcoats no longer as pristine as they might once have been. It is also curious how old the guests are, with only a handful of younger women and no young men at all except for Vane, Billy and himself. He comments on it to Billy, remembering Moira Wilson's remark from earlier.

'Most men my age have gone elsewhere. There's nothing here for us now, in the country at least, and it's not safe either. I hope being Maud's brother is some protection, but it's hard to be certain. The general was held up for his guns by Volunteers just before Christmas. Everyone knows a family whose house has been burned to the ground or someone who has been told to leave the country on pain of death or murdered as a police informer. We've been lucky.'

Harkin thinks about the smouldering cottage he passed that morning, and the tortured Volunteer left dead at the crossroads.

'It will be over soon,' he says, but he knows that things will never go back to the way they were.

# CHAPTER 16

It might be tiredness, or Sir John's generosity with his wine, but Harkin's head is not quite with him when he slips out of the drawing room. It is quiet in the long hall and the candles are no longer lit. He is just wondering how he is going to make his way up to his room when the door opens behind him. He turns to find Lord Kilcolgan holding a brass chamber-stick, its candle already lit.

'You'll need this.'

Harkin remembers passing a table of them as he left the room, but Harkin having electricity in his small suburban home, their purpose hadn't occurred to him in his befuddled state.

'Thank you for coming down.' Kilcolgan's voice is even gruffer than usual; the candle's flame lights him from below so that the contours of his face are deeply shadowed. 'Maud would have been pleased.'

For a moment Harkin thinks Kilcolgan is going to add to this, but instead the older man, flustered, thrusts the chamber-stick at him and retreats so quickly into the drawing room that there is no time to say anything in reply. Harkin looks at the door and considers following him back in, but then decides it is too late – and what, after all, would he say? Instead, he turns and makes his way across the marble floor towards the staircase and hopes he can remember where his room is.

As the noise of the others recedes, the sounds that Harkin makes – his footsteps, the rustle of his clothes as he moves, even his breathing – become more pronounced. The house has a thick silence which seems to magnify them. The shadows stretch out around him, across the chequered tile floor, illuminating the animals that line the walls, their eyes seeming to follow him as he moves.

He has felt like a stranger most of the evening, conscious of the hundred ties that bind the others while excluding him. At least he managed to speak to the Eustaces, but they could tell him nothing about the card evening – or Maud – that he didn't know already. Now he finds that the long day has caught up with him, and left him exhausted.

When Harkin begins to climb the staircase, each step creaks in a different key and he is conscious of a murmur of wind coming through the window alongside which he passes. It sounds like a warning whisper. He clings to the thick banister, his dead man's clothes like a weight on his shoulders. He stops on the landing, looking back down along the hallway despite his better judgement, and sees, at the far end, the amber glow of the fireplace grow bright for an instant as a gust of wind comes down the chimney. If it is giving out any warmth, it does not reach this far; the air is chill upon his skin.

When he eventually reaches his bedroom at the back of the house, he closes the door behind him and leans against it, breathing heavily. The room is smaller than he remembers, almost claustrophobic, as though the walls are closing in on him. It has been used as a place to store old luggage when not putting up the likes of him. A stack of cases and trunks stands along one wall, with faded hotel labels and military destinations still stuck or chalked on their cracked leather exteriors. But there is a fire in the grate that is still lit, just about, even though the candle flickers when the wind, with a plaintive whistle, slips through a gap in the window frame. His breathing gradually slows and he does his best to clear his head. There is a key in the door and he turns it, locking himself in, though he has nothing to be afraid of. He is just tired. There is nothing more to any of this that a good night's sleep will not fix.

Harkin pulls back the curtains and finds the gap between the sash window and its frame and finds a sock in his suitcase to plug it with. There is a stillness now in the room, despite the occasional laughter that echoes up from below. Outside, the wind is pulling at the trees and, in the distance, waves roll onto the shore.

He leans his forehead against the glass, closing his eyes. How long he stays in this position, he has no idea, but the creak of a floorboard somewhere reminds him that he is in a house full of strangers. He closes the curtains and begins to undress in the light of the single guttering candle and the feeble fire, and he remembers the stories Maud would tell about the house and its past. Then he remembers the ghost that Driscoll says Billy saw before Maud's death. His mind wanders back to the last time he stayed in Kilcolgan, before the war, but he cannot think about that visit or Maud now. He is not strong enough. Instead he takes a few minutes to write a brief letter about Vane which he hopes Driscoll will be able to forward to Dublin then lies down, blows out the candle and pulls the blankets up around his chin.

He does not fall asleep immediately, instead watching the swirling shapes the fire throws up on to the ceiling. He does not let his eyes close. He is not ready to brave sleeping yet.

A motor car arrives outside, the latecomers complaining loudly about Volunteers making even funerals impossible. He listens as the last of the guests make their way upstairs to bed and hears someone laugh nearby, then there is only the moan of the wind, the slow creaking of the house's timbers, like a ship at anchor, and an occasional low metallic clang from somewhere in the pipes.

If he sleeps, he fears he will dream of the war. So he lies there in his narrow bed, watching the last glow on the ceiling. Eventually, however, the sounds of the house, the sea and the wind pushing against the window combine into a strange music in which he loses himself.

# CHAPTER 17

*A* night-time road stretches ahead of Harkin like a long, twisting hangman's rope. He is in the passenger seat of a car which is being driven at breakneck speed. The car's headlamps are like searchlights that flick back and forth across the low, rough country, turning the stone walls that line the road white. The car is going too fast, but he can't hear any engine, only the swish of its tyres as it navigates the bends and turns. Somehow he knows that the journey ends with a death and he finds himself pushing back into the leather seat, his hands rising up of their own accord to cover his face. It is cold in the car and he feels it creeping through his veins, turning them to ice.

Ahead he sees a low fog, bare trees reaching up from it like bony fingers. Then they are inside it but the car does not slow down, the driver somehow knowing when to turn and when to slow. Then the car passes through stone gates and they are travelling along an avenue of closely overhanging trees. They have no leaves, only bare thin branches. He reaches up to touch them as they pass but they are out of reach, and then the trees are behind them and the house is up ahead, black against the dark night sky.

The car comes to a halt and the driver gets out as lights begin to appear at the windows. At first he thinks the lights are candles, but *then the windows explode outwards, the glass glittering like welding sparks as it falls to the ground, while great tongues of flame reach up towards the sky. He can hear the fire roar. It consumes the building. He can smell the burning flesh. He can hear the screaming.*

*And now he recognises the house.*

# CHAPTER 18

Harkin is awake, the cotton of the pillowcase damp against his cheek. He gathers himself.

The house was Kilcolgan, of course, and he recognises the road as being the one that runs to it from the town. He goes back over the dream's sequence again and again, and each time the feeling of dread in the driving car almost overwhelms him. He doesn't like to think about the time before, after Passchendaele, when dreams and reality intertwined, but he can't help but think that his present situation, with day visions of wounded soldiers and constant nightmares, is beginning to feel familiar. Harkin thinks back to Flanders and the mud, and how it could swallow a man who lay down for a moment's rest. He feels like that now – that if he sleeps, the darkness will swallow him and he will never surface from it.

Harkin reaches for the brass lighter he left beside the stub of the candle, running his thumb back across the flint wheel. An orange flame spills out, along with the reek of petrol. The flame, like his hand, is unsteady, but he manages to light the candle. He checks his watch – a few minutes past five. He must have slept, which is something. The sky, when he pulls the curtain back, is

119

black, and all that can be seen is his own faint reflection in the glass. Even with no electricity because of the curfew, there is always light somewhere in Dublin. Here, there is nothing. For a moment he is overcome by a sense of his own insignificance, the void that surrounds him reaching out into the universe, and he swallows so hard it turns into a half retch.

He needs to get out of this room; it stinks of his own fear. Harkin decides he will take the candle and the novel he brought down from Dublin and he'll sit in the dining room until morning. Bridget will be up soon, if not Mrs Driscoll or Murphy, and they will surely give him a cup of tea. In the meantime, the book will focus his scattered mind. He dresses quickly, then closes the bedroom door behind him with the softest of clicks and feels out each step as he makes his way to the staircase, straining to make no noise. He doesn't want to wake anyone. He just wants to sit for a while and bring his senses into line. When he reaches his destination, he sits himself down in the same chair he sat in the night before, and places the candle on the table in front of him.

He opens the book at the page he has marked. The hero has been spending a lot of time being chased around Scotland by German spies, if he remembers right, while being rescued by people he half knows at convenient moments. It is all nonsense, of course, but enjoyable all the same. Apart from the circle of light around the candles, the room is dark, except for the reflection of its flame on the cutlery and plates that are already laid out for breakfast. Somewhere in the room a clock ticks – fat, whirring clicks. He sighs, and something – a slight movement perhaps – makes him look up. There is the outline of a man sitting at the far end of the table, who seems to be examining Harkin in turn, before he looks away.

Harkin's breath shortens but the man seems real enough. He must have been there all along, sitting quietly, watching him come into the room and making himself comfortable; one of the late arrivals from the night before, perhaps, here for the funeral and delayed by dug-up roads and barricades. He cannot quite see his face in the darkness but there is just enough light to make out that he is wearing an officer's tunic and the faint gleam of three pips on the sleeve indicates he is, or perhaps once was, a captain.

Harkin opens his mouth to say something, to apologise for disturbing the man's solitude, but there is something about the man's stillness that stops him speaking. It's conceivable, after all, that Harkin isn't the only one who revisits the trenches and their horrors in the sleeping hours. He decides to leave the other man in peace. He'll talk to him when the girl comes in to light the fire.

Harkin feels the outline of the cigarette case in his pocket, extracts it and lights one from the candle. The smoke hangs in the air, gently turning over on itself in the half-light. He didn't smoke before he joined up. He didn't even smoke when Maud gave him the cigarette case. His brother Martin told him that he would when he got to France. Martin wasn't always right about things, but he was right about that. Harkin exhales a small cloud of smoke.

The book draws him in. He likes the way the story twists and turns – how no one is quite who they seem to be. He glances up from time to time at his fellow insomniac, but after that first cool examination, the man ignores him. He just sits with his hands folded on the table in front of him – a little like a priest. There is something familiar about the profile but he cannot place it.

The approaching dawn begins to colour the sky and the room takes on a pale grey light. Dawn is the coldest time of the day and Harkin can feel it nipping at his cheeks and nose. He turns another page and hears the sounds of movement in the house as the inhabitants begin to stir. Somewhere footsteps walk along a corridor and a toilet flushes. He can hear water moving though the pipes and the sound of an oven door opening and then closing somewhere in the back of the house. He smells bread baking, and lights another cigarette. At last, he hears shoes climbing the staircase from the kitchen. He places a finger on the page he is reading and turns to smile at Bridget when she enters.

'Mr Harkin, are you up already?' she says breezily. 'Good morning to you. Can I get you anything?'

'I'd love a cup of tea.'

'Of course. Let me just get the fire lit and I'll bring you up a pot.'

She walks quickly to the fireplace, kneeling down to clear the grate.

He wonders why she has not greeted the officer, but when he turns his gaze in his direction, he has left.

It is only later, when Harkin is going upstairs to his bedroom, when he glances at Arthur Prendeville's portrait in its black-ribboned frame, that he recognises the man from breakfast.

# CHAPTER 19

Later in the morning, Harkin, still unsettled by the experience in the dining room, takes advantage of the lull before the funeral to walk out along the coast road. The Protestant church where Maud is to be buried sits on the rise that overlooks Kilcolgan Strand, halfway between Mrs Wilson's guest house and Kilcolgan, sheltered from the worst of the weather that comes in from the Atlantic by a small clump of trees, and it seems as good a place as any to head for. The walk will clear his mind, he hopes. As he walks along the drive, he looks inland to see the lower slopes of the hills blurred by the rain that must be falling over that way, while the upper parts are shrouded in cloud. The wind sends a shiver through his bones but the countryside – a mixture of bog, rock and gorse – is real and tangible and it's what his mind needs at this moment and he loses himself in the rhythm of his feet.

'A penny for your thoughts.'

Harkin turns, alarmed, but relaxes as he sees Sean Driscoll emerge from beside a whitewashed cottage, its walls pressed up against the road like a small bastion, his gleaming shoes picking a cautious path through the muck. He is wearing a black armband in anticipation of the funeral, and his hair seems to have been cut and oiled specially for the day. His limp is, if anything, more pronounced when he moves slowly.

He's a good-looking man, Harkin thinks. I can see how a woman might fall for him.

'I'm sorry if I startled you,' Driscoll says, falling into step alongside him.

'Did you get a hold of the priest?' Harkin asks, disconcerted. He wonders what he must have looked like.

Driscoll gives a slight scowl.

'He won't even talk to me. Says he wants nothing to do with the business. Says he'd never have got involved if he'd known it would lead to murder.'

'Is there another way to identify the source?'

'I have some lads keeping an eye on him to see who he talks to. With luck that will throw up something.'

'Let's hope so.'

Harkin wonders, if the priest isn't talking to Driscoll, that he might not be taking the same course of action with the source. A more direct approach might be necessary. A man like Vincent Bourke would be handy, he thinks.

'What are your thoughts at this stage?' Driscoll asks.

Harkin does his best to give a confident smile.

'I've a few things to follow up on. What about Egan?'

'I haven't had a response as yet. But I can take you to Patrick Walsh, the gatekeeper, this afternoon.'

Harkin nods his appreciation.

'There's one more thing,' Harkin says, feeling his way into the question. 'There are some discrepancies between your account of the evening's events and Billy's.'

'Go on,' Driscoll says, frowning.

'You say you were just behind Billy when you went into the house, but Billy says you were a couple of minutes behind him.'

The frown deepens, almost theatrically, and Driscoll's eyes seem to take on some kind of affected stupidity. Except that Harkin doesn't think, for one moment, that Driscoll is stupid.

'He must just be a bit confused, what with all that happened. I was right behind him. No more than a few yards.'

Which is possible, Harkin supposes, and he still can't think of any reason why Driscoll would want to kill Maud, even if he had the opportunity to do so. At the same time, he has the sense that Driscoll is not telling him the whole truth.

'Billy said you were together earlier in the evening, when he saw whatever he saw?'

Driscoll meets his gaze and again there is the sense of something being withheld.

'Look, I saw him out by the stables. He was shaken.' He hesitates, as though considering his words. 'He can get a little jittery from time to time. It's not that unusual. He's better than he was.'

'When was this?'

'Earlier,' Driscoll says, his irritation clear now. 'I saw nothing but I walked him back to the house. Around eight o'clock. It's the time the family normally eat.'

'Maud used to tell me the house was haunted,' Harkin says, trying a different approach.

'My mother might agree with her. She says the house takes getting used to. But it's just an old house with not enough people in it. It's easy to imagine things in the dark.'

Like seeing Arthur Prendeville sitting at the dining room table.

125

'What I'm wondering is, if maybe you went down to the car before you came up to the house. I'm not accusing you of anything but it would explain that discrepancy.'

Driscoll stops, holding his ground.

'I didn't go anywhere near the ambush until I went down with Billy and the others. You can ask my mother. There was no time.'

Harkin smiles, attempting to reassure the other man.

'I tried to talk to her this morning, but she was busy.'

'The funeral has to be done just so, you see.'

'But you're not helping her?'

'Best to stay out from under her feet, and Sir John's people are better at this sort of thing.'

'Anyway, I just wanted to understand why there was that difference in timing?'

'Look,' Driscoll says, eventually, 'I should make my way back. Even if I'm not needed, I probably shouldn't be missed.'

Harkin nods, wondering if Driscoll has even heard his question.

'Any more news from the town?'

'They burned the creamery last night and a few houses and they've been beating lads in the street, but no more killings. Teevan's funeral is tomorrow, though.'

'If you'd take my advice, you'll be careful,' Harkin says, after a moment's hesitation.

Driscoll's face loses some of its dissatisfaction, replacing it with an alertness that Harkin remembers from that other time.

'Why do you say that?'

Harkin feels his tiredness dragging at him, but he's also aware he must tell Driscoll about Vane and the danger he might represent.

'Have you met Major Vane? I understand he's a cousin of the Prendevilles.'

Driscoll shrugs.

'He's stayed at the house a couple of times. He buys horses for the army, I'm told.'

'Did he pay any attention to you?'

Driscoll's concern is more apparent now.

'I don't think he even noticed me.'

Harkin takes a moment to put his thoughts in order.

'I had a conversation with him last night and there's something about him I don't much like.' Harkin reminds himself he can't specify his concerns, given the necessity of keeping Driscoll in the dark about the guns. 'I'd be very wary of him.'

'Why?'

'He might be more than he says he is. If we know him, it's under another name. They're more cautious these days, since November. But I think we might have enough to identify him. How do you communicate with GHQ?'

Driscoll looks confused for a moment, then nods in the direction of the town.

'One of the guards on the Dublin train acts as messenger.'

'Is he working today?'

'He is. He's taking a package up for us.'

'Good. I'd like to add this to it.'

Harkin hands Driscoll the letter he wrote the night before.

'I think Vane must be his real name – if he's people to the Prendevilles, he can't have given them a false one. What he's called in Dublin may be a different matter. Still, we have people in Dublin Castle who should be able to identify him.'

'What did he say to you last night?' Driscoll says, and Harkin can imagine how his mind is working.

'I don't think he knows I'm a Volunteer, but he asked some awkward questions.' Harkin weighs his words and decides they are probably accurate, although he can't shake off his uneasiness. He breathes out slowly. 'If Sergeant Kelly knows about your involvement, then you might be known to the police in general. If that's the case, then he might be after the column. So, I'd suggest you keep an eye on him. If you think he is suspicious, act quickly. Better making a mistake killing him than losing one of ours.'

Driscoll nods and Harkin has the sense that he is only speaking aloud what Driscoll had already decided. They stand in silence for a while.

'Do you think he might have been close to Maud?' Harkin asks.

'Vane, do you mean?'

'Yes.'

'Not to my knowledge,' Driscoll says, although he seems hesitant. 'To my knowledge she wasn't seeing anyone at all.'

Harkin nods but he is not convinced by Driscoll's response.

# CHAPTER 20

The funeral is a modest affair, given the part Maud played in 1916 and her connections to the locality. If she had died in some other way, rather than in an IRA ambush, it's likely there would be thousands here, with an honour guard of Volunteers and shots fired over the grave. The eulogies, such as they have been, have avoided mention of the rising, and there have been no symbols or flags to indicate her history. Instead, her passing is marked by columns of black smoke rising from the town where the Auxies and RIC have burned half the main street in revenge for Teevan.

Harkin looks around at the assorted relatives, gentry, and local tradespeople – sombre and long-faced, wearing dark clothes and with the surprised look of people accustomed to holding sway who find themselves on the losing side of a hedgerow war. When considered from that perspective, he supposes, it's a not a bad turnout at all. It could even be considered impressive, given that there can't be a person here who mustn't wonder, with the fires burning in the town and the Auxies shooting left, right and centre, and the IRA no doubt planning to do pretty much the same in retaliation, whether it is sensible to attend. Even grief is a political statement these days.

He finds he is sympathetic to the subdued crowd waiting for the coffin to emerge from the church, wondering if they might be next, but he reminds himself that this is, as much as anything, a war about land. For every big house like Kilcolgan that was built, there were a hundred small homes taken. The land that supports the big houses is, as often as not, rented back to the people whose land it once was. Maud and her like will always carry the burden of their settler ancestors. Even after hundreds of years, they are still seen as foreigners in their own country, trapped by their past and facing a bleak future. It occurs to Harkin that his sympathy might be as much for himself as for them. He is also standing at the edge of a past, looking into a future that is uncertain – if not terrifying.

Harkin swallows and acknowledges that he is not, by any object-ive standard, well. Sweat has drenched his shirt and yet he is shivering with cold. It is not just the physical symptoms that concern him. A dark, swirling current lurks just below his con-sciousness, and he fears that at any moment it may tug him down into a black place that he does not want to go to. He bites the side of his lip, welcoming the pain. The pain helps him focus on staying above the surface.

'We meet again.' The voice is quiet, level with his ear – almost a whisper.

Harkin recognises the voice and tries to gather himself, even as he feels the strength in his legs receding. With a final effort, he turns to face Hugo Vane, and is surprised by the major's pallor. He doesn't know what he expected, but he didn't expect such obvious grief.

The major examines him and Harkin sees another emotion surface that he hadn't expected: concern.

'Are you all right?' Vane asks.

'I've felt better,' Harkin admits, seeing no point in denying it. He's also alarmed to feel a surge of gratitude at the unexpected kindness. He has to get a hold of himself.

'I didn't know you were so close to Maud,' Harkin says, and it comes out like an accusation but at least it came out. The major's smile takes on a bitter tinge.

'Am I a suspect?'

Harkin swallows, and attempts to shake his head.

'That kind of investigation would be the RIC's responsibility.'

'Ah yes. The RIC.' The major looks across at the columns of smoke that rise from the smouldering town. 'I rather think that investigation has been closed, don't you? In the circumstances I welcome questions being asked about Maud's death. Whoever chooses to ask them.'

Harkin does not trust himself to speak. He feels the ground reaching up towards him and it is all he can do to stay on his feet.

'If Maud survived the initial ambush,' Vane says, 'and it seems she might have, then I suppose someone must have had a reason to want her dead.'

'Indeed,' Harkin manages to say.

'I can think of one possible reason,' the major continues. 'What did you say the name of the insurance company you worked for was again?'

'The All-Ireland Insurance Company,' Harkin says, the words heavy on his tongue.

He can see the recognition in the major's eyes, even before he says anything. When he does speak, it is with a careful detachment.

'Yes, I thought that was the one. I believe I have come across the name. I did wonder if Sir John was the only beneficiary of

131

the policy. But perhaps, now I think of it, that is an unlikely motive.'

Harkin says nothing and the major nods, as though in agreement with himself.

'I suppose another reason someone might have killed her is if she had some information that might have been compromising to them.'

It doesn't seem that Harkin is expected to give a response, so he doesn't.

'Of course, there is another possibility,' Vane continues. 'That the IRA considered her presence in the car to be an act of treachery. It wouldn't be the first time such a thing has happened.'

The suggestion takes Harkin aback, so that he almost surfaces from the bleary sense of dislocation into which he is slipping. The approach of an Auxiliary officer in his tam o' shanter cap and dark green tunic provides a convenient, if not very welcome, interruption. A reversed holster sits on the officer's thigh, the leather gleaming black.

'Vane,' the officer says, nodding to the major, then looks at Harkin expectantly, as if anticipating an introduction. He's a small man, wiry, with the jutting chin of a martinet. A clipped moustache lurks under an aquiline nose. His eyes are grey and there is a challenge in them.

'Mr Harkin, this is Major Abercrombie. He commands the Auxiliary unit in the town. I'm sure you must know him by repute?'

Abercrombie responds to Vane's introduction with a look of mild amusement.

'I know all about Mr Harkin.' Abercrombie places an emphasis on the word 'Mister'. 'I'm told you intend to interfere in police business. It would be most unfortunate if you were to do so.'

132

Abercrombie's words are like a splash of cold water, reviving Harkin to some extent and causing him to wonder who has told Abercrombie about him, before deciding it is a question for later.

'The insurance company I work for has a liability as a result of Miss Prendeville's death,' Harkin says, pleased that his voice remains low and more or less in control. 'It is customary in such cases for us to look into the circumstance of the loss.'

Other mourners have turned to look in their direction – he can see Moira Wilson's pale, concerned face, her arm caught in the elbow of an older man. He wonders if it is her father. The last thing he wants is to get involved in a shouting match at a funeral. He's fairly certain it isn't the done thing.

'"The insurance company I work for",' Abercrombie growls. 'I don't care who you work for. The only investigation into this matter will be carried out by the Royal Irish Constabulary, namely by me and my men. Is that clear?'

'I'm afraid you have no legal authority to prevent me going about my employer's lawful business.'

Abercrombie steps closer, staring up at him, his teeth clenched. More faces are turning towards them, but if Abercrombie is aware of them, he shows no sign that he cares.

'Go back to Dublin, Mr Harkin. We have martial law in this part of Ireland. Don't tempt me to demonstrate the extent of my legal authority and the limits to your legal protection.'

Something about the man, haranguing him at a funeral, in his own country, has pushed Harkin to the point of resistance. He nods towards the burning town, continuing to speak quietly but his anger giving his words force.

'Is there a particular reason you don't want anyone else to investigate murders in this part of the country, Major Abercrombie?'

Harkin can feel the blood thumping in his ears, and he wonders what he must look like, standing there, toe to toe with the Auxiliary. When Vane speaks it sounds as though he is far away. His voice is calm, but firm.

'Abercrombie, this is my cousin's funeral. If you would like to continue this discussion, it will have to wait for another time. That is an order. Do you understand?'

There is a moment of indecision, then Abercrombie's eyes seem to lose some of their intensity, although the anger still simmers in them.

'I know whose funeral it is, Vane. A rebel's. No loyal officer should be present.'

He turns and walks away, the quiver of his rage apparent in each jerky movement. They watch him leave the churchyard and climb into one of the two Crossley Tenders parked on the road outside, and then drive off. The Auxiliaries in the back unsling their rifles as they do so.

'He seems to be a very angry man,' Harkin says.

'I hesitate to offer advice, Harkin—'

'But you think I should take the first train to Dublin?' Now that his anger has passed, Harkin finds it has left him drained. 'You're probably right.'

'May I ask a question?' Vane says, and Harkin finds himself sighing. He is tired of the pretence.

'Isn't that what men like you do? In your line of work?'

Vane shrugs.

'Sometimes.'

Harkin's suspicion hardens to a certainty. If he isn't a British intelligence officer, how can he order Abercrombie around?

'My question is whether you have a good enough reason to believe the IRA didn't kill Maud? This five-minute delay before the single shot. Is it enough to risk your life, do you think?'

'Yes,' he says. 'I think it is.'

'I see.'

Vane looks down at the ground for a moment, as though considering the implications of Harkin's answer. When he looks up, it appears he has made a decision. He nods curtly.

'I'll have a word with Abercrombie. However, I suggest you avoid him where possible.'

Harkin opens his mouth to say something but Vane is distracted by a commotion at the door of the church as the coffin, carried by assorted Prendevilles, slowly makes its way across the churchyard, weaving in and out among the scattered tombstones and gathering in its wake a flow of black-garbed mourners. Vane and he follow, although Harkin feels as though he is moving in a kind of dream-like state.

The open grave around which they gather brings another memory he can't trifle with. The dark earth is flecked with human bone and it reminds him so strongly of the trenches that he can hear what sounds like the rumble of gunfire in the distance. He hopes it is thunder, but when he looks up it is night and the mourners have been replaced with soldiers from his battalion. Their faces are grey, lit intermittently by the orange muzzle flashes of nearby artillery, and the pale red of signal flares. He recognises each one of them, despite their injuries. All of them, he knows, are dead. They stare at him with blank expressions, their faces immobile, as stiff as photographs. A building is burning nearby and he thinks it must be the church. He can hear the cracking of its rafters and smell the bodies that are burning within. It reminds him of the dream the night before, and he is, once again, very cold. He wonders what his dead comrades want from him, and then he looks into the grave and sees that the corpse that lies there, wrapped in a groundsheet except for the face, is his own.

He shouldn't have come to this funeral, or down to this place. He should have stayed in Dublin, no matter what the boss said.

Harkin thinks this even as the last of the strength seeps out of his legs and he feels his knees buckle, aware suddenly that Moira is beside him with the older man she had been arm in arm with. He feels their urgent hands pulling at him to keep him on his feet.

They are too late.

# CHAPTER 21

Harkin doesn't fall into a complete void. He is conscious, at one stage, of a circle of concerned faces looking down at him, the grey sky above them and the spatter of raindrops on his face. At another point he is placed on the back seat of a motor car, his head in someone's lap. He thinks it might be Moira Wilson's, but he is not certain of anything except that his head hurts and he has a strong desire to be sick. Later, he surfaces to find himself being carried up a wide staircase and it is Billy's face looking down at him, as he sways from side to side with each step the bearers take. He is looking up at the windows that run the length of the ornate ceiling above Kilcolgan's long central hall, noticing the damp patch that deforms a laughing cherub. He knows he is unwell because he is shivering. Then he is placed in a very soft, but cold, bed.

He warms it with his fever.

When he awakes, it is night. The curtains have been left open and he can see, through the large sash windows, a silvered swirl of stars. He is no longer in the small room with the suitcases and trunks. He is lying in a wide bed with thick, carved pillars at each corner. A chest of drawers sits against the wall to his right and there is an armchair beside it. He is wearing pyjamas and they are a soft, thick cotton, better than his own; he presumes they must belong to Billy. His throat is dry and he reaches for the glass he sees on the bedside cabinet. A woman is sitting beside the bed and, when he moves, she stirs. She lights a candle and he recognises Mrs Driscoll, wearing black, her grey hair pulled back into a bun.

'You're awake?'

'I seem to be.' His voice is hoarse, more of a croak than anything.

'Would you like some water?'

He nods and she reaches to fill the glass from a small jug. He takes it from her, but his hand is shaking and he spills some of it as he drinks it, sideways. It dribbles down his cheek. She tuts and reaches forwards to dry his face with a linen napkin, taking the glass from him.

'What time is it?' Harkin asks.

'I heard the clock strike three a few minutes ago.'

He must have slept but he is still exhausted. He rests for a moment, the effort of reaching for the glass and returning it having spent much of his energy, then, with an effort, pushes himself up to a sitting position. He tries to make some sense of his situation, gathering together the few snatches of memory he has.

'I fainted?'

'You did. At Miss Prendeville's funeral.'

He can't say that he's surprised by the hostility in her voice. Everything is clear up until when he met Vane and Abercrombie; after that less so, except for the dead soldiers staring at him from across the grave, their sunken eyes regarding him without emotion, or even interest. He feels his stomach contract, recalling enough to realise he must have passed out beside the grave, just as Maud was about to be interred.

How can he have done something so . . .? He searches for a word and can find none that accurately encapsulates it. It is certainly worse than 'embarrassing'. A silence falls between them.

'I wanted to talk to you before,' Harkin says eventually.

'Why?'

'I wanted to ask about the night Maud was killed. About the days leading up to it. About her state of mind.'

'Why should I tell you anything about Miss Prendeville?'

He sighs.

'It will get me out of here more quickly.'

Mrs Driscoll considers this.

'Ask me your questions.'

'You heard the gunfire?'

'I couldn't help but hear it.'

'What did you do then?'

'I got out of bed, got dressed and ran up the house.'

'And Sean?'

There is a momentary hesitation, so brief he isn't certain it was there at all.

'He did the same.'

'Where did he go to?'

She is irritated with the questions now.

'Didn't I say? The same as me. He went straight up the house.'

'You didn't stop him leaving, thinking it was dangerous, perhaps?'

Mrs Driscoll looks at him, her eyes black in the candlelight.

'His place was with the Prendevilles,' she says. 'The same as mine.'

'Who reached the house first?'

'He's a young man. Who do you think got there first?'

Which isn't really an answer. He feels sleep tugging at him.

'What about Maud?' he asks. 'Did anyone have a reason to kill her?'

His eyes have closed of their own volition, but when he opens them briefly he sees that her eyes are wet.

'Get some rest now,' she says, getting to her feet. 'That's enough with your nonsense questions.'

Harkin watches Mrs Driscoll stand and walk towards the door, taking the chamber-stick with her. After she's left, he's uncertain she was ever there at all.

Later – he is not sure when – he surfaces from a troubled sleep to find that his hand is being held. Instinctively he feels his fingers tighten around the hand that holds his. He opens his eyes to see Moira, her pupils dark circles in the candlelight. He opens his mouth to speak but she reaches over to place a finger on his lips.

'Don't try and talk. I'll talk if there's talking needs doing. Close your eyes and I'll tell you a story about a woman who loved a man and he didn't know it.'

He closes his eyes and listens as she tells her tale.

The characters are familiar, but the story is new to him.

# CHAPTER 22

When Harkin wakes for the third time he thinks there is a little more light in the sky. He lies there looking out through the window, savouring the warmth of the bed and the taut cotton pillowcase. He listens to the house but hears nothing. It is as though it is deserted. The guests must have left after the funeral. He wonders how they managed to carry on with it, after the show he made of himself. He pushes himself up, then swings his legs from under the covers. When he tries to stand, the carpet seems to move under his feet, as though the house were afloat. He has to sit back for a moment before allowing his legs to take his weight once more, using them to carefully push himself upright. He keeps a hand held out towards the bed in case he needs to steady himself. He wonders what he must look like, standing there in the silvered dark, bent over like an old man reaching for his walking stick. The thought makes him smile and he feels the better for it.

He takes stock. There's a door beside the chest of drawers which must lead somewhere. He sees a candlestick and a box of matches on a small side table, although he doesn't feel the need to light it; the room is dark, but he can make things out well enough in what little light there is. Paintings look down at him from the walls, their subjects just visible: landscapes; horses; ships; buildings. He can make out pale faces in the gloom – more Prendevilles, he suspects – and imagines their cold eyes regarding him in turn, finding him wanting. Once again Harkin remarks to himself on the strange stillness the house has. He places his hand against the pillar at the foot of the bed and turns slowly to examine the rest of the room.

Near the first of the windows there is a dressing table and at the foot of the bed a chest. Finally, there is a second armchair beside the far window, and someone is sitting in it. A woman, lit by the starlight so that she seems to glow. She stares out at the sea beyond, her expression unclear from where he stands.

At first he thinks it must be Mrs Driscoll, or perhaps Bridget, but the woman is younger than Mrs Driscoll and wears a long dress of a quality that neither she nor Bridget will ever wear. Her dark hair, a luminescent silver in the half-light, is braided to hang in a thick rope that rests on her left shoulder, before falling down over her chest. She holds it in her right hand, like a club. Her nose is straight, her lips full and for an instant he thinks it must be Charlie, but it isn't. Charlie doesn't wear the perfume his nostrils are filled with. Only Maud did . . . and the woman who helped him across the bridge in the Dublin fog.

The carpet beneath his feet seems to slip away but he doesn't fall. Harkin grips the pillar with both hands and holds on to it, using it to pull himself onto the bed, where he sits. He doesn't take his eyes off the figure in the armchair. He knows she can't be there, that she is either imagined, or something altogether outside any reality he understands. He watches her uncertainly, wanting to confront whatever she is. He locks his elbow around the pillar, as though escorting it, and feels himself begin to shiver. She doesn't move, not even to breathe. He stays there, his eyes fixed on her, until the cold creeps further into his bones and the shivering becomes uncontrollable. He tries to summon the energy to walk over to her – to try to touch her, to confirm to himself that she is not real. But what if his hand touches flesh?

When she turns to face him, the emotion Harkin detects is, to his relief, one of compassion – perhaps even sympathy. She holds his gaze and he loses himself in it. Memories flood back, as well as regret for what might have been. Then her gaze shifts, but he cannot take his eyes away from her to see what has attracted her attention. Then she looks back to him once again, something like a question in her expression. To his surprise he finds that he is no longer afraid. It is as though they have come to some sort of agreement.

He sits there, watching her for a long time, expecting something more, but there is no change to her steady gaze and tiredness tugs at him. Eventually, he reaches a decision and pushes himself back along the bed and gets beneath the covers, allowing the warmth to seep back into him.

He continues to look at her for a while, then he closes his eyes.

# CHAPTER 23

The next time Harkin wakes, it is because of the light of a new day. He doesn't open his eyes, not because he is afraid of what he might see – he seems to be past that – but because he wants to avoid the world for a little longer. He listens to the house wake; tasks being performed, people going about their business. At the thought of the day before, his guilt returns. He will have to face the Prendevilles soon enough, but, for the moment, he turns on his shoulder, away from the bright windows and towards the dark of the furthest corner of the room. He pulls the blankets up around him and remembers Maud sitting in her armchair, and how beautiful she was. He finds the strange experience has brought forth memories of their time together that have not surfaced for years. A breathless, laughing run to catch a tram. A dance in some grand Dublin house, her cheek warm against his. A morning they had spent crammed into his single bed in his rooms in Trinity, whispering in case they might be overheard. He allows himself to be taken over by the remembered happiness.

Later, when he wakes again, he is aware that someone else is in the room. He can hear their slow and steady breathing; the slight rasp of someone with a blocked nose. They are close, then a hand lifts his, feeling for his pulse. He opens his eyes to find a stocky, bearded man is leaning over him. One hand has his, while the other holds a silver pocket watch on a chain which he examines.

'You're alive,' the man says, without looking away from the watch.

'So it seems.'

'Always better than the alternative,' the man says, placing Harkin's hand back on the pillow. 'How do you feel?'

Harkin's body feels, he decides, halfway to being a corpse. But his mind seems to be clear for a change.

'Not too bad,' he says.

'You got a good sleep, anyway. Would you like me to help you drink some water?'

'I can manage, I think.'

He lifts himself up on to his elbow and finds the glass from the night before.

'Better?' the man says, when Harkin places the empty glass back down.

'Yes, thank you.' Harkin squints up at him. He recognises the voice from his half-memories from the previous day. 'Are you Dr Hegarty? If you aren't, would you mind putting my hand back down?'

The man smiles, a flash of teeth in among the beard.

'Pleased to meet you.'

'What time is it?' Harkin asks.

Hegarty gives Harkin back his hand, and then writes something in a notebook he has open on his lap.

'Just past eleven. Do you mind if I ask some questions?'

Hegarty takes Harkin's silence as consent.

'Has this happened before?'

146

'Has what happened before?'

'A prolonged period of involuntary unconsciousness. Alcohol-related incidents apart.'

'In the war,' Harkin says, reluctantly.

'Concussion?'

'Everyone at the front suffered concussion at one time or another.'

It was true. High-explosive shells shook the brains inside soldiers' skulls so hard sometimes they would be found dead, with no visible wounds.

'Billy told me some of your medical history and I've spoken to your doctor in Dublin as well.'

Harkin's alarm at this is more for his mother's sake than this. He's always been careful what he has told the family doctor for fear he would tell his mother. Now he wonders how Hegarty got hold of him. If it was through his mother, she'll be worried.

'My mother knows about this?'

'No. Your employer gave me his details.'

'Good. She worries about me enough as it is,' Harkin says, wondering if he spoke directly to the boss or one of the men who actually deals with insurance. Not that it makes any difference.

'Why is that? That she worries about you?'

Hegarty reminds him of the doctors in Scotland. The steady, persistent questioning.

'What kind of doctor were you during the war?'

Hegarty smiles, as if pleased with his patient's perspicacity.

'I started at the front, in forward dressing stations, but I was really too old for that. As the war proceeded I moved to hospitals in the rear and specialised in what we then called war neuroses. Shell shock, in other words.'

'And now you're back being a family doctor in the Irish countryside?'

'Well, I was always that. The war was a break from it, that's all.' He examines Harkin. 'Does that concern you? What I specialised in during the war?'

Harkin thinks about this, then shakes his head, deciding to lie. It does concern him, and not least because he remembers that this man's daughter is Moira Wilson.

'No.'

'Good. The thing to take comfort from is that I have experience in matters of this nature which may be useful. If you'd like to talk to me, to tell me what led up to this, then I'm happy to listen. And to help if I can.'

Harkin doesn't know how to respond.

'What matters are you referring to?'

'Well, it seems likely that an episode like this has been building for some time. You haven't been a quiet sleeper here. You served through Gallipoli, the Somme, Passchendaele and God knows where else. I understand you suffered a severe concussion at Passchendaele, but I imagine you had your fair share of similar concussions beforehand. Repeat concussions of this nature can cause lasting physical damage. Aside from which, the experiences you had during the war will have had emotional effects. It may well be that your condition is a combination of the two.'

Harkin shifts uncomfortably in the bed.

'I can guarantee confidentiality, of course,' Hegarty continues. 'I know it is difficult to discuss these things, but in my experience it is often the case that talking to someone like me can help. I think you probably know that.'

Billy must have told him about Edinburgh. Harkin can't be angry. He would have done the same if he'd seen Billy faint at a graveside. He thinks about the encounter in the Dublin fog, the gassed soldiers in the train, Arthur Prendeville sitting at the dining table, and all the other times he has seen something he shouldn't be seeing: corpses floating in the Liffey; wounded soldiers strewn across Grafton Street; Maud sitting in her armchair. Even now, looking at Hegarty, he isn't entirely certain this is happening.

Harkin takes a deep breath, shrugs, then meets Hegarty's gaze, composing his features into something approaching puzzlement.

'It's nothing like that. I haven't been sleeping well, that's all.'

Hegarty smiles once again, sighing in a contented fashion.

'Very good. I should say Billy told me a little bit about a hospital you both were patients at. Near Edinburgh?'

Harkin is hardly surprised at the confirmation of his suspicions.

'Which is why I know it's only insomnia.'

Hegarty's left eyebrow rises.

'I've no doubt there could be an element of insomnia. On the other hand, if a relapse of some description is taking place it is often a result of stress. What is it you do for a living, Mr Harkin?'

Harkin decides to proceed with caution.

'I work for an insurance company.'

'I'd have thought, seeing how your condition has worsened, that you might have a more stressful occupation. Is there perhaps something else in your life that might be causing anxiety?'

Harkin says nothing. He thinks of the clandestine war he has been engaged in – about the things he's done and witnessed over the last year and a half. Hegarty, meanwhile is examining him intently. It doesn't take a mind-reader to detect the doctor's train of thought.

'My daughter tells me you're down here investigating Maud Prendeville's death.' Hegarty pauses. 'For your insurance company.'

The implication is unmistakable. Harkin feels as though he might as well be sitting here with a tricolour wrapped round him, singing 'The Soldier's Song', as far as the doctor is concerned.

'That's right.' Harkin can hear the unease in his voice. He watches as Hegarty's frown deepens.

'As a doctor, I would advise you to give up this business. To return to Dublin or, even better, take a holiday in foreign parts. Somewhere far away from the Troubles we find ourselves in the midst of.'

'And if I ignored that advice?'

'Well, at least avoid any activity that is likely to agitate you. In addition, I'd recommend regular exercise – at least twice a day. And I'd suggest you remove yourself from this house. The Prendevilles are used to the place, and the place is used to them. The rest of us need to be cautious. I'd not spend the night here for pleasure. Not for a hundred pounds.'

'I hope not to have to stay too long.'

'Are you determined to pursue your investigation?' Hegarty continues, after a long pause.

'That is my intention.'

Hegarty inhales deeply, as though preparing to dive into an icy lake.

'Am I right to say you suspect Miss Prendeville was not killed by the rebels? That she may have been killed by someone else?'

'It's possible.' Harkin is reluctant to commit himself once again. 'There are certainly some questions that need addressing before I'm satisfied one way or the other.'

'You are probably aware that the local authorities require a post mortem to be performed when a death occurs in this kind of circumstance. The police were reluctant, considering a post mortem to be a formality, but in any event it was carried out. By me. Now, out of consideration for the Prendevilles, my examination was not as invasive as it might have been, because the cause of death was clear. A single bullet entered her skull just above her left eye and did not exit her body. It was fired at close range – there were powder residues around the entry wound, so within two feet, I would say. Not, in other words, by someone firing on the car during the ambush. There was also a separate contusion to the forehead, not caused by the bullet, but more likely by her hitting her head shortly before death.'

Harkin digests this information. It chimes with the column's version.

'There is one piece of evidence I thought might interest you in particular.'

Hegarty reaches into his jacket pocket and brings out a small brown envelope, the type used for weekly wages. He hands it to Harkin, who opens it. There is a brass bullet, distorted by impact. It is small in his hand, its weight barely noticeable.

It makes his stomach turn.

'I took this out of Maud Prendeville's neck. It was pressing up against the skin. It's not unusual for a bullet to ricochet around inside the skull and then through the body, and that's where it ended up. I was able to extract it with a small incision. As you can see, it's quite small calibre – my guess would be .25. Probably a pocket pistol with an effective range of about the length of this room. I haven't come across many bullets this size and I've extracted a fair few in my time, from both the living and the dead.'

'Did you show it to Abercrombie?'

'I've sent him my report. Major Abercrombie probably used it to light the fire. I doubt he values any opinion that isn't his own.

With Teevan in charge, there was some hope for the loyalist cause down here. Not anymore.'

Harkin replaces the bullet into the envelope and returns it to the doctor.

'Thank you.'

'You're welcome. There's something else. I presume you would be interested in any information that might point towards a motive.'

'That would be correct.'

'There is something I left out of the report.'

Again there is a hesitation and Harkin wonders if the doctor is about to change his mind. Instead, he runs a hand across his face and closes his eyes, as if praying. When he speaks, his voice is very quiet.

'If I tell you this, you must promise me your absolute discretion.'

'I will be as discreet as I possibly can.'

The doctor nods.

'I suppose that is all I can ask for in the circumstances.'

Hegarty pauses again, then closes his eyes. When he opens them again it is clear that he has made a decision.

'Maud Prendeville was pregnant. About three months gone.'

# CHAPTER 24

When the doctor leaves, Harkin gets out of bed and walks over to stand beside Maud's armchair. He looks out at the dark, smouldering grey sky, its clouds rolling over the house in a constant stream. Beneath it, the heavy grass of the home meadow is frosted by recent rain. Harkin takes stock of himself. He feels a little weak but he supposes that is to be expected after a long time in bed. His mind, however, seems sharp enough. It is as though the doctor's information about Maud has given him a sense of purpose that has papered over, at least for the moment, the sense of unreality and dread that has confused his waking hours these last few days – indeed, weeks.

Maud had not been prudish about these things – she and Harkin had been lovers before the war, after all – but she had always been careful. Her reputation would certainly have been damaged if a pregnancy had been made public – and perhaps also her lover's? But even if the pregnancy was the reason behind the killing, it still doesn't explain how whoever was responsible knew Maud was going to be in the car.

Harkin watches as Billy comes into view, walking across the front of the house, a turned-up tweed jacket buttoned tight across his chest and neck and a flat cap pulled down low across his fore-head. He swishes at the grass with a blackthorn stick as he goes, each swing sending an arc of grass and water into the air. Even from this distance, Harkin can tell Billy is worried. It occurs to Harkin that perhaps Billy is worried about him.

Harkin turns back to the room. There is a collection of framed photographs on top of the chest of drawers and, curious, he takes a moment to examine them. Almost immediately his gaze falls on a photograph of himself with Maud. They are standing in front of high black railings that separate them from the trees and bushes of a park. It could be Stephen's Green, but he isn't sure. He looks young, and Maud even younger. He remembers the afternoon. 1912 – just after he left university.

It still astonishes him, seeing the two of them together. The Honourable Maud Prendeville, the daughter of a lord, mixing with the likes of Tom Harkin – a solicitor's son and a Roman Catholic. No wonder Lord Kilcolgan never warmed to the idea. Harkin reaches out to place a fingertip on the photograph, touching his younger self. He would like to be back at that moment – to have all that has happened since then to be in a future that might or might not come to pass. It's not hard to remember, looking at the Maud in the picture, why he loved her – although why she might have loved him is less clear. He seems naive, uncomfortable in his suit and tie, while she seems amused by herself, and perhaps by him as well; there is a mischievous slant to her gaze. They are looking towards the camera with affection and he remembers it was Billy who took the photograph. He remembers how Billy was back then, before the war.

There is another photograph of Maud beside it. She is older in this one, and much changed. She is wearing the dark uniform of the Cumann na mBan, the women's auxiliary organisation that supports the IRA. He thinks it must have been taken after the 1916 Rising. There is a sombreness to her gaze that he recognises from the trenches, a turn to the mouth that suggests experience, and not all of it pleasant. There is still that intelligence he remembers, but the mischievous amusement is no longer there.

There are photographs of other men and women and he recognises many of them – the makers of an attempted revolution. Some of them are dead, some still living, and then it occurs to him – the bedroom must be Maud's. There is no other room in the house in which these photographs could be on display.

He looks around at the armchair, remembers the figure sitting in it, staring out at the night, and shivers once again. What can have possessed the Prendevilles to have put him in here?

Harkin walks slowly to the bed and sits, considering his options. The sensible thing to do, in his condition, is probably to take the doctor's advice, cut his losses and return to Dublin. He probably has enough, with Hegarty's information, to confirm to the boss and Sir John that the column's story is credible. As for the wider world believing in their guilt, the column has broad shoulders. It's not as though they have been saints this last while. It's a dirty war and they have all of them, himself included, had to get down in the dirt to scrap it out with the British. If it weren't for Sir John's guns, and if Maud had not been one of the survivors of the GPO, no one from the boss on down would have given more than two seconds' thought to the matter.

He goes to the chest of drawers and picks up the photograph of the two of them together and looks at it once again. The last few years have been full of events outside either of their control, and it occurs to him that Maud's death is something that perhaps he *can* control, or at least find some justice for. He remembers Maud from the night before, sitting in her armchair, and the way she looked at him. He presumes what he saw was a manifestation of his imagination. The alternative – that it was some kind of spectral apparition – is a possibility he would rather not consider. In any event, whatever it was, he feels sure there was some kind of communication between them. He knows she is dead – indeed, he'd held the bullet that killed her in his hand only a few minutes earlier – but he also suspects that something passed between them, inexplicable as that may be.

Harkin's eye falls on the small davenport desk beside the left-hand window – an embossed green leather writing slope on top of a four-drawer pedestal. It must have been where Maud wrote her letters. He looks back to her armchair, remembering the way her gaze shifted when she looked back towards him for the first time, and he feels a sudden sweat chill on the back of his neck. He looks again at the davenport. Logic suggests that if she received any letters, perhaps from a lover, then there's a good chance that they will have been kept in one of its four drawers. Was it the desk her gaze shifted to? Had she been sending him some kind of message? No police detective has searched this room, but there's no reason Harkin can't, so long as no one walks in on him. The morality of the act doesn't bother him too much. It is the nature of his work these days to pry into other people's secrets, and in this case Maud is dead and the benefits seem clear.

Which isn't to say that he plans on getting caught doing it. He lifts the chair that sits in front of the davenport and carries it to the door, wedging it under the handle. He can't hear anyone nearby but, if someone should come to visit him, the chair should give him a moment or two's grace.

He walks back over to the desk and tries the top drawer. It's locked, as are all the others, and he leans down to examine them. Each drawer has its own small round keyhole and, he suspects, they will have the same relatively simple mechanism, served by a single key. He has spent a few afternoons waiting around in the insurance company offices with Vincent Bourke, who has shown him how to pick a lock. If Harkin can find a hairpin or something similar, there's a good chance he'll be able to open them. He listens to the house. There is some new movement and noise from downstairs but the upper part remains quiet.

His eye is drawn to the dressing table. He walks over to it quickly and begins his search for a hairpin. The table's drawers are well organised, with make-up in one drawer, handkerchiefs in another, and so on. They smell of powder, patchouli and, he realises in a hot flush of memory, Maud's cologne. In the fourth drawer he opens, he finds hairbrushes and, as he had hoped, a small glass jar of hairpins. It is not, however, the presence of the hairpins that makes him smile but rather the brass key attached to a thin gold chain, exactly the kind of chain a young woman like Maud might wear around her neck and more or less the size of key that would fit the davenport's locks. A moment later Harkin is trying it in the top drawer of the desk. There is a slight resistance and then the key turns and the drawer is open.

He pauses to listen once again. Downstairs in the long hall someone is walking across the marble floor, the sound echoing up through the house. He takes a deep breath, lets it out slowly and pulls the drawer towards him. It contains pens and pencils, two ink bottles and a pad of blotting paper. He takes everything out carefully, checking each item, before replacing them as he found them and closing the drawer gently. He listens. Nothing at all this time, except for the sound of his own shortened breathing. He rebukes himself for his nervousness. If he's caught there will be embarrassment, but he's up to his neck in that already after his performance at the funeral. A little more won't make any difference.

Harkin opens the next drawer. It contains correspondence, although mostly of a commercial nature. There are letters from a dressmaker in Dublin, informing Maud of new arrivals and a dress that has been made for her, and a reminder about an unpaid bill from a Bond Street milliner. There is some legal correspondence about a will in which she was named as a minor beneficiary, and a description of a horse that a farrier in the town wanted to sell to her. He flicks through each of them, page by page, listening as he does so for any sound on the stairs or landing that might announce an imminent arrival. Then, satisfied there is nothing of significance in the contents, he again replaces them exactly as he found them. It's unlikely anyone other than Maud has ever seen the inside of the drawer, and Maud is past caring, but it feels the right thing to do – to examine, to remember, but not to disturb.

The third drawer is more promising. It is stuffed full of letters from friends and relatives, dating back several years. There are invitations to dances and hunt balls, newsy updates from a god-mother in England and a cousin in India. They decline in number sharply after 1916. Harkin wonders if Maud was no longer welcome at the house parties and afternoon teas after her involvement in the Rising. It seems likely. At the bottom of the drawer, wrapped in a dark green ribbon, he finds a small stack of letters with a handwriting that he recognises as his own. Some are dated from before the war, and some from the training camp in the Curragh and then more from France. He turns over the pages, hearing his own voice in his head, speaking of events he barely remembers.

He knows they won't be the whole truth, because you never told people at home the truth of the trenches, but they bring back the smell and the feel of the war. One letter is marked in places, brown blotches that he suspects must be mud, or maybe blood. Another must have become damp at some stage, the paper bleached by water and the ink blurred where it ran. He looks at the dates – 1915, 1916. There are even some letters from after the Rising, which he reads more carefully. Although officers' letters weren't censored in the way that those of the other ranks were, his words are carefully chosen. He would have known, even then, that a policeman or intelligence officer would want to know who was writing to a known rebel from the front, particularly from an Irish regiment. Reading between the lines, it is clear that he was not against the Rising – far from it – although it seems he considered it badly executed. His opinion hasn't changed since then. It was, however, a necessary step and a lesson about the futility of directly engaging the greatest military power in the world that was well learned.

The last letter is in response to her calling off the engagement. There are no harsh words – only a hope that when the war is over and their situations are different, they will find some means of rekindling the love he believed that they had shared. A tear takes him by surprise when it runs the length of his nose and lands just beside his signature.

When he finishes reading, he ties the letters back up into the stack in which he found them and weighs them in his hand. He thinks, for a moment, about keeping them. They're no use to Maud now, and of no interest to anyone but him. He could put them in his pocket and no one would ever know. But what would he do with them? Take them out and think about what might have been? He puts them back where he found them, as before. He's wallowed in the past for long enough. From this point on, he'll look to the future.

The last drawer is a disappointment – a collection of diaries from Maud's schooldays. He checks each one in case there might be a more recent entry, but there is nothing. Then he hears footsteps climbing the staircase, along with an accompanying scratchy cavalcade of canine paws, so he closes the drawer, locks it, and quickly crosses the room to take the chair from underneath the door handle and return it to its usual place. The footsteps are approaching along the galleried landing, so he returns to sit on the bed, placing the key underneath the pillow as an afterthought. The steps stop outside his door.

There is a pause and then a soft knock.

'Come in.' Harkin can hear the croak in his voice. He reaches for the now empty glass, filling it with water.

Charlie Prendeville enters accompanied by her hounds, who immediately explore every corner of the room, before returning to the door and curling up at her command to be still and not bother them. Once again he is struck by her resemblance to Maud.

'You're awake, Mr Harkin. Dr Hegarty said you might be, but we've become quite accustomed to you slumbering away. I hope you feel better?'

Her smile seems genuine and, given the circumstances, he is grateful.

'I feel much better,' he says. 'Although I can only apologise. Not the kind of thing I would have ever wanted to do – fainting at your sister's funeral.'

Her smile doesn't falter; in fact he thinks his statement somehow amuses her.

'You have nothing to apologise for. Dr Hegarty tells us you're likely still suffering from concussion. As a result, I believe Father is quite reconciled to you, given that your passing out was a result of you doing your bit for the Empire and the Union. As for Maud, I don't think she would have minded a former beau collapsing at her funeral. In fact, I think she would have been delighted.'

He smiles, wondering about that other beau, the father of Maud's unborn child, and whether he was at the graveside, too, and what he felt when Maud was put in the ground.

'I'm sure I must have outstayed my welcome, no matter what you say. I should make arrangements to depart.'

'I'm afraid you can't. Dr Hegarty said you are not fit to travel just yet. He wanted to send you over to his daughter's establishment, but we felt that would place us in a shabby light. You are to stay until you are able to leave.'

Harkin can't help his gaze straying to the davenport.

'I might stay for a day or two,' he says, although he can't disguise his discomfort. 'There are a few people I still need to talk to.'

She considers this for a moment.

'Am I one of them?' She sets her chin at a determined angle. 'I wouldn't worry about offending me.'

Harkin finds it momentarily difficult to gather his thoughts. He wants to ask her about Maud's lover, but he doesn't know where to begin with that.

'It might help,' he says, hesitantly, 'if you could you tell me what you remember from that night. The sequence of events.'

Charlie walks slowly to the chest of drawers and picks up the photograph of Maud in her Volunteer uniform.

'I was in my bedroom when I heard the gunfire. I hadn't undressed. I was reading. I often read late at night. It's the quietest

161

time. It was two minutes before midnight. I have a bedside clock and it is accurate to the station clock. The shooting was very intense for about ten seconds and I knew it came from the direction of the gate lodge. We knew Harry had hoped to be dropped back that evening, and as there is no traffic to speak of along the road at that time of night, I feared the worst for him.'

'You had no idea Maud was with him? Or that Teevan was driving.'

She looks down again at the photograph and he can see that her eyes are wet.

'No. No idea. She was meant to be staying with Uncle John. Harry had wanted to come back because he was leaving in the morning. I suppose it is possible that he knew Abercrombie would be there but Maud didn't, otherwise she wouldn't have gone.'

'So what happened then?'

'I came out and found my father in his dressing gown on the landing, then we joined Murphy and Bridget downstairs in the hall. She'd been waiting up for Harry.'

'And Billy?'

She glances towards the bedroom door, as though concerned that Billy might walk through it.

'Billy was outside. He likes to go out walking at night. It's been that way since he came back from France. He came in a few minutes after the shooting started. Perhaps five.'

There's something she's holding back – he's sure of it. A slight hesitancy, as though she might be checking over her response before she speaks.

'He goes out every night?'

She nods, more confident now.

'In all weathers. I sometimes see him making his way across the home meadow in the moonlight and I know he goes down to the stables on occasion. He's not the same as he was before the war. No one who came back is.'

She gazes at him calmly and it's clear she thinks that he has also changed and Harkin can't but agree. He also knows that there have been more than a few nights when he, too, has walked the streets of Dublin, preferring to take his chances with the curfew than lie in a sleepless bed. He returns to the matter in hand.

'And when did Sean Driscoll arrive?'

'A little after Billy.'

Harkin tries to remember the timing. Billy said he had been just walking up to the house when the final shot was fired, with Driscoll not far behind him. Driscoll said that he was also just walking in when the final shot was fired. There's a question that has to be asked.

'They weren't together?'

She sends him an enquiring glance but when she answers her voice is flat.

'No. Sean was a little after Billy.'

He rubs at his morning stubble. 'How long after Billy, would you say?'

'I should think two minutes.'

Another discrepancy. But he knows how hard it is to keep track of time in such a situation. An hour can seem like a few moments, while the briefest wait can seem to stretch forever.

'There was a separate shot, a while after the main ambush. Did you hear it?'

Charlie gives a fairly good impression of someone searching her memory, but Harkin has the sense that she's gone over the events of the evening more than once, and that there is something about it that she doesn't quite like.

'Yes.'

'And when was that in relation to Sean and Billy's arrival?'

She hesitates once again.

'Neither Sean nor Billy had arrived when we heard it. Father was anxious – he was worried Billy might have been caught up in the shooting. If he'd been down by the strand, for example, the Volunteers might have picked him up. Maud's brother or not, he's a former British officer, and if he blundered into their ambush, they would certainly have taken him prisoner – the same as they did with Patrick Walsh the gatekeeper – or worse . . .' She pauses, and he can see her face tightening with remembered emotion. 'When we heard the gunshot, we thought they might have shot Billy. They have shot others for less.'

The Prendevilles were right to be worried. Given the brutality of British reprisals against the families of Volunteers, his death would have been more than likely if Billy could have identified anyone in the column.

'What did you do?'

'What could we do? Father called the station in the town and told them about the ambush and they promised to send a patrol, but we knew it would take time for them to come. The rebels knew which road they'd come along, so the police had to be careful in case they were ambushed. It took an hour in the end, and we thought that was pretty good.'

It says something about the state of the country, he thinks, that polite young women are well versed in guerrilla tactics.

'But Billy was all right.' Harkin feels relief when he says it, as though he hadn't known this until he spoke the words aloud. 'How long after the single shot until Billy arrived, would you say?'

Charlie shrugs as if the timing is of no importance to her, but he doesn't believe that. Her hands are clasped together and her knuckles are white. Her nervousness makes him wonder why she chose to talk to him in the first place.

'Two or three minutes, I should think, but it's hard to be certain. And when Billy did come in, we weren't entirely sure it was him, he was so pale. It was only that his coat and boots were wet and he was so solid that we knew he wasn't a ghost. And then he told us what he'd seen.'

'The White Lady?' Harkin says, with an attempt at a laugh. His attempt sounds so false that he feels his cheeks warm with embarrassment. She looks at him sharply in response, but then her expression softens.

'I know you won't mock,' she begins. 'Because you're kind. But my family has been here a very long time and not all of us pass on when they are supposed to. The White Lady, we think, is one of them. She's always seen before a Prendeville dies. Billy saw her earlier that night.'

She looks at him, as though expecting some kind of reaction, which he does his best not to give. She shrugs.

'I don't expect you to believe me.'

She isn't joking – far from it. He opens his mouth to ask her a question, but he can't find the words.

Who, after all, is he to be sceptical, after having seen Maud Prendeville sitting in the armchair by the window only the night before?

There must be something in his expression that amuses Charlie, because she smiles.

'You get used to them.'

'You see them?'

'Not so often these days, but when I was younger I did. There was one who sometimes came into my bedroom. I would wake up and find an elderly woman looking down at me. She wasn't frightening – more reassuring, if anything. Billy used to say she was our great-grandmother, looking for the child she lost to cholera, but he was just teasing. There is another in the kitchen, a cook, we think, who used to give Mrs Driscoll all sorts of trouble, moving things about. But once Mrs Driscoll left them where the old cook preferred them, things became much quieter.'

Harkin sees that she is regarding him expectantly, as though he might be about to say something. He finds his mouth opening.

'I think I saw Maud last night,' he says abruptly. 'She was sitting over by the window.'

Charlie walks over and places her hands on the back of the chair. She seems unsurprised.

'She did like to sit here,' she says, leaning forwards, as though looking for traces of her sister's presence. 'Do you think she wanted something?'

'From me?'

'You're the one she came to see.'

Harkin thinks back to the Ha'penny Bridge. It was a few minutes after the bells of Christ Church rang for midnight. If Charlie is right about the ambush being at two minutes before, then whatever guided him across the bridge did so at the very moment that Maud died. Perhaps they were saving him for a purpose. He wants to laugh at the idea and finds he can't. Instead he shakes his head in the negative.

'I don't think so.' He allows a brief silence to develop. 'Do you think she might have had a lover? Or someone who wanted to be her lover?'

He can see Charlie's shoulders stiffen.

'Why do you ask?'

'Because I'm looking for a reason why someone might have killed her.'

166

Charlie's head drops a little lower. He thinks she might be crying.

'She was different, recently. She was almost her old self. She would go on little trips. She even went to Paris with a friend from school and when she came back, we would talk about moving there, the two of us. How many Frenchmen would fall in love with us. She said she had come into some money – she wouldn't tell me how . . .' There is a sob in her voice and she breaks off.

Harkin wonders about the money; the solicitor's letter had concerned a bequest for a few hundred pounds, no more. What is more interesting is her plan to leave. Might that have been what drove her lover to despair?

'And now we're left here, Billy and I. We'll be like the house, slowly falling into ruin, getting older and more threadbare. There'll be no French admirers, only bailiffs and rats in the kitchen and begging for money from Uncle John to keep the walls half standing. And the people around here will hate us because we will represent a past they would rather not remember. Or, worse still, they will pity us.'

Without thinking, he walks over and places a hand on her shoulder. She covers it with her own and then, without another word, she straightens herself and walks quickly from the room.

Harkin stands looking out at the sea and the barren rocky shore across the bay. It is a hard beauty. It is the type of place a man might end up when he has looked everywhere else for whatever it is that he seeks and discovers there is nowhere else to go. Perhaps that was how the original Prendevilles found it.

He has not noticed it before but, in the corner of one of the panes of glass someone – he presumes Maud – has etched her initials and a date. *M.J.A.P, 4th February, 1911*. He reaches out a finger to run it along the chipped, overpainted putty that holds the glass inside the window frame. He can feel it shift under his touch. One more gust of wind might be enough and then Maud's mark will be gone.

He takes a step back, noticing how the wallpaper underneath the window frame is peeling away and that the ceiling above him is stained by damp in several places. Even Maud's chair sags, although he imagines it might still be quite comfortable. Perhaps that's it. This house, for all its faults and decrepitude, is always going to be comfortable for the Prendevilles. Otherwise he cannot for the life of him understand why an intelligent person like Charlie Prendeville – or, for that matter, Billy – feels tied to the place. Here, they still have stature; they have their ascendancy friends and family and a place in their faded parade. Or perhaps they feel that nowhere else will have them, at least not on terms they could accept. And then there are the Prendevilles that came before them, and the house that contained them . . . and what would come of it if the last of the living left?

Harkin dresses slowly and as he does so, he contemplates the davenport desk. It has a high base and sits flat to the ground rather than on wheels, as is more usual. It occurs to him that if the base were hollow, and it is very unlikely to be a solid piece of wood, there could be a void within it. He fetches the key from where he placed it underneath the pillow and unlocks the lowest drawer, this time pulling it all the way out and placing it to one side. He peers inside, hoping to see a space within, but if there is, it is sealed by three wooden planks, on top of which the drawer must rest.

He is about to replace the drawer when he notices there is a small gap between the middle plank and the others. The plank is thin, and when he gets a fingernail underneath it, it lifts and beneath there is a space. He breathes out slowly and reaches inside.

His hand brings out, first, a ribboned stack of letters and, then, a small black automatic that fits neatly into his hand. A pocket pistol. Just like the one the doctor said was used to kill Maud.

The gun is an evil little thing, made by a French manufacturer. There is a date on the barrel – 1920 – and it appears, as the date suggests, brand new. He turns it over in his hand, feeling the weight of it, then pulls out the magazine to reveal four shiny .25 calibre bullets, a match for the one Hegarty showed him. It can't be the gun that killed Maud but it poses some interesting questions, not least of which is that Maud may have thought she needed it for protection.

Harkin considers whether to return it to the cavity, but remembers the way Maud had looked in the direction of the small writing desk. Perhaps he can consider it a gift of sorts and, having made his decision, he finds its weight in his pocket reassuring.

He turns his attention to the letters and immediately realises that they are of an intimate nature. They are not dated and there is no postmark or stamp. He skims the first.

*My beloved Maud,*

He skips through the banal endearments, a little embarrassed, until he comes to the last paragraph.

*The barrier that stands between us exists only in your mind. If you will trust me, and we take our courage in our hands, then we can be together forever in a place where we will not be judged, or even remembered.*

*With all my love*

*Sean*

Harkin can hear Charlie Prendeville's quick steps clip across the marble floor below and then begin to climb the stairs, but he does not move from his position. It is only when she is on the landing itself that he hurriedly replaces the bundle of letters and then the drawer, keeping only the letter which he has just read. He stands so quickly that he feels unsteady, his vision temporarily blurred, but he takes the few steps to the window, leaning on its frame for support. There is a knock on the door.

'Are you decent, Tom?'

'I think so,' he says, and hears her open the door.

'I am sorry about earlier,' she says with a tight smile.

'Not at all. She was your sister. You're allowed to grieve for her. We're all grieving for her.'

'Are you quite all right?' she asks. 'Your face is very pale.'

'Is it?' he says. 'I'm sorry.'

She smiles at him, and he can see a trace of embarrassment.

'I shouldn't have disturbed you. Only Sean Driscoll heard you were up and, seeing as Dr Hegarty said you should take some exercise, he's asking if you might like to take a jaunt along the coast a little. One of your colleagues is staying at Moira Wilson's and would like to see you.'

Harkin has to think for a moment – this comes as such a surprise.

'And when would this be? This jaunt,' Harkin says, curious as to who this colleague might be.

'Sean is putting a horse to the buggy as we speak.'

'I'll be down directly.'

# CHAPTER 25

Charlie insists that Harkin take a thick travel blanket for the journey and, although he does his best to reject the kindness, by the time Driscoll has guided them out from the shelter offered by the house, and the buggy is exposed to the icy wind from the sea, he is grateful for it. He wraps it tight around his legs and lifts the collar of his coat, feeling the skin on his face tauten in the chill.

'It's fresh enough,' Driscoll says, seeing how Harkin is huddling into himself.

'It's bloody freezing is what it is.'

Driscoll chuckles, his gloved hands flicking the traces at the black horse's back. The buggy creaks and sways on the uneven surface.

'Anyway, you'll soon be out of this. GHQ have sent a man down for you. He's waiting for you at Wilson's.'

Harkin doesn't say anything for a moment, wondering who the boss has sent down, and what it might mean.

'What kind of a man?'

'A big man. He drove down in a motor car.' Driscoll looks at Harkin. 'It wasn't me as let them know. About you at the funeral.'

'I know,' Harkin says. 'It was Hegarty trying to get a hold of my doctor.'

171

In fact, if his visitor is who he thinks it is, then he has reason to be grateful to Hegarty. Although Driscoll, it occurs to him, may not.

'Did he mention his name, this visitor of mine? Might it be a Mr Bourke?'

'I think that was his name,' Driscoll replies. 'Looks like a prize-fighter. Hands like shovels.'

Which sounds exactly like Vincent Bourke.

They travel in silence, while Harkin puts his thoughts in order. The journey is an opportunity for him to calculate the distance from the house to the gate, and the time it might take a man to walk it, and he thinks that it is a walk that could be made in a couple of minutes – faster if a man ran. Enough time for Driscoll, who arrived several minutes after the single shot, to have fired it. And then he is reminded about the letters. And the child Maud Prendeville was carrying inside her when she died.

'Did Maud know about you?'

Harkin detects his sudden distaste for Driscoll in his tone. He makes a note not to show it again. He must play this very carefully.

'You mean about my being a Volunteer?' Driscoll says, giving him a sideways glance. Before Harkin can reply, Driscoll continues. 'We never discussed it, if that's what you mean. I was only dis-charged in June 1919 and she was no longer active by then – down here, at least. I didn't tell her when I took the oath because I thought I should keep my involvement quiet, as regards the Prendevilles at least. She may have known anyway. She knew a lot of the local Sinn Fein and Volunteers from before. They might have mentioned it to her, but she never heard it from me.'

'But you were close?' Harkin allows himself the slight emphasis on the final word to see what kind of reaction it might provoke.

Driscoll involuntarily tugs at the traces and the horse comes to a half-halt before Driscoll urges it forwards once again. When he speaks, he sounds guarded.

'How do you mean *close*?'

Harkin feels his irritation bubbling up, despite his best intentions.

'What do you think I mean? Were you friendly with her? Would you say you were good friends?'

Driscoll takes a moment to respond, and Harkin can see confusion and also anger in his expression, despite his efforts to maintain a neutral facade.

'I knew Maud Prendeville all my life. We got on well enough. There was a distance, of course. I was born to a servant in this house, and so that's what I'll always be to the Prendevilles. So I wouldn't say we were close. No, not close.'

Harkin knows he's right about the distance but, then again, surely the letter to Maud had referred to this very issue.

'There's a barrier, would you say?' This time Harkin manages to keep his voice clear of any emotion.

'That's exactly what I'd say.'

There's a thick vein visible on Driscoll's jawline that wasn't there a few moments ago, and a bitter thinness to his mouth that Harkin suspects might match his own. He takes a slow breath.

'Look,' Harkin says, deciding to try a different tack, 'I'm sorry. I'm a bit out of sorts.'

Driscoll seems to relax a little.

'You don't look the best,' he says. 'Maybe you should let this business go. Let some other fellow look into it, by all means – maybe your Mr Bourke?'

Harkin feels his anger rise up once more but this time he allows it to dissipate. It might be Driscoll doing his best to put him off from pursuing the matter, or it might be honest concern. Driscoll, after all, didn't know that Maud was in the car. Unless, of course, Maud had always intended to return that night, perhaps to meet with Driscoll. He muses on this as the horse's gait increases to a brisk trot, almost as though Driscoll is keen for the journey to be over.

'Did you arrange a meeting with Commandant Egan?' Harkin asks. 'If Bourke has a motor car, we could go wherever he feels comfortable meeting us.'

Unless, of course, Bourke has orders to take Harkin directly back to Dublin.

But even if he does, Harkin thinks he can persuade him to stay for a day or two.

'Are you sure you're in a fit state?'

'With Bourke driving I wouldn't be exerting myself too much.'

Driscoll looks across at him.

'The likelihood is the commandant will be somewhere near the gap on the other side of town.' He points to the far side of the bay, where there is a break in the hills. 'If that's the case, there's a village called Ballycourt. If you go into O'Brien's beside the church and ask for a bag of sugar and three candles, they'll point you in the right direction. I'll let you know in the morning if there is a change of plan.'

They are approaching Moira's guest house and Driscoll begins to slow the horse down. Harkin wonders if he intends to drop him at the gate. He examines the gentle slope of the drive and decides he will be firm.

'Take me to the door, Driscoll,' he says. 'There's no need to wait around, Bourke will drive me back.'

# CHAPTER 26

Harkin is sitting beside the fireplace in the residents' sitting room, watching as Vincent Bourke wedges his considerable frame into a leather armchair and reaches for the tea the young maid, Mary, has brought him. The cup seems small in Bourke's big hand and Harkin watches as he places the saucer delicately on his knee and then, little finger extended, raises the cup to his lips.

'Lovely,' he says, smiling up at Mary. 'This is as fine a cup of tea as I have had this many a day.'

His blue eyes twinkle as he speaks and Harkin is not surprised to see Mary blush in response. For a moment, she seems to lose control of her feet, which point first one way, then the other, as she tries to decide what to do with herself.

'Would you like some cake?' she says, inspiration striking.

'I would love some cake,' Bourke says, grinning at her. 'Cake would be delightful. Wouldn't you love some cake, Mr Harkin?'

'Some cake would be good,' Harkin agrees, giving Bourke a warning look.

Mary, to his surprise, snorts but it seems to be a sound of pleasure, rather than disapproval. She walks quickly from the room, leaving them alone.

'A lovely girl,' Bourke says. 'If I'd known there were so many attractive women down here, I'd have come sooner, orders or no orders.'

'But you do have orders.'

'I do,' Bourke says. 'I certainly do.'

'And they are?'

'To place myself at your disposal. If you want to fuck off out of here, I'm your man. If you want to stay around, I'm also your man. It's up to you, but the boss wants you to make your decision based on some new information that has come to his attention.'

Bourke speaks with a studied eloquence, without altering his deep Dublin accent one iota, although there is an undercurrent of mischievousness.

Which is strange, Harkin thinks, because Vincent Bourke is a very serious individual when it comes down to it.

'Tell me.'

'Firstly, your Major Vane is indeed known to us. He is known to you also, but as Mr Tomkins. Does that name ring a bell?'

It does. Tomkins is a relatively new arrival, coming to the attention of the intelligence directorate in the late summer of the previous year. He'd made his presence felt before the shooting of a sizeable number of British intelligence officers the previous November, and he had avoided their fate largely because the intelligence directorate had still not, at that point, known where he was living or what he looked like. After the November operation, Tomkins – or rather, Vane – had become more cautious still, remaining in the background when it came to active British operations. Nonetheless, the intelligence directorate had obtained two physical descriptions of him from those who had been in his company. Harkin remembers them now, and while they aren't an exact match to Vane, he curses himself for not making the connection earlier.

'That *is* an interesting piece of information,' he says.

'Isn't it, though? Here's another thing. He's currently in charge of Paddy Malone's interrogation. No sign, as yet, that Malone has told him anything, but the boss is taking steps to limit the damage if he does. Which is one of the reasons I'm here. To look after you.'

'I see.' It makes sense. Malone is currently a minor loss. But if Malone gives up Harkin or any of the other senior members of the intelligence directorate or, indeed, the boss, then the damage would be significant.

'And there's more. I'm only passing on the message, so don't be at me for more details because I don't have them.' Bourke pauses, as if trying to recall the exact words that he's been told. 'The boss says there are signs the British are aware of a shipment, which he says you know about. He says if Vane is snooping around down here, then the chances are it's to do with the shipment. He says you can tell me about it if you think you need to but you'll know best.'

This is a development that poses all sorts of questions, but if Bourke says he doesn't have the answers then there is no point asking them aloud.

'Did the boss have any thoughts as to how we should proceed?'

Bourke nods gravely, although his twinkle has returned.

'He said if I got a chance I should shoot the fucker. Unless you had any objections.'

Most of Harkin's colleagues are idealists and, like Harkin himself, suffer the emotional and psychological strain of their clandestine war. Vincent Bourke is different. He doesn't have qualms or nerves the way the rest of them do. If anything, he takes enjoyment from the whole business. He's pleasant company – charming, even – and a good friend, but he's also a killer. If Bourke wasn't fighting this war, he would find another one.

'I'd better tell you what the current situation is, then,' Harkin says, and begins to fill Bourke in on what he knows about Maud's death and the surrounding circumstances. After some hesitation, he tells Bourke about the shipment, without mentioning Sir John Prendeville's involvement, but revealing that Maud knew about it and was involved. When he finishes, Bourke sits back and closes his eyes for a moment. When he speaks he is to the point.

'So you think Driscoll plugged her?'

'It's possible. But it doesn't entirely make sense. I mean, why would he kill her? What reason might he have?'

'She was up the duff.'

'I haven't read all the letters, but they could be from years ago, and there was nothing in the one I read about a pregnancy.'

'Were there envelopes? Postmarks? Have you compared the writing?'

All good points.

'That's one of the things. There were no envelopes and no postmarks, which could mean they were hand-delivered. That might point to Driscoll but, no, I haven't compared the handwriting yet.'

'You say Maud Prendeville had something to do with the arms shipment. Did Driscoll?'

'No. I'm fairly sure he knows nothing about the guns.'

'But what if she told him about them? If they were lovers, she might have.' Bourke scowls, as though thinking over a particularly complex problem. 'What if he's a British informer? What if he's playing a double game?'

Harkin considers this, then shrugs.

'You've met Driscoll, Vincent. What did you make of him?'

Bourke considers the question for a moment, his scowl twisting his mouth still further.

'Smart enough. A bit arrogant with it, which is no bad thing. Tough, I'd say, if he went through the war. I didn't much take to him, but then I'm very particular in my choice of friends.' He nods cordially to Harkin. 'All in all, he seemed straight and if he is a spy, he's not having any effect on Egan's activities. I've one thought, though.'

'Go on.'

'We'd know better what was what if we knew who tipped off the column about Abercrombie. If Driscoll had nothing to do with it, that might let him off the hook and give us a name to talk to. If he did, it might be a different story.'

'A trip to Father Dillon?'

Bourke smiles, but there isn't much humour in it.

'As it happens, I'm in need of confession. Two birds with one stone.'

'Three birds,' Harkin says. 'You can take a letter to Sir John for me. He's not far out of your way and I need to tell him what I've uncovered so far.'

Later, when Bourke is leaving, Harkin wonders, absent-mindedly, if the boss has told Bourke to shoot Harkin if it looks likely he'll be arrested.

It's a possibility, he decides.

# CHAPTER 27

Harkin sits in the unlit room, watching the last of the light wash out of the already dark sky and listening to the sound of Bourke's car disappearing in the direction of Sir John's house. He finds himself to be in a sombre mood, although it lifts when Moira Wilson enters.

'Where are your memsahibs this evening?' he asks, gathering together a smile.

'They're playing cards with the Eustaces.' Moira's monocle glints as she lights a candle. 'They won't be back until the morning. I'm all alone.'

'What about Mary?'

'Her evening off. There's a dance in town and I believe Mr Bourke has just been kind enough to provide her with a lift in. Her intention is, I believe, to stay with her mother and be back in the morning.'

Harkin remembers the burst of feminine laughter just before the departure of the car. He smiles. The chances of Bourke accompanying Mary to the dance would seem to be high. He wonders how he will get back to Kilcolgan.

'Mr Bourke asked for the key to the front door. Just so you know.'

He looks up to find that there is suppressed amusement in Moira's expression. It seems as though the conversation is heading in an unexpected direction, one that Moira has control of.

'That is disappointing. He was supposed to drive me back to Kilcolgan later on.'

'So I believe. However, I have solved that problem. You are to stay the night here.'

His surprise must show.

'It is perfectly respectable. You are feeling unwell and I am the daughter of a doctor of medicine, so practically a medical professional myself.'

'Do I have any say in this?'

'No. It's all arranged. I informed your Mr Bourke of my decision, so that he felt under no obligation to return too early, and called Kilcolgan and spoke to Mrs Driscoll.' She leans towards him, as though worried she might be overheard. 'I don't like to mention this, but she did not sound disappointed in the slightest.'

'Well, I must hope for my speedy recovery.'

'Quite so. Mrs Driscoll hopes for it, too, in that it will lead to your return to Dublin. Anyway, I hope you like stew.'

'I'm very fond of it.'

'That's just as well, because the alternatives are very limited. An omelette at best.' She walks over to sit in the chair that Bourke recently vacated. Her face is orange in the firelight, her hair touched with gold. 'My father tells me you intend to stay at Kilcolgan for a little while. Is that true?'

'It would seem so.'

Moira nods. Her face is half-obscured but in the flickering flame of the candle her lips seem fuller than usual. A mouth that curves upwards.

'I'm pleased. It is good to have you around after all these years.'

Harkin remembers snatches from the story she told him the night before – about a young woman who loved a man, only he had loved another – and finds that his chest is suddenly empty of breath. If Moira notices his state of mind, which he suspects plays across his features like a newspaper headline, she covers it with a breezy demeanour.

'Now we have to decide where to eat. I will give you the alternatives. There is the kitchen, which is warm, well lit and convenient, but perhaps a little domestic. Or there is the dining room, which would mean I should be traipsing up and down the corridor most of the night, seeing as you are an invalid and incapable of movement. On balance, I think we should be more comfortable in the kitchen, but the decision is yours.'

He wonders what she means by 'comfortable' and can't help but allow his imagination to speculate. This she somehow notices and taps his knee in reproof.

'I am not sure what is going through your mind, Mr Harkin. But it should get out of your mind and behave itself.'

'I didn't mean—' he begins but she interrupts him.

'The kitchen, then?'

Her smile seems to indicate she is not offended, and Harkin knows better than most when to stop digging himself into a hole.

'The kitchen it is.'

He follows her and the candle through the house, its reflection glittering from the glass and polished wood and, for an instant, the black and white photograph of Robert Wilson. As they walk, Harkin has the sense of the shadows gathering in behind them, but this house is not like Kilcolgan. There is no sense that the very walls are listening and watching.

183

The kitchen is a square room, which must once have kept several people employed. A long table with eight chairs stands in front of a large cream-coloured oven; a tendril of steam leaks from a covered pot. Around the walls there are dressers loaded down with plates, pots and the other necessities of a large kitchen.

The oven gives off a warmth that is almost solid, and Harkin finds himself making his way towards it to sit on the rail that runs along its front. The table, he sees, is set for two, the silver cutlery gilded by the light of two candles.

'I anticipated your decision,' she says, lifting the lid of a pot with a towelled hand and staring into it intently. 'Not long now. Will you have some soup to start with?'

'What kind of soup?' he says. She shakes her head reprovingly.

'You'll be getting no clues from me. You'll have to make up your own mind as to what breed of soup it is. Anyway, it's very early yet. I expect a man of your refinement won't want to be eating until eight o'clock at the earliest.'

His spirits sink at the prospect of sitting in the kitchen, making small talk, with the smell of the stew in his nostrils, for another three hours.

'Unless, of course, you are half-starved after your sleep-enforced fast.'

'I could be tempted to stray from my years of refined late evening dining.'

She considers him with a quizzical expression.

'Sit down before you fall down, then.'

'You're very good to me,' he says, and means it. He wonders at his sudden emotion. Perhaps she sees how affected he is, because her smile returns.

'You were with me last night,' he says, to break the silence.

184

'I was.'

'And you told me a story.'

'You were asleep. How would you know what story I told or didn't tell?'

'Perhaps I am mistaken.'

'Perhaps.'

'Thank you for looking after me, anyway.'

'I like to have someone to look after, but really I'm a selfish woman. I am starved for intelligent conversation, particularly with an attractive man, so I mean to feed you up, let you drink a little wine and then hope you will entertain me.' She points to the chair. 'Don't look so alarmed, only sit down and rest and let me see to the feeding and watering. I expect no entertainment until you feel yourself once again.'

He obeys her, walking around the table to sit down. He watches her move around the oven, retrieving a round soda bread loaf and placing it on the table between them. She glances at him sharply as she does so.

'I expect this kind of informality is deeply shocking to you, Mr Harkin, with your high society Dublin ways, but I won't have you sit in judgement on me, do you hear?'

'You'll hear no complaints from me, Mrs Wilson.'

She sighs, squinting at him through her monocle.

'I think you need a glass of wine. I'm not sure I can bear being called Mrs Wilson all evening.' She fetches an open bottle with a faded label from the china-laden dresser and splashes the bottom of his glass before pausing. 'Unless you'd prefer beer. Perhaps beer is the fashion now? In Dublin? In high society.'

'Are you going to tease me all evening?'

She seems to make a half-hearted attempt to appear offended.

'I might. Anyway, we don't have any beer. Really you're doing me a favour – we haven't had many guests since the start of the Troubles and the memsahibs don't drink as much as I'd like them to. It's a real shame as they are much more agreeable when they are slightly sozzled. Anyway, I don't know how long wine keeps and for all I know this may have gone off.'

He tastes the wine. He can feel its glow sliding down his throat to his empty stomach. He places his glass back on the table, wary of his almost instantaneous light-headedness.

'It's very good,' he says, then, after a pause, 'Moira.'

Her eyes twinkle in the candlelight. It seems she has removed her monocle while he wasn't looking. He decides he doesn't miss it.

'I thought you'd like it, Thomas.'

She stands behind him and he feels the touch of her hand on his shoulder, tracking the scars of old wounds through his clothes. He finds that his breath is coming more quickly than usual.

'I helped my father when we brought you back to Kilcolgan,' she says in a quiet voice. 'He said your injuries were mostly shrapnel but they made me sad to see.'

Harkin thinks about his body when he looks at it in the mirror. The bone-white shapes and swirls that hot metal carved into his pale flesh, the curls of hair around his breastbone. Moira will have seen the dark pink scars where a bullet entered and exited his thigh. To his surprise, he finds he does not mind that Moira Wilson has seen him naked.

'Thank you,' he says, reaching up to take her hand. 'Once again. For looking after me.'

She exerts the smallest of pressure on his fingers.

186

'Later I watched you sleeping. You looked very peaceful, but then I thought about the war and what you must have seen. I held your hand sometimes. It was heavier than I expected.'

'I remember that.'

'I didn't mind, Thomas,' she says, shaking her head as though he has said something silly. 'I wanted to look after you or I wouldn't have bothered.' She hesitates. 'My father says you should make a full recovery. So long as you keep yourself out of trouble. I wonder will you be able to, though?'

He wonders what she knows about him, or suspects, but he is not worried that she will betray him.

'It may be difficult,' he says.

Part of him wishes that Hegarty had told her nothing about his condition, but now that he is sitting across from her, her hands holding his, it seems to him she has a right to know.

She squeezes his fingers. Part of him wants to pull back his hand but he forces himself to leave it there, to submit to the stroking of her thumb. He looks down, fascinated by the movement.

'Shall we eat our soup?' she asks in a low voice and he nods.

When they've finished the meal, she takes him by the hand and leads him upstairs.

# CHAPTER 28

Afterwards they lie on their backs, looking up at the shifting glow that the single candle's flame casts on the ceiling, their fingers entwined. Harkin's breathing is laboured and, despite the chill in the room, he finds that he is covered in a sheen of sweat. He savours the feel of Moira's skin against his; the warmth of her alongside him.

'There are some things I think you need to know,' he says.

After a pause to organise his thoughts, he tells Moira about his involvement with the IRA, and something of his activities. Even now, lying here with her like this, he holds back anything specific. It is not that he doesn't trust her. It is that the information might place her in harm's way. He also does not tell her about the visions and the apparitions. He thinks there is enough for her to digest already, without adding them. When he finishes, Moira says nothing at first but pulls the blankets over them and nestles into his side.

'And Maud's murder?' she asks. 'Will you carry on with that?'

'I feel I have to.' He can hear the apology in his words.

In response she places her hand on his chest.

'Well, I'm not sure it is what my father had in mind when he wanted you to stay out of trouble.'

He takes a deep breath.

'Did he tell you about Maud's condition?'

He can feel the shake of her head.

'About her being pregnant? He didn't.' Moira pauses. 'Maud told me herself. Once I knew he was to do the post mortem, I spoke to him. I asked him to keep it out of the report, which he agreed to do. After all, at that time, it didn't seem her being pregnant had anything to do with her death. I know he told you, though. He came by this afternoon.'

'If I said to you the father might have been Sean Driscoll, what would you say to that?'

She considers the question carefully.

'Do you have any reason to think that?'

'I might do. But at the moment it doesn't quite hang together. I'll know more tomorrow but I wanted to get your opinion before that.'

She doesn't speak for some time.

'You need to understand what it is like down here, for women like Maud and me. We aren't young girls anymore and we have had some experience of the world. If we lived in Dublin or London, we might have some more freedom, but here engaging with a man outside of marriage is very difficult, and marrying even more so. She obviously slept with someone, and I suppose in theory it could have been Driscoll. He's a good-looking man. He is a rebel, which would have appealed to her. On the other hand, he isn't from her class, or her religion, he works for her family, and I am not sure there was . . . how shall I put it? . . . an attraction. It's unlikely, I think.'

'He's a rebel?' Harkin asks, attempting to sound perplexed. She sighs in response.

190

'The reason I know he is a rebel and don't much care for Sean Driscoll is that my husband's guns were taken from this house and he led the men that did it. He wore a mask but I knew him all the same. Anyway, you're not fooling me, Thomas Harkin. I watched you talking to him and I watched him talking to you. You know very well he is one of yours.'

He leans down to kiss her forehead.

'I'm sorry. Old habits die hard. But it's as well if you know as little as possible about my business.'

'You don't want me to join you storming the battlements, my breasts bound in a tricolour?' she says, amused.

'I like them unbound.'

Moira smiles across at him.

'I don't want you to be hurt because of me, that's all,' he says.

'There is that,' she agrees, her voice languid. 'It's not myself, of course, that I'm worried about. It's the poor memsahibs. They wouldn't last a week on their own.'

He is conscious that she hasn't asked him about his intentions or affections. He runs a finger along her arm.

'And what of us, Moira Wilson?'

'What indeed?' Her voice is dismissive, but not unkind. 'You're a good-looking man and I'm a desperate woman tied to a house on the edge of the world. I'm sorry but I've taken advantage of you. Your chaste reputation is all torn asunder.'

'My reputation is as a renowned ladies' man.'

She snorts into his armpit.

'If you'd like me to throw you a crumb of reassurance, then I will tell you that I like you, Tom Harkin. I always have. More than I should have and I shed a tear or two when Maud swept in and took you for her own. I think you're brave and honest and

191

kind and true. They say these Troubles will pass over soon, that things can't go on the way they are, that the Americans won't stand for it. Well, all I'll say to you, Tom, is that you will always have a warm welcome in this house. When that comes to pass.'

'Not until then?'

He hears her sigh.

'I'm not suited to waiting around for soldiers to return from war. I tried it once and the poor man didn't come home at all. Anyway, I know your sort – I'd only be an impediment. I wasn't born to be an impediment. So, for now, you had better leave my room before your Mr Bourke returns. There's one towards the front I've made ready for you.'

She pats him on the chest, kisses him and stands. He watches her walk around the room, gathering his clothing, her skin golden in the candlelight. She hands the clothes to him, then pulls a dressing gown from a hook behind the door and puts it on. She smiles and there is no shame or sadness in it.

'I'm going to go and wash but first I'll show you to your room.'

'Thank you,' he says, putting an arm through his shirtsleeve.

She takes a candle from a drawer in her bedside table and places it into a small round holder. She lights the candle and hands it to him. Then she leans forwards and kisses him on the cheek. As a gesture it feels chaste, almost sisterly.

'Come on, then, Tom Harkin. You need a good night's sleep.'

# CHAPTER 29

Harkin does sleep well, at first. A solid, black sleep in which there is no horror or memory or indeed anything. This absence of his surroundings and even his own self is how he imagines death must feel, if death can be felt. His waking consists of him leaving the nothingness and becoming aware first of himself, then of the bed and the room and then the nagging sense of an approaching danger.

Before he is even fully conscious, he has pushed back the blankets and has rolled himself out and is standing. The carpet is cold under his feet and the house is silent. He crosses to push aside the curtains to look out, but he can see nothing in the darkness except for the faintest outline of the trees that shield the house from the sea and the suggestion of a mist. He places a hand against the window, hearing the sound of wood against wood as it shifts in its frame, and leans close to the glass, but there is no light to be seen anywhere and even the sea is quiet. But something has woken him.

Then, after a few moments, he hears it. A sound in the distance, and as it grows louder, Harkin becomes certain it is an approaching vehicle. At first he thinks it must be Bourke coming back from the town, but as the noise comes closer, he recognises the distinctive rattle of the Crossley Tender lorries used by the police and army and realises that it is more than one vehicle. No sooner has he come to this conclusion than three sets of headlights cross the rise that separates the guest house from Kilcolgan, searching through the misted hedges and fields like greedy fingers. He hurriedly pulls on his trousers and his shoes and gathers his shirt and jacket in his hands, but they are already almost outside and coming to a halt. Harkin can see the shapes of men jumping down onto the road and fanning out around the house. One of the tenders turns in through the gate, its headlights turning the short drive yellow, and he steps away from the window as they light the room as well. Harkin stands there, thinking about the gun he took from Maud's room, not because he might use it but because if he is caught with it they will likely shoot him on the spot. He looks around for somewhere to hide it, and then Moira has entered the room and crosses quickly towards him. Her face seems tight with tension in the reflected light, her eyes shining.

'Have you anything needs taking?' He can hear her anger, although is not certain whether it is directed towards him or the police outside.

Mutely he hands her the small pistol from his jacket pocket. She weighs it in her hand without comment and then leaves.

'Harkin!'

The voice comes from outside. He recognises it as Abercrombie's. Without conscious thought, Harkin crosses to the window and looks down, a part of him attempting to stop the movement but seemingly unable to. Abercrombie is standing in front of the lorry that has turned in, silhouetted by its headlights. He is carrying a revolver in his hand. He imagines the other Auxies and RIC men out there with their guns trained on him. He must make an easy target in his white vest.

Abercrombie raises his pistol and aims it at Harkin, then slowly raises the pistol further and fires it twice into the air. Harkin knows he should move away from the window but, as before, it is as though his body belongs to someone else. He feels a distance from the events that are unfolding around him, uncertain as to what has just passed. He watches Abercrombie as though the major is an actor on a backlit stage. Then he sees a silhouetted figure, who must be Moira, come from the direction of the house and stand in front of Abercrombie, who lowers the pistol and smiles at her. The smile seems to be polite, even gentle, and seems out of place given the shooting. The sense of being a powerless member of an audience watching a perfromance is stronger than ever. Harkin wants to call out to Moira, to tell her to come away, but he is not able to. Instead, someone comes to stand beside Abercrombie and Harkin sees in the headlight's glare the flash of a sergeant's chevrons against the dark green uniform of the regular RIC.

There is a pause, during which the sergeant leans towards Abercrombie. Harkin thinks he recognises the shape of Sergeant Kelly, the RIC man who questioned him on the journey from the station, but it could be anyone. If there are words, Harkin cannot hear them. The only sound he can hear is the beating of his own heart and nothing else – not even the sound of the tenders' engines.

Perhaps someone gives orders then, as the shapes and shadows of RIC policemen and Auxiliaries begin to move through and around the patterns of misted light. He notices that their rifles are slung now, whereas before they were held ready. After a short pause, the semi-silence Harkin finds himself in is broken by the sudden, harsh grind of gears as first one of the tenders and then another drive off. Only the sergeant and Abercrombie are left standing in front of the last tender, facing Moira, their shadows stretching out towards the house, until finally the major nods curtly and the two policemen walk out of the headlights' glare.

After a moment, there is the metallic clang of the tender's doors closing. Then the tender reverses down the drive and follows the others along the road to the west.

# CHAPTER 30

When the last of the glow from the final Crossley's headlights disappears over the hill, Harkin makes his way down to the hallway, where a single lit candle sits on a small table. As he descends the last step, Moira Wilson enters, her long hair wild around her shoulders, her face pale. Seeing him, she runs the last few steps and holds up a hand to his cheek. He leans his head into her hand and then he finds he has her in his arms, or perhaps she has him in hers. The only sound in the hallway is the tick-tock of the grandfather clock and the only light the swirling shadows from the candle's flame. She pushes away from him, her eyes catching a glitter from the candle's flame.

'I thought they were shooting at you.'

'They were just a warning,' he says, the words sounding calmer than he feels.

She places a hand behind his neck and kisses him.

'If they were a warning, maybe you should pay some heed to it.'

'I'll think about it.'

He wants to say something reassuring, but they are interrupted by the sound of another approaching engine. They look at each other with apprehension for a moment but whoever is coming, it isn't the RIC.

'It's not Abercrombie,' he says. 'It sounds more like a motor car. Perhaps it's Bourke.'

'I'll go and get dressed. You can meet him like this, but not me, I don't think.'

It isn't Bourke, however. When Harkin walks outside to greet the visitor, it is clear that the motor car is approaching not from the direction of the town but from the west, and when it pulls into the driveway, it is Sir John Prendeville's blue Daimler, not Bourke's nondescript Ford. Sir John steps out, pale and anxious.

'Is everything all right? I heard shooting and drove straight over.' He looks at Harkin.

Harkin reaches up to rub at his chin.

'It was nothing. Major Abercrombie came visiting and fired a few shots in the air, that's all.'

'Abercrombie?' Sir John looks along the road that leads toward the town, his concern apparent.

'Where is Mrs Wilson?' Sir John says, seeming uncertain for a moment how to proceed but having asked the question, Harkin can see finds himself on safer ground, his indignation swelling him. 'Is she harmed? And the ladies? I shall report Abercrombie directly to the Commissioner of the RIC first thing in the morning.'

'The ladies are away playing cards and Mrs Wilson went to get dressed when she heard you coming. I'm sure she'll return directly.'

Sir John looks at him in confusion and then he sees another emotion enter the older man's expression. A quick glance towards the doorway.

'But what are you doing here, Harkin? I thought you were at Kilcolgan.'

'The boss sent a man down to assist me. I came over to talk to him this afternoon and was taken unwell.' He can see Sir John is less than convinced and decides to stretch the truth a little. 'Dr Hegarty insisted I stay here until I felt better and I only woke up when Abercrombie came calling.'

He listens back to his words and is unconvinced. They sound too detailed, too rehearsed. He wouldn't believe himself and Sir John's confusion has disappeared, replaced by something more like wariness. He decides on a quick change of direction.

'Mr Bourke brought you my message?'

'Yes. Some interesting developments. The letters, for example.'

He can see that Sir John is uncomfortable discussing his niece's love affair.

'We have a few moments before Mrs Wilson gathers herself,' Harkin says. 'Shall we discuss the matter as it stands?'

Harkin leads Sir John into the dining room, lights one of the oil lamps and places it on a table before sitting down facing the older man. He repeats the information he put in the letter but with more detail. Sir John says nothing until Harkin has finished. His expression is as bland as if he is being told yesterday's weather.

'You kept one letter, you say. May I see it?'

Harkin reaches into his pocket and passes the envelope across to Sir John. He notices that his hands shake when he takes it.

'Is the writing Driscoll's?' Harkin asks, once Sir John begins to examine it.

Harkin notices that Sir John's blue eyes are so pale in the candle-light they might almost be white. He seems to have aged since he stepped from the car.

'I believe it is,' Sir John says, after a moment. 'Would you mind if I keep this? I wouldn't want it to be circulated more widely and this doesn't seem to be a matter which we would want to bring to the police, given the circumstances. I will talk to Dr Hegarty, thank him for his discretion so far and do my best to ensure the matter is left there.'

Harkin nods his agreement.

'What will you do now?' Sir John asks, his gaze focused on his upturned hands, as though he holds an answer in those long fingers of his.

'That depends on you. The evidence is mainly circumstantial and, to be honest, confusing. But I think he needs to give an explanation.'

'I think it is more than circumstantial. He would have lost his job if the matter came to light,' Sir John says quickly. 'His mother would have lost hers, also. What is more, it seems clear to me that this RIC source is a nonsense. Driscoll must have known Maud was coming back that night. He set up the ambush and killed her when she somehow survived.'

Sir John's face sags after he finishes speaking, as though overcome by the horror of it. Harkin notices the older man swallow hard, then he seems to gather himself. When Harkin speaks, he keeps his tone calm.

'We'll know more when my colleague has spoken to Father Dillon. Once we have as much information as we can gather, Driscoll will be given a chance to explain himself. Mr Bourke and I will talk to him tomorrow. If we are not satisfied with his explanation, he will be dealt with by a court martial.'

Sir John's face is white, even in soft light from the lamp. When he speaks it is slowly and quietly, but with a gathering conviction.

'I am not certain there is a need for something so official,' he says. 'His guilt is clear. It would be preferable if it were dealt with much more . . . how shall I put it . . . efficiently. No more talking. No more dragging Maud's name through the mud.' He pauses and when he resumes, there is a grating menace to his tone. 'I would

200

go further. My continued co-operation with your superior and your organisation depends on absolute discretion in this matter.'

There is something repellent to Harkin about the coldness in Sir John's expression, but he remembers the boss's instructions about the guns being the most important element of this whole business. He can hear Moira coming down the staircase, approaching the dining room.

'I will consider your suggestion.'

Once Sir John leaves, Moira walks Harkin back to his bedroom and leaves him there, closing the door behind her with a whispered but firm 'goodnight'.

He stands, thinking, for a moment, and it occurs to him that Sean Driscoll is almost the only person who knew he was here and not in Kilcolgan. It also made the major's visit all the more suspicious. It's a thought he decides he will address with Driscoll in the morning, possibly with Vincent Bourke's assistance.

Eventually he gets into bed and lies there for a while, unable to sleep. He stares up at the ceiling and listens to the waves on the long shore and the sounds of the house. He tries to relax, to slow his heart rate, to trick his body into slumber, but nothing seems to work, even though he is tired. Bone-tired. Eventually, in desperation, he lights the candle and decides to go downstairs to find a book to read by it.

He descends the stairs slowly, not wanting to wake Moira, placing his weight on each step with care. The candlelight barely reaches his feet and he holds on to the banister with one hand, its wood chill to the touch.

He is halfway down the staircase when he has the sense that he is being watched. He stops, lifting the candle higher, looking down into the hallway for a waiting shadow or an unexpected movement, but there is nothing. Yet the feeling will not go away. He stands there, holding the candle aloft, feeling slightly foolish. He takes two more steps down the staircase, before coming to another halt. He takes a moment to breathe, admitting to himself that while his mind is telling him there is nothing to worry about, his body is taking a different view. Adrenaline swirls through his veins like a long electric shock, while the hair on his head and the skin on his shoulders seem both to be stiff with anticipation. He tries to swallow, but he can't, and all the while his heart is pumping blood around his body at a furious rate, the sound of it so loud in his ears that he isn't sure he would be able to hear danger approaching even if it were right beside him.

Another step. And now he smells an almost overpowering stench as if something is rotting nearby. He lifts the candle once again, conscious that it is shaking in his hand, the hot wax shaking down on to his bare skin, and looks down to see if there is a vase of decomposing flowers on the side table in the hallway. But the table is clear.

He doesn't know, afterwards, what makes him look up at this point. He turns slowly on the staircase, the light thrown by the candle advancing slowly along the wall, reaching upwards until he sees the shape of a woman, her features indistinct, standing at the top of the staircase, a long, old-fashioned white dress falling from her bare shoulders, nearly as pale as her face. She holds in her hands a bouquet of white roses, the petals withered almost to brown, and he remembers the story about their smell, which now fills his nostrils, being a warning of death. Transfixed, he realises he can see the wooden panelling on the far side of her.

He swallows, or tries to, and then closes his eyes. When he opens them again, the woman has gone, although the corrupted perfume of the roses remains.

# CHAPTER 31

It is long after morning light penetrates the half-drawn curtains that Harkin wakes fully. He lies there, thinking back to the night before – to Moira Wilson, and Abercrombie's arrival, and the terrifying incident on the staircase. At first he is uncertain that any of it was real, but when he looks at his hand it is still mottled by the wax, now stiff and flaking, that dripped from the candle while he stood frozen on the staircase. He has no idea how he returned to his bedroom, and yet he seems to have slept.

He dresses quickly, only pausing when he hears the sound of an approaching motor car, but this time, to his relief, it is driven by the returning Vincent Bourke. They meet in the dining room, where a somewhat subdued Mary has sat the big man at a table with a pot of tea. She leaves with the promise of breakfast. Bourke is unreadable, his demeanour one of jovial bonhomie despite a whiff of stale whiskey on his breath and the air of a man who has not slept much.

'You stayed the night in town, then?' Harkin asks, his gaze following Mary as she leaves the room.

'I didn't have much choice, what with the peelers on the warpath. I holed up at the hotel.'

'And Mary?'

'Anyone would think you were her mother,' Bourke says, raising an eyebrow in mock affront. 'Anyway, you don't need to worry about Mary. She knows all about the likes of me.'

'You didn't go to the ceilidh?'

'There was no ceilidh. The police imposed a six o'clock curfew and it was just as well they cancelled it. Our lads burned out two big houses the evening before in retaliation for the death of Matt Breen, and the Auxies lost two men yesterday up the hills going after them. The Auxies were after blood last night and God knows what would have happened if they'd had a ceilidh to fix their attention on.'

'Our friend Egan again?'

'I presume so.'

Harkin rubs his chin with the palm of his hand.

'It wasn't only in the town that Abercrombie and his men were throwing their weight about last night.'

Harkin tells Bourke about the major's visit.

'Jesus,' Bourke says, cheerfully. 'You're a man in demand. Do you think Vane tipped him off?'

'I'm not sure. I think if Vane had, though, I'd be dead, so maybe Malone has held firm after all. I think it's just that Abercrombie doesn't want me poking around in his business. I'm more worried about how he knew I was here.'

'One of the Prendevilles?'

'Or Sean Driscoll.'

Mary returns with toast and two plates of eggs and bacon. Harkin find that he is hungry.

'Did you talk to Father Dillon?'

'He wasn't there,' Bourke says, through a mouthful of toast. 'His housekeeper said he would be back later in the evening, but by that stage the Auxies had the place battened down. Anyway, I thought we could visit him on the way.'

'On the way?'

'Well, the residents' bar stayed open and our friend Sean Driscoll came in.'

'And . . .?'

'And he said the bold Commandant Egan would be delighted to make your acquaintance. He said if you were to go to the establishment he told you about, you'll be given directions. Which I took to mean you knew what the hell he was talking about.'

'What time did he tell you this?'

'Around eight in the evening, I'd say.'

Abercrombie's visit had been at just after two. If Driscoll was in town the night before, might he have told Abercrombie he was staying at Moira's guest house?

'Did he stay long?'

'No, he was in and out. Said he needed to be back at Kilcolgan for the morning and had a man he needed to meet. The barman told him to stay because of the trouble, but he said he'd be careful.'

Harkin ponders this statement for a moment or two, watching Bourke make short work of the last of his breakfast. Bourke helps himself to another slice of toast and then looks at the remnants on Harkin's plate.

'Do you want a hand finishing that?'

Harkin pushes it across the table and the big man smiles in anticipation.

'I wonder about Driscoll,' Harkin says. 'I wonder how come he felt comfortable going about the town on a night when the Auxies were on the rampage. There are a lot of things to wonder about when it comes to Sean Driscoll.'

He tells Bourke about Sir John's confirmation that the letters came from Sean Driscoll. Bourke's expression darkens while he speaks.

'It's not looking good for our Sean.'

Harkin nods.

'It's not. Let's see Father Dillon first, and then it would do no harm to square things with Egan before we deal with Driscoll. In any event, whether or not there was a message about Abercrombie passed on through the good father is something we need to know.' Harkin takes a moment to consider his next question, knowing its implications. 'Are you armed?'

'If needs be,' Bourke says, his mouth thin and hard. 'I have a Mauser in the motor behind a panel. It takes no time to get it out.'

Harkin takes a deep breath, preparing himself for the day ahead.

'Let's see what the day brings.'

After breakfast, Harkin goes in search of Moira and finds her in the kitchen. When she sees him, she smiles and turns to Mary.

'The gentlemen seem to have finished their breakfast. Will you go and clear the room for lunch? The ladies will be back from the Eustaces' soon.'

When Mary leaves the room, he takes a step towards her and slips his hand around her waist. To his surprise, she lets him, turning up her mouth to him to be kissed.

'Did you sleep well?' she asks.

'Not too bad.'

He wants to tell her about the apparition, but the words don't come and then he thinks she knows enough to frighten off any sensible woman already.

'I'll be leaving with Mr Bourke in a little while.'

She regards him steadily.

'You owe me nothing, you know. I am not a damsel in a fairy story that needs taking care of. If anyone needs taking care of, it's you.'

'That's good to know.'

She reaches up a hand to pull at his tie.

'I'd better take that litle gun back,' he says.

She looks at him, then turns and leaves the room. When she returns, less than a minute later, she is carrying the small pistol in her hand. He takes it from her, checks the safety catch and puts it in his pocket.

'Thank you.'

'I would like you to be careful, Mr Harkin. Whatever you are getting up to today.'

'I'll do my best.'

'That,' she says, 'will have to do.'

# CHAPTER 32

St Ann's is a small, recently built church on the outskirts of the town, the granite from which it is constructed still retaining a fresh polish that the sea air and the weather have not yet dulled. Bourke slows the car and brings it to a halt just past the entrance, indicating a detached house made from the same cut stone, set in a newly laid-out garden.

'Does the housekeeper live in?' Harkin asks, examining the building.

'She was leaving when I was here last night, but she could have been just going out for the evening.'

Harkin pulls out his watch. It's just past ten o'clock. He takes another look at the priest's house. The curtains are still drawn across the windows.

'Let's take a look around.'

They step out of the car into a fine misty drizzle, barely visible on a day that is so overcast. Harkin walks over to the entrance to the church. There is a mass scheduled for eleven o'clock, which makes the house's curtains still being closed all the more strange. He can tell from Bourke's narrow mouth and alert air that he has the same presentiment.

'Will I fetch the Mauser from the car?'

Harkin looks along the street, first towards the town and then along the road that leads towards the hills. He has a bad feeling about the house but, on the other hand, he knows he is not quite his normal self.

'No,' he says, after a moment's further thought. 'I'll go and have a look. You stay back. I'll let you know if I need you.'

'Would it not be better if I went?'

Harkin looks at the big man and smiles. Bourke is good at persuading people to do what he wants them to do, but he's not subtle. Harkin wants whatever information the priest has, but ideally without breaking any of his bones.

'Best if I go, I think. You keep an eye out for trouble.'

Bourke nods his agreement but there is a part of Harkin that wishes the big man would insist on coming with him.

There is no pavement and the run-off from the verges has caused a layer of mud to spread across the road. Harkin has no choice but to walk through it, and the suck of it on his boots and the anticipation of danger send him back to the memory of a slow straggling night march up into the line – the sound of his company moving step by step through the dark, their boots scraping on duckboards and squelching through mud, the soft clang and bump of their equipment and the sound of the guns along the front a dull rumble that gets louder with each step. He feels a familiar dullness come over him. It is the deliberate suppression of emotion and hope. What will be, will be. He reaches the gate to the priest's garden and lifts the cast-iron latch, the creak of the metal against metal bringing back another image of a German trench, and along it the strewn corpses of the dead. The image is so clear that he feels his body become damp with sweat. He swallows and takes a

210

step onto the path that leads to the house. There is no sound or sign of life, only the cawing from the spiral of crows circling the field beyond. Harkin concentrates on walking, but even his best efforts can't stop the nagging certainty that the house ahead of him does not harbour a warm welcome.

He reaches the door, pulls the bell and waits, hearing it echo within, imagining a tiled hallway with religious paintings and a clock on the wall that someone has forgot to wind up. There is no immediate response and he turns to look at Bourke, who is leaning against the motor car, his hat pulled low, a cloud of cigarette smoke hiding his face. Harkin nods to him and tries the bell again then, tentatively, puts his hand on the door knob. He turns it and the door opens inwards.

He finds himself looking into a hallway that is almost exactly as he has imagined it, except that there is no clock. He allows the door to swing open fully and stands there, taking in the small side table with a set of keys in a bowl and a statue of the Sacred Heart. He does not call out. There is no point. He can tell from the perfect stillness that no one will answer him. Somehow Maud's pistol is in his hand, even though he doesn't remember taking it out.

The house smells of patchouli and peat and something else that he prefers not to think about. He follows the short corridor that runs alongside the staircase towards the back of the house, where the kitchen door stands open. A half-eaten plate of food sits on the long table, beside it an overturned glass, red wine pooled around it, and in front of it an open book, the page held open by a red ribbon. A solitary supper interrupted. Harkin makes his way around the table and finds a chair is lying on the floor behind it, along with a single slipper.

He considers the scene. If there was a struggle, it was brief. A kitchen dresser stands against one wall, a set of porcelain plates on display. A double Belfast sink stands in front of the window that overlooks the rear of the house, with dishes and cutlery long dried on the rack beside it. There is a pantry and a laundry room leading off the kitchen, but both are empty of anything but the usual. Harkin checks the range. It is still warm, but when he opens the lower door to look at the grate, there are only ashes.

An evening meal, an interruption. And then what?

Harkin walks back out into the hall and stands for a moment, considering whether to call for Bourke, but as he is passing the doorway on his left, his hand, as if of its own volition, comes to rest on the handle. He nods to himself. He has been in houses like this before. This will be the priest's study. He turns the handle and the click of the mechanism sounds shockingly loud in the silence. He concentrates now on his senses. The smell he avoided addressing when he entered the house is coming from inside the room, and he makes his breathing shallow to avoid as much of it as he can. He knows the smell. He feels his stomach turn slowly and his eyes begin to water.

'Come on,' someone says, and he knows it is his own voice even if it sounds as though it belongs to someone else. He pushes the door and it swings open.

A body hangs from a cassock rope that has been tied to the ornamented corner of a huge wardrobe, at least eight feet high.

A single slipper still clings to the body's left foot, which hangs in space, six inches above the floor.

The stench of death is almost overpowering.

# CHAPTER 33

Bourke enters the room and stands in front of the priest, examining the dead body, his face impassive.

'He wasn't a big man, was he?'

Harkin hears him speak as though from a distance. He is searching through the drawers of the priest's desk, looking for something – anything – that might give some clue as to why the priest died. It's true, though, Dillon was a small-boned man, not much bigger than a child. The priest's eyes are closed, for which Harkin is grateful.

'What time is it?' he asks Bourke.

'Just coming up to a quarter past.'

Harkin remembers the mass that is due to be said at eleven. He should have left as soon as he found the body, but here he is, going through Dillon's papers as fast as he can.

'I take it you didn't find the housekeeper?' Harkin says, relieved that Bourke didn't return with news of another body.

'No. It must be her day off,' Bourke says, the distraction in his voice suggesting his mind is on other things. 'She's well out of it. Find anything?'

'His appointment book.'

'Anything useful in it?'

'Might be,' Harkin says, wondering if Bourke will ever be quiet and let him finish.

'I'll tell you something, though,' Bourke says, sounding satisfied, as though he has solved a problem. 'He didn't hang himself up there, the little priest. He was dead before the rope was put on him.'

Harkin looks up to find Bourke reaching up to lift the priest's eyelid. After a quick examination he lowers his hand to press a finger into the corpse's neck.

'Why do you say that?' Harkin asks.

'I've seen a man hanged himself before. There was spit all down his front.' He taps at a long wooden library ladder beside the wardrobe, which the dead man had probably used to reach the upper shelves of the fitted bookcases that stretch from floor to ceiling on two of the study's walls. 'I'd say someone knocked him on the head – look, you can see he's taken a knock – then hung him up there to make it look like he killed himself. I doubt the peelers will be fooled. Your Dr Hegarty won't be fooled anyway.'

Bourke taps the priest's body so that it sways for a moment, like a sluggish pendulum.

'I'll tell you something else,' he says. 'Rigor mortis. That doesn't set in to this extent for around twelve hours. The priest wasn't here when I visited at about six o'clock last night, and it's ten in the morning now. So that's my guess as to when it happened, between six and ten last night.'

'How do you know all this?' Harkin asks.

'I used to work for an undertaker.'

Somehow this doesn't come as a surprise to Harkin. He shuts the last of the drawers. He leaves everything except for the appointment book, which he places in the pocket of his overcoat.

'Come on,' Harkin says. 'Rigor mortis or no rigor mortis, we don't want to be found here with a corpse.'

They walk into the hallway, where Bourke holds up a hand to stop Harkin while he looks out through the side window beside the hall door.

'The coast is clear.'

They walk briskly down to the road and Harkin lets out a long breath of relief when Bourke closes the garden gate behind them. Perhaps it's the relief that causes him to stop walking, suddenly overwhelmed by the scene back in the priest's study, his legs shaking as he struggles to stay standing.

'You're grand,' Bourke says, taking his elbow and almost lifting him up from the ground as he pushes him forwards. 'You can rest in the car.'

The next thing Harkin is aware of is sitting in the Ford's passenger seat and the car moving slowly away from the side of the road. Bourke is looking in the rear mirror, where something has caught his attention. Harkin looks over at him and notices the sudden sharpness in his expression.

'Peelers,' Bourke says. 'A trip out to the country for us, I think.'

Harkin turns with the last of his energy and sees a Crossley Tender turning in to the road that leads out from town to the church, about half a mile back. It disappears from view as the Ford follows a bend in the road.

'I doubt they saw us,' Bourke says. 'And even if they did, we were moving by that point. Just a coincidence.' He looks across at Harkin and frowns. 'You look like a dead man.'

He reaches inside his jacket to the breast pocket and produces a thin silver flask, unscrewing its top with the hand he keeps on the wheel, sniffing it and then passing it across.

'Have a drink of this. It'll fix you up or nothing will.'

Harkin takes a sip. It's as though he's poured fire down his throat.

'Christ almighty,' he manages to say when the coughing subsides.

'Fella in the bar sold me a bottle of it last night. You could run a car on that stuff.'

Harkin does feel better for it, though.

'Don't be hogging it, now,' Bourke says, retrieving the flask and drinking deeply. In contrast to Harkin, his only reaction is a quick intake of breath and a tiny, pained grimace. 'The man who put that through the copper piping knew what he was doing. Are you feeling better?'

'Yes, sorry. Just felt a bit dizzy for a moment.'

'If we're being sensible here,' Bourke says, his concern apparent, 'we shouldn't stop this car until we get to Dublin. Someone will have seen the car parked while we were inside. There aren't so many cars in this part of the country that a passer-by won't have taken notice of it.'

Bourke has a point, and Harkin is on the point of agreeing with him until they come to a crossroads and he sees a signpost for Ballycourt.

'Stop here for a second,' Harkin says.

Bourke obeys, although he looks over his shoulder, back along the road, in case the police lorry comes into view. Harkin considers the sign and then thinks about Bourke's suggestion that they cut their losses.

'Take the left to Ballycourt.'

'You're sure?'

'I am.'

Bourke shrugs as though to say 'at least he I tried'. The car moves forwards and then turns the corner.

'What's in Ballycourt?' Bourke asks, after they have driven for a short distance.

'Egan.'

Harkin takes the appointment book out of his pocket and opens it at the last entry.

'When you saw Driscoll last night, did you tell him you'd been out to see the priest?'

'I did.'

'And you'd be going back the following day?'

Bourke thinks back, then nods. Harkin holds up the open page of the appointment book. On the left-hand side of each page is a column of times. Driscoll's name is written in for nine in the evening.

'According to this, that meeting he told you about? The one he was so anxious to attend? It was with Father Dillon.'

Bourke gives out a low whistle.

'He didn't mention it.'

'No.'

'You think he killed him?'

'I'm saying it looks like he was in the house within your time frame.'

'On top of everything else.' Bourke snorts.

'The only question is, why?'

Bourke emits a dry laugh.

'Maybe because Father Dillon would have told us there was no anonymous source of information – that Driscoll set the whole thing up. If you ask me, he's the one tipped off the peelers about Matt Breen as well, to cover his tracks. The same way he probably pointed Abercrombie in your direction last night.'

Harkin flicks back through the pages of the appointment book until he reaches the day of the ambush. The initials B.M. are written in for an 11 o'clock appointment. B.M., reversed, could easily stand for Matt Breen, the column's recently deceased intelligence officer. Harkin can feel his frown deepening as he sees another set of initials written in for the day before: K.R. He checks back through the pages and nearly all the appointments have the full name written out. The only exceptions are these two sets of initials. If B.M. really is Matt Breen, then perhaps Egan will know who K.R. is. Harkin turns to Bourke.

'Killing the priest doesn't stop us thinking Driscoll set up the ambush and Egan can tell us where the information came from one way or another. Also, the way we found Father Dillon doesn't make sense. If it was Driscoll, why would he leave the appointment book behind? Why stage it as a suicide but leave signs of a struggle?'

'Maybe he was disturbed?'

'Maybe,' Harkin allows. 'And maybe it wasn't about the informer. Look, Dillon has written B.M. in on the day of the ambush. My guess would be that it stands for Matt Breen. If Matt Breen was there the morning of the ambush, then the likelihood is he was picking up information and it came from the anonymous source. The information didn't pass through Driscoll.'

'So Driscoll's in the clear?'

'Not at all. He was the last person to see Dillon alive. Perhaps the priest knew something about Driscoll and Maud Prendeville that Driscoll didn't want to come out – or something else. Once Driscoll knew you'd be visiting Dillon this morning, perhaps he felt he had to act.'

'So we need to talk to Egan?'

'Yes. And then Driscoll. Either way, he has some explaining to do.'

# CHAPTER 34

Ballycourt is more of a gathering of dwellings than a village – a scattering of ramshackle houses and cottages and a small thatched church, with a crossroads as their focus. The road that has brought them this far carries on through the village up to the gap in the hills beyond it. There is no pavement in the village, and the road itself is more of a long muddy streak of gravel than anything else. The only other vehicle on display is a dilapidated, horseless cart that stands beside the church.

'This could be a one-horse town if only they had a horse,' Bourke says, slowing the car to little more than walking pace. The sound of the car's engine brings wary men and women to their doors and windows, and a handful of shoeless children gather to watch them, their feet caked brown.

'You can stop here,' Harkin says, indicating the entrance to the church, and Bourke slows still further till the car comes to a halt.

'That will be your pub,' Bourke says, indicating the long low-slung thatched cottage from which men are coming out to stand watching them. It doesn't look as though the villagers are inclined to welcome strangers in a motor car with a Dublin registration. Harkin suspects Bourke is enjoying the situation.

'I hope you've put dubbin on your boots, Tom. I'd say it's three inches deep.'

'So I'm the one going in, is it? I thought you were concerned about me.'

'I scare people – isn't that what you said? Anyway, someone needs to keep the car's engine running if we need to get out of here quickly and you can't drive.'

'I can.'

'Too late to be telling me that now.'

Bourke leans down to press twice at a panel, which drops down to reveal a Mauser automatic pistol held in place by two leather straps. He undoes them and holds the gun low between his knees.

'If you want me to go in, I'll go in. But if Driscoll set this up, he'll likely have given your name and description, not mine. Are you up to it?'

Harkin sighs. The truth is he feels better for the drive, even though that doesn't mean he wants to get out of the car. He reaches for the door handle all the same, thinking, as he does so, that if Driscoll is a traitor, then this could be a trap.

'If this goes badly,' Harkin says, 'I want you to pass on my annoyance to Sean Driscoll.'

'You can count on it,' Bourke says, sliding back the safety on the Mauser.

Harkin steps out of the car into a stagnant puddle. He looks down to see how deep his boots have gone in. No more than two inches. Bourke was wrong on that, at least. He takes his time to look around at the scattering of men and women who have gathered to examine him. No one has thrown anything so far, or even said anything, and he takes this as a good sign. He nods to them, but no one acknowledges this, so he takes a breath and begins to walk across the road, stepping carefully.

As he does so, a young man in a long black overcoat and a flat cap, like every other man he can see, comes walking along the road. He walks an unsteady, weaving path and the other inhabitants step back to give him a clear passage. He seems oblivious to Harkin and, as he comes closer, Harkin can hear that the man is singing to himself. Harkin continues his slow walk, changing direction slightly to avoid the singer, at which point it seems he finally notices Harkin, comes to a halt and, still swaying, examines him.

The young man has a sharp face, all edges and points, as pale as a sheet of paper, that reminds Harkin of a saint in a religious painting, except that the young man is most likely drunk. The black hair that curls out from under his cap is caught by the breeze, and the young man reaches up to slowly push it away from dark blue eyes that seem to have a touch of madness about them. He has not shaved and the collarless shirt beneath the coat is dark with dirt. At first he seems confused by Harkin's presence but then he looks closer, and his mouth curls in a sneer, revealing the yellowed stumps of rotten teeth.

Harkin also stops, close enough now to see crusted blood on one of his ears, a scuff on the young man's cheekbone and a fat, broken lower lip. The young man has a thin neck and a prominent Adam's apple which bobs as he swallows. Harkin can smell him now. The sour smell of old drink and ancient sweat. The contempt in the man's expression is almost a physical force. They look at each other and Harkin is conscious of his ironed suit and leather boots, his trench coat and his hat. He sees himself, for a moment, from the viewpoint of the people in the village. He thinks back to the burning cottage on the first day and doesn't like the version of him he suspects they see.

'Good morning,' Harkin finds himself saying, and immediately wishes he hadn't spoken.

'Good morning,' the man answers in exaggerated imitation.

Harkin begins to walk towards the bar, deciding to ignore him. But the man leans back, then flings his head forwards, spitting into the long puddle in which they both find themselves. It isn't aimed at him, or if it is, it's aimed poorly, but the intention to offend is clear and Harkin decides that, from the perspective of the people in a place like this, he probably deserves it. The young man stands, swaying, as though offering Harkin a challenge, before scowling once again, and turning to walk away.

Harkin glances at the retreating figure one last time, then walks forwards towards the bar. The men who have gathered in the doorway move slowly out of his way, except for one of them, a stocky older man in an apron who leads the way inside.

Harkin has to stoop to enter and, as he does so, he is greeted by the smell of old drink and ingrained cigarette smoke. It's as familiar to him as baking bread. The man in the apron moves behind the counter to stand at the cash register and Harkin pauses for a moment, looking into the empty unlit interior, and then glancing over the shelves of branded tins and boxes. The man behind the counter says nothing.

'Mr O'Brien?'

'The same.'

'A bag of sugar,' Harkin says. 'And three candles. Please.'

To Harkin's faint surprise, there is a telephone on the wall and the publican turns to it, winding the handle. When the operator comes on, he asks for someone called O'Mahony. When he comes on the line, O'Brien tells him that the items he asked for have arrived, and asks if he wants someone to bring them out or will he collect them himself. He listens to the answer and rings off. He turns back to Harkin.

'You're expected. Carry on up the road and there'll be someone waiting for you. They'll direct you from there.' Then O'Brien's grave face breaks into a smile. It takes Harkin by surprise. 'Is there anything else you need before you go?'

Harkin, bemused, points at a shelf of Sweet Afton cigarettes, while rooting in his pocket for a shilling.

'Give me a packet of those.'

By the time Harkin gets back to the car, the panel in the door is back in place and the Mauser out of sight.

'All good?' Bourke says.

The men and women who were watching them earlier have gone on about their business and the village seems almost deserted once again, except for the children, who have gathered by the gate to the church. They look hungry, like everyone else in the village except, perhaps, Mr O'Brien.

'I think so.'

Harkin passes on the publican's directions. The children watch them as they leave the village and when Harkin looks back over his shoulder as the car begins to climb the road to the gap, he sees them standing in the muddy road until eventually they can be seen no more.

'Imagine living in a place like that?' Bourke says, and Harkin is surprised by the spurt of anger that twists inside his stomach.

'Imagine what that place would be like if Irishmen owned the land on which they stood,' Harkin says. 'And made their own laws.'

Bourke laughs without humour.

'You think it will be any different if that happens?' he says. 'You're an optimist, I'll give you that.'

'Maybe not right away,' Harkin says, 'but one day.'

The road begins to snake back on itself as they climb higher, the landscape around them barren and covered by gorse and rock, broken up in places into small fields with thick stone walls. What grass there is stands stiff in the wind. Harkin looks behind them at the sea and the white-edged coast. On the far side of the bay, he can just about make out Kilcolgan.

After about ten minutes' driving, they crest the rise and begin to descend the other side of the hills, the countryside below them opening up to view.

'Have we gone too far?' Bourke says, perhaps sensing that Harkin has begun to worry they have missed whoever is to meet them.

Harkin doesn't answer, his attention focused on a young red-haired boy of about fourteen, in a black woollen jumper and a grimy cap, leaning against a stone wall. As they approach, he nods to them and stands up, stepping forwards onto the road. Bourke slows the car and the youngster leans in when he rolls the window down. He looks from Harkin to Bourke and then back again.

'Mr Harkin?'

'Yes.'

'Any chance of a lift?'

'In you get.'

The boy directs them along the road for about another mile and then tells Bourke to take a left turn along a narrow lane which doesn't look as though it has seen much traffic in recent times, and certainly not a car. Trees soon surround the lane, and Harkin is sure he sees two men with rifles standing in among them. He looks across to Bourke, who nods that he has seen them also. Soon the boy tells them to stop beside a small farmyard. Another two men stand in front of it, bandoliers of ammunition across their long coats, one wearing a flat cap and the other a fedora.

'Stay here for a minute,' the boy says, and goes to speak to the two men, before waving them forwards. They are patted down for weapons and then taken into the farmhouse.

They find themselves in a long low room and both Bourke and Harkin have to lean down to avoid the low-slung beams. Harkin takes off his hat and looks around, his eyes slowly adjusting to the gloom. An elderly woman is busy at the open hearth at the far wall and young men are gathered around it, sitting on the few chairs and stools, on the ground and against the walls. The smell, a mixture of wet wool and the sour odour of men who have not washed for some time, is familiar to Harkin. The men that he can make out have two- or three-day beards, and their tired eyes look back at him without much interest. Tough men. Harkin wonders how the message came over the hill from Ballycourt, because there has never been a telephone in this house.

'Our guests from Dublin.' A small, wiry man sitting at the only table in the room waves them over to sit with him.

Their interest satisfied, most of the Volunteers in the low room look away and begin to converse in low voices. Those who have a plate of food are eating; the others, waiting. The noise reminds Harkin of early evening in a pub. The small man's blue eyes sparkle, although it isn't clear to Harkin if it's with amusement or something less friendly.

'I have orders to assist you, of course.'

'Mick Egan?'

The small man nods.

'You'll be Tom Harkin and you –' he gives Bourke an appraising glance – 'will be Vincent Bourke.'

Harkin looks around, uncomfortable to be speaking in front of so many men he does not know.

225

'Don't worry about them. If they want to listen in, they will. If they don't, they won't. Whatever we have to say to each other is for everyone's ears. That's how we operate. No secrets in this unit. Well, not many, at least.'

Harkin explains why they are there, which seems to come as no surprise to Egan. Egan takes them through the column's activities on the day of the ambush, from Matt Breen's arrival with news of Abercrombie's likely visit to Kilcolgan, through to the ambush itself and then the final pistol shot, heard when they were already some distance away from the smoking car.

'Miss Prendeville was unconscious but we left her comfortable enough. Other than that, all we did was take Teevan's revolver and a rifle that we found in the boot. We didn't wait around – I wanted to be back in the hills before the light came up.'

'Driscoll told us the information for the ambush came through Father Dillon.' Harkin decides to hold the news about the priest's death back for the moment.

'That's right,' Egan says, frowning, and Harkin wonders if it's at the memory of Matt Breen, or perhaps because he is thinking ahead to what Harkin may say next.

'Do you know who gave the information to Dillon?'

'I say we have no secrets, but Matt would keep some things to himself. That source was important to us and Matt was careful to protect him. If all of us knew who he was, it would have put the source at risk.'

'Any suspicions?'

'None I would put my name to. Why do you ask?'

'If Maud was killed by someone other than the men of your column, they probably knew when the ambush was due to take place. It's unlikely they were there by coincidence.'

Egan leans forwards, interested.

'Go on.'

'But Sean Driscoll wasn't anything to do with the ambush?'

'No.' Egan speaks the word slowly. Harkin can see his mind working behind those cool blue eyes.

'But might he have known about it?'

Egan examines Harkin intently.

'He might have done.'

'You're not certain.'

'I only know Matt met him after he met Father Dillon, to pick up whatever news Sean might have had for us. I don't know if Matt told him about the ambush. I doubt it, but he may have.'

'Why?'

'Because Sean wouldn't have been happy about an ambush so close to Kilcolgan. It might be Matt decided it was safer for him and for us if Sean didn't know about it. Sean is a reliable man, but he would have a loyalty to the Prendevilles as well.'

'But you're not certain?'

'In all the rush to get there in time, I never asked Matt what Sean knew and what he didn't. To be honest, I didn't want to ask him in case he'd tell me something I didn't want to hear. We had a great opportunity to deal with Abercrombie. I knew there would be a risk to Sean Driscoll but it was a risk I was ready to run.' Egan lifts his eyes to gaze steadily at Harkin. 'To tell the truth, I would have shot up that car even if I'd known Maud Prendeville was in it, so long as I thought there was a good chance I could plug Abercrombie at the same time. I've no regrets. In case that isn't clear to you.'

'I would think the chances of Lord Kilcolgan letting the Auxiliaries have the house as a base are significantly greater as a result of the ambush.'

Egan looks up at him sharply, as though assessing the statement for a criticism, or something else. He smiles.

227

'I wouldn't like the Auxies to be based in Kilcolgan House. It would suit them very well and it wouldn't suit us at all. But it's a factor I took into consideration.'

The intent in the words is clear.

'What about afterwards? You didn't ask Breen then?'

'I didn't speak to Matt after the ambush. He peeled away from the column after an hour or so – he had business to attend to – and you know what happened to him after that.'

Harkin nods, thinking the information through.

'All your men were with you when the single shot was fired?'

Egan nods once again, but there is a question now, Harkin can see, that the commandant wants to ask, and it's about Sean Driscoll. Harkin takes the appointment book out of his pocket and opens it on the table at the date of the ambush.

'This is Father Dillon's appointment book. I'm guessing 'B.M.' is Matt Breen.'

Egan leans forwards to examine the initials and then nods.

'That would be the time Matt met him.'

Harkin turns back to the page before.

'Any idea who "K. R." is? It might be the source of the information.'

Egan thinks for a moment.

'I suppose I always suspected the source was someone in the RIC barracks in town. The only person I know of in there with initials similar to that would be Richard Kelly. Dicky Kelly. A sergeant.'

'I've met him.'

'It's a possibility, anyway,' Egan says. 'Do you mind me asking how you come to have Father Dillon's appointment book?'

'We found him hanging from a rope this morning. Someone tried to make it look as though he'd hung himself. We think he was murdered.'

Egan nods slowly, and Harkin turns the pages to yesterday's date. 'He had an interesting visitor last night.'

Egan leans forwards and reads Sean Driscoll's name. Then he leans back and, apparently absent-mindedly, takes a tobacco pouch from his jacket pocket and begins to roll himself a cigarette.

'Come out for a walk with me while I smoke this. Our hostess doesn't like us smoking inside.'

Outside they stand in the small, rocky farmyard, watched by an ancient sheepdog and, at a distance, by the two guards. A few lethargic chickens peck at the ground around their feet.

'Tell me what else you've found out about Sean Driscoll. I can tell there's more.'

Harkin fills him in about the inconsistencies in Driscoll's account of the ambush, the letters to Maud Prendeville and about her pregnancy. Then, a little reluctantly, he tells him about Abercrombie's visit to Moira Wilson's the night before.

'Sean Driscoll was the only person apart from the Prendevilles who knew I was there.'

'And what time was this?'

'Two in the morning or so.'

Egan takes a long pull on his cigarette and looks out at a cow that stands, watching them, in the adjoining field.

'That's interesting,' Egan says. 'Because Sean Driscoll didn't show up for a meeting with the brigade quartermaster in town last night at ten o'clock. I'm told they found his horse, still with the saddle on, in a field beside the road first thing this morning. Make of that what you will.'

# CHAPTER 35

There is not much conversation between Harkin and Bourke on the drive back to Kilcolgan. Every now and then Bourke looks across at him and shakes his head, and eventually Harkin can't ignore the silent reproofs any longer.

'Leave me at the back gates and head back to Dublin. Egan can look after me if I need to go to ground.'

'It's not Egan's job to look after you, it's mine. I only wish you'd make it easy for me.'

'There's an ironmonger's in town called Lanigan's. I'll tell you what the password is and the man to talk to. You can send a message to GHQ from there. Ask for instructions – for both of us. You'll have an answer on the morning train. If we're ordered to leave, we'll leave.'

'If we make it to the morning.'

Harkin opens his cigarette case, lights one and hands it to Bourke, then lights another for himself.

'There are four possibilities, as I see it, for where Driscoll has disappeared to. First, he was lying drunk in a ditch or in someone's house when they found the horse, and he's back at Kilcolgan by now.'

'That's a possibility I like.'

'Second, he panicked, maybe because he killed Father Dillon, and has gone on the run. In which case, he isn't a danger to us. We're a danger to him.'

'Go on.'

'Third, he was picked up by the police. If they know he's an intelligence officer, things will have gone hard for him, but he's tougher than he looks. And then again, they may not even have questioned him. He could be sitting in a police cell now, waiting for his cup of tea.'

'Or be in a bog with a bagful of bullets in him.'

'Indeed. The fourth possibility is the one I don't like.'

'Nor me. If he's been working with Abercrombie all along then we're in trouble.'

'Except that Driscoll knows who I am and I'm still walking around. Do you think, if Driscoll had told him, that Abercrombie wouldn't have taken me away last night? He may have let Abercrombie know where I was, but he can't have told him who I was. On top of which, if he did know about the Abercrombie ambush, and told Abercrombie, why was it allowed to go ahead?'

'Maybe Abercrombie wanted Teevan dead for some reason? Or Maud Prendeville. Or maybe the English fella.'

Harkin looks across at him, but Bourke isn't being serious. Harkin settles himself into the seat, watching Bourke think the situation through. Eventually the big man nods.

'All right, then. I'll take you to your back gate and leave you there, and then I'll go into town to this place Lanigan's and send a message through. I warn you, I'm not holding anything back.'

'I wouldn't want you to,' Harkin says.

'You can be sure I'll be waiting to meet the morning train to see what he says.'

232

'That's all right with me.'

'Very good, then. Is there anything else you need me to do?'

Harkin thinks for a moment, then looks across.

'Your contact is Peter Lanigan. Your password is Excelsior. Ask him if he knows where Sergeant Kelly lives.'

'Are you joking me?'

'The chances are he lives in the barracks, but he might still live in the town. He is Mrs Driscoll's first cousin. I don't see any reason I shouldn't visit him, given Driscoll is missing. If he is the source, then we will know where we stand on that, at least.'

'I'll ask.' Bourke's unhappiness is more than apparent. 'Afterwards, I'll be at Mrs Wilson's and you are to call me if there is even a hint of trouble. Or if you need me to drive you into town.'

'Thank you, Vincent.'

'You're very welcome.'

Harkin's eyes are heavy and he allows himself to slip forwards so that he can rest his head on the back of the seat. Soon the rhythmic thrum of the engine begins to take effect and he feels sleep dragging him under.

*His view of his surroundings is framed by the glass eyepieces of a gas mask, fogged by his own breath, like twin portholes looking out on to a storm-struck sea of mud.*

*Everything is brown; the ground is brown, pockmarked with ragged holes torn from it by the shells. He looks down at the rifle he is holding. The stock and strap are thick with mud; the bayonet and the strap are caked with it, and he cannot even see the skin of his hands. Everything is the same: the scraps and fragments of abandoned kit and shattered wood; the tangles and twists of barbed wire and metal. Even the dead are brown, almost indistinguishable from the ground into which they slowly sink.*

233

*The only sound is the rasp of his breathing through the respirator. He sounds like a steam engine on its last legs. His breath wheezes and sucks and there is an irregular rhythm to it, as though it is about to come to a juddering halt at any moment. He can taste the mud; it must have been inside the mask and now it is in his mouth. Outside the mask there must be noise. He can see the slow fountains where shells are exploding and he watches as a line of small splashes comes towards him – machine-gun bullets losing themselves in the soft mud one after another, stitching a seam across the liquid earth. He knows he cannot avoid them but they stop three feet away and he stumbles past them, tasting his own vomit.*

*He picks his way forwards, moving from tuft of seemingly solid ground to half-submerged duckboard to sandbag, and onwards. Some of the fog is outside the mask, he realises – a low-lying bank of thick yellow gas about thirty yards ahead of him. Not much of it, though, and it turns slowly in the breeze and the wake of the other men who are advancing through it. Up ahead he can see the flash of the machine gun as it starts up again, and he watches men tumble, one after another, to his left.*

*And then a hand takes his elbow, shaking him hard, and he hears someone speaking to him urgently.*

'Wake up now. Slowly now. There's a checkpoint a couple of hundred yards ahead.'

The voice is Bourke's. Harkin struggles up in his seat, the taste of mud and vomit still in his mouth. He looks across to Bourke, who smiles back at him, fortifying him with his own confidence.

'Are you all right?'

'Yes,' Harkin says, and hears the thickness in the word. 'Never better.'

In the distance a line of men stands in front of an armoured car, wearing a jumble sale of military and police uniforms. Auxiliaries. The car moves slowly towards them, Bourke keeping their pace steady.

'I'll do the talking,' Harkin says.

He rolls down the window to turn his head away from the Auxies and spit away the taste of the dream, grateful for the cold haze of misty rain that clings to his face.

Ten yards from the checkpoint, a tall, thin man in the glengarry cap of a Scottish regiment, the red and white check bright above his pale face, holds up his hand to stop them. Harkin leans his elbow out to greet him.

'Everything all right?' he says, in his best officer's drawl, arranging his mouth into a stiff smile.

'Your papers, please.' The thin man doesn't sound Scottish, but then there's no reason he should. Nearly half the Dublin Fusiliers in the last year of the war had never set foot in Ireland, let alone Dublin.

Harkin hands his papers over and watches as the Auxie examines them carefully, looking up first at Bourke, then at Harkin.

'Mr Harkin?'

'Yes.'

'Do you have business up ahead?'

'I'm staying with Lord Kilcolgan. I served with his son in France.'

The Auxie looks down at the papers again, and then at Bourke.

'Is Mr Bourke staying at Kilcolgan House also?'

'A colleague. I work in insurance these days. He's staying elsewhere.'

'Where would that be?'

'Mrs Wilson's, out the other side of the town. Is there something the matter?'

'There's been some trouble in the town. Nothing to worry about. It's under control now. Where are you coming from?'

For a moment, Harkin's mind is blank, then he mentions a town some twenty miles away, the other side of the hills.

'Did you see anything suspicious on your journey? There is an active column of rebels in the area.'

'Nothing, I'm afraid. Is this the same group who ambushed Miss Prendeville and Inspector Teevan?'

The Auxie doesn't reply at first, handing back the papers. He holds up his hand and there is a burst of noise from the armoured car as it reverses with a series of jerks into a gap in the hedge.

'Yes. Some of them have been dealt with already. It won't take us long to catch up with those who remain. Have a safe journey.'

Bourke drives slowly forwards and Harkin runs his gaze over the Auxies – men hardened by years of war, with blank faces and dark, fatalistic expressions. They likely weren't much bothered with taking prisoners in France and he doubts they see much need to change that policy in Ireland.

'I fucking hate checkpoints,' Bourke says, when they are through.

Harkin nods. Then a question occurs to him.

'Do you think Sean Driscoll was one of those they dealt with?'

# CHAPTER 36

It's a short walk from Kilcolgan's back gate, where Bourke drops him off, to the main house, although not one that Harkin has taken since his last visit, over seven years before. Whereas the home meadow and the drive to the front of the house are maintained to some extent, here Kilcolgan's decline is clearer. As Harkin makes his way past the stables, he finds the cobblestones in the yard are almost invisible under the grass, and many of the doors of the individual stalls stand open or hang from their hinges. The only sign of life is in the corner, where three horses look out at him without much curiosity. They have cleared with their hooves a path that leads out to the arched gate that still supports a rusting bell. He stands beneath it for a moment, looking around him, remembering the crisp white-wash on the walls of the main block before the war, now stained by rain and damp to a pale yellow, darkening to charcoal where the water drips from a broken gutter.

Past the stables, the rows of vegetables in the once neat walled kitchen garden are weed-strewn and barren. The trees of the small orchard are surrounded by the brown husks of rotted fruit. There is an air of desolation about the place.

It is a similar story when he approaches the rear of the house. The walls are slick with damp in places, and the windows ivy-choked and frosted by grime. His feet crunch across the grass-hidden gravel and climb the granite steps that lead to the small stone portico that guards the back door, his footsteps seeming to echo in the silence. When he lifts the knocker, the door opens before his hand; somewhere within, a dog barks.

'Hello?' he calls out and, when no one answers, he steps inside the small hallway.

The room smells of damp wool, old leather and salt, and his presence disturbs a mouse that runs out from underneath the skeleton of an umbrella. The room is hung with long-abandoned coats and scarves while the floor swarms with cracked riding boots, stringless tennis rackets, fishing tackle and a shattered box containing an ancient croquet set, the balls so faded by use and age that their colours are mere suggestions.

'Hello?' he calls out again.

He walks through to find himself standing at one end of the long hall that runs along the middle of the house. The only light comes from the smudged gallery windows far above, and he makes his way along the hall like a ship proceeding through a fog: pictures, furniture and dead animals looming out at him like landmarks he does not recognise.

'Tom.'

The voice is quiet, barely a whisper, and he turns to find Billy standing in the doorway to the dining room. He is wearing a tweed jacket, the lapels turned in so that it is buttoned up around a roll neck jumper; his jodhpurs are tucked into mud-flecked riding boots. His pallor gives him the look of a corpse.

'Sean didn't come back last night.'

'So I heard. There's still no sign of him?'

'None. A man found his horse in a field near the mountain turn. I've ridden every field and lane near it but there's no sign of him.'

'Could he have fallen?'

'He could, but the horse didn't open the gate to the field itself.'

Harkin reaches out to place an arm on Billy's shoulder, surprised by how upset his friend is.

'I'm sure there is an explanation,' Harkin says.

Billy turns away, taking three or four steps to stand in the middle of the long hall, a pool of light around his feet from the windows high above.

'I think the Auxiliaries must have taken him.' Billy looks over his shoulder at Harkin with a hunted expression. 'To go through the war, all of that, and then to come back to your home . . .'

'Has he anything to fear from them?' Harkin chooses his words with precision.

When Billy speaks, it is as much a sigh as a sentence.

'Jesus, Tom. Of course he does. I'm surprised they haven't picked him up before.'

Harkin looks at his friend and wonders if his anguish is as much for himself as for Driscoll.

'Might he have been involved in the ambush, do you think? Is that why they've taken him?'

'The Auxies might think it, but he wasn't. I know that for a fact. That won't bother them, though. They snatch a man and that's the end of it. They're not from here and they don't care if they make a mistake or the damage they cause. One of them told me if the fellow they shoot didn't do the crime they suspect him of, then he likely did another. That all the Irish were disloyal. The thing is, though, Tom. I'm Irish, too.'

'You're certain he had nothing to do with it?' Harkin presses. 'He would have had time.'

Billy looks at him as though seeing him for the first time. Harkin wonders if he has pushed too hard.

'I mean, there was time for him to be with the ambushers.'

Billy shakes his head.

'Your timings are wrong. He couldn't have shot Maud and nor could he have been present at the ambush. There is no possibility of it. I know where he was before the shooting started and I saw him after.'

'Where was he?'

Billy gives him another long look and it is difficult to make out what it signifies. Then Billy shakes his head.

'I saw him leaving his mother's cottage and I saw him go in as well.'

'Why didn't you tell me this earlier?'

'You asked me when he came into the house, not whether I saw him before that. Anyway, he grew up with Maud. He has always been a part of the family. He'd never do anything to put any of us at risk. On top of which, he was cute about his involvement. He keeps the IRA away from here. We have never even been raided for guns, and there's barely another big house for fifty miles can say that.'

Harkin remembers Driscoll's consciousness of the divide between the family and those that work for them and wonders, if he were desperate, what he might and might not have done. The mathematics of fear – what a man is capable of doing for his own survival – are much clearer to those who have lived with them on a day-to-day basis.

Perhaps Billy has forgotten this. The Prendevilles and their kind have always struggled to understand that loyalty springing from economic dependence is not something that survives much testing.

'Have you telephoned Abercrombie?' Harkin asks. 'If he has him, a word from you or your father would surely give him some protection.'

'We've tried. The major is unavailable, or so they say. Mrs Driscoll has a cousin in the station, Sergeant Kelly, and he swore on his mother's grave they hadn't Sean, but that means nothing. It will be the Auxiliaries who've taken him, if anyone, and they're accountable to no one but Abercrombie, what with Teevan dead and his replacement not yet arrived. Charlie is trying the army barracks in case they can help, but it's a long shot.'

'What about your uncle?' Harkin asks.

'He's on his way over.'

As if summoned by the mention of her name, Charlie emerges from a door further along the hallway.

'Any luck?' Billy asks.

'The captain says it is a police matter and that Abercrombie is unco-operative at the best of times. He'll see what he can do, however.'

'A police matter?' Billy says. 'And isn't that the whole problem? Abercrombie and his crew are as bad as the rebels.'

A silence falls. Billy paces back and forth.

'What about your cousin, Major Vane?' Harkin asks. 'Have you called him?'

Charlie shakes her head.

'He's in Dublin.'

'He'd be no use to us anyway,' Billy says. 'He only buys horses for the army. He has no influence over the likes of Abercrombie.'

'That isn't all he does, Billy.'

Charlie glances at him, a question on her lips. Harkin indicates the door she has just come out of.

'Call him in Dublin, if you have a number for him. Try the Castle if you haven't. If they don't recognise Vane, ask for Mr Tomkins. But they'll know who he is all right. If anyone can help you, he can.'

Charlie gives him one final look of puzzlement, before turning to follow his instructions. Harkin turns to Billy.

'Does his mother know he's missing?'

Billy nods, his puzzlement about Vane still apparent. It's not, however, the moment to explain how he knows about Vane's alias.

'Where is she?'

Harkin follows Billy down the narrow dining room staircase to the kitchen. It is a long, low-beamed room with two wooden tables running most of its length. Like the exterior of the house, it seems largely unused and uncared for, except for the area around the large enamel stove, where Mrs Driscoll sits in a black dress, her face composed, a line of jute buttons rising to a crisp white collar. Murphy the butler sits alongside her, holding a glass of whiskey out in his large, bony hand. It isn't clear if the whiskey is for Murphy or the housekeeper. Harkin decides, from Murphy's rosy cheeks and wet eyes, that it is probably the former. When they enter, Mrs Driscoll looks up, her anxiety momentarily apparent, before she composes herself once again, her shoulders stiff and her back straight. Harkin notices how her gaze slides past Billy, as though avoiding him, before coming to a rest on Harkin.

'Mr Harkin,' she says. 'Have you word of my son?'

'Not yet. I have a car and a driver at my disposal. We'll go looking for him directly.'

She says nothing, as though waiting for the question he is about to ask.

'Is there anything you could tell me that might be useful? Any reason you think he might have been taken.' For a moment he sees a quickly suppressed emotion, which he takes for anger. 'Anything at all. You can rest assured it won't be passed on if it is prejudicial to him.'

She looks at Murphy, then Billy, and finally back to Harkin, as though asking each of them in turn what she could possibly tell him.

'I know he's an active Volunteer, Mrs Driscoll,' Harkin continues, wanting to shake her into answering him. 'Have there been any previous threats to him? From the RIC, or anyone else? Since he lives here, it may be the police think he was responsible for the ambush.'

'Mr Harkin, my son would never intentionally cause harm to one of the Prendevilles. Above all, not to Miss Prendeville.'

Harkin considers this in the light of the letters.

'Why Miss Prendeville in particular?'

She sighs, and when she speaks it is like a teacher explaining something to a particularly stupid child.

'On account of the actions she took during the rebellion.'

The older woman looks at him and for a moment it seems he is the one being interrogated, not the other way around.

'Are you certain he had no involvement in the ambush itself? That he was with you the whole evening?'

She looks from Harkin to Billy, and then back to Harkin. Her look is one of scornful contempt.

'My son was well regarded by all who knew him,' she says in a steady voice, as though reading from a prepared speech. 'I have no idea what people have said about him but, if you'll excuse me, I won't answer any more questions of this nature. If there is any news, I will be in my house.'

'I meant no disrespect . . .' Harkin begins to say, but she has already got to her feet and is walking from the room.

He turns to Billy, but his friend is leaning back on the long table, a hand shielding his eyes. Harkin turns to Murphy who, as Harkin watches, drinks the glass of whiskey he has been holding in his hand in one long swallow, before wiping his mouth with the back of his hand.

'He'll turn up. A fine young man. You couldn't help but know it as soon as you looked at him.'

The doorbell jangles from upstairs but Murphy ignores it.

Then, from somewhere upstairs, comes the sound of a long, wailing scream.

# CHAPTER 37

Billy is moving before the scream ends, running towards the narrow staircase that leads up to the dining room. Harkin follows him and they make their way through the house until they find Lord Kilcolgan in his slippers and a moth-eaten cardigan, standing in front of the still open front door. Sir John is with him and their expressions are grave. A red-eyed, sobbing Bridget is holding Sir John's hat and umbrella, and it seems the weight of them is almost too much for her to bear. None of them pay any attention to the sudden squall of rain that drives in, spattering the marble tiles.

'Go down to Mrs Driscoll, Bridget,' Charlie says, walking towards them from the shadowed hall and assessing the situation. 'I'll look after Sir John.'

Bridget bobs her head and puts Sir John's belongings into Charlie's waiting hands. They listen to her sobbing as she walks quickly away. The others do not speak, waiting until she has left.

'They've found him,' Lord Kilcolgan says. There is no need for him to add that Sean Driscoll is dead.

'Where is he?' Billy asks, his voice washed smooth of any emotion.

'At the far end of the long strand, towards town.'

245

Sir John looks directly at Harkin and, for an instant, it occurs to him that the older man might think he has something to do with Driscoll's death. Billy steps forwards towards the door, but his father blocks his path. This is a side of the man Harkin has not seen before, because he takes hold of Billy's arms and pins them to his side, speaking to him with an absolute authority.

'You will not go down to him, Billy. Mr Harkin will oblige us by attending to Sean. You must stay here, Billy. You must promise me this.'

Billy looks shocked by the fierce resolve in his father but, after a moment, he nods. Harkin sees that his friend's face is wet with tears.

'I'll go down with Tom, Billy,' Charlie says, putting her arms around him. 'We'll look after him. There will be a time and a place.'

'You know it is for the best, Billy,' Lord Kilcolgan says. 'Let Harkin handle the police and whoever else is there.'

Billy leans into Charlie's embrace. He looks over at Harkin.

'Thank you,' Billy says in a whisper, composing himself. 'I will go to my room.'

Harkin watches him walk along the long hall, his shoulders slumped.

'It seems Driscoll was a member of the IRA,' Sir John says into the silence. 'It appears the police discovered this.' He looks at Harkin for a moment, gauging his reaction. 'We must presume they believe he was responsible for the ambush. Perhaps for Maud's murder as well.'

The others look at Sir John and he seems uncomfortable under their gaze.

'Where is Mrs Driscoll?' Charlie asks, as if to change an embarrassing subject. 'She will have to be told.'

'I could tell her,' Sir John says, but Kilcolgan responds to this with an impatient shake of his head.

'I will. It would be best if you were to stay clear of Mrs Driscoll.' Then when he sees his brother's look of confusion, he adds in a softer voice, 'For the moment. You must see it is my responsibility to break the news to her.'

'She left to go to her cottage,' Harkin says.

Kilcolgan nods, turning to walk towards the back of the house without further ado. Charlie looks after him, then turns to Harkin.

'I'll get a coat and then I'll be with you,' she says. 'I should call Hugo back as well, if I can get through. He was going to come down, but I don't think there is any point now.'

Harkin finds himself alone with Sir John, who is once again gazing at him with an intensity that is making him feel uncomfortable.

'I didn't kill Driscoll,' Harkin says.

Sir John gives a strange, tight smile that suggests he is unconvinced by the denial. There is something repellent about his misplaced knowingness.

'Might your colleague have taken matters into his own hands? I am not complaining, by any means.'

'Nor did Mr Bourke.'

'You've heard about Father Dillon, I take it?' the older man asks, almost as an aside.

'Father Dillon?'

'He hanged himself . . .' The older man hesitates. 'Apparently. Last night or this morning. Before eleven o'clock mass, in any event, as that's when they found him. Did your man speak to him beforehand?' Again there is an insinuation that Harkin doesn't much like. 'You said that he intended to.'

'No,' Harkin says, deciding that their encounter with the priest could be described as many things, but there was no speaking involved. 'But Driscoll did. Last night at nine o'clock.'

Sir John digests this new information, his face turning a little pale.

'Do you think Driscoll killed him?'

'He would seem the most likely person. I don't understand why, though.'

Sir John considers the question.

'Does it matter? We know he killed Maud. Perhaps it was the war? One hears things about soldiers being unable to adjust to civilian life. Perhaps he went to confess about murdering Maud and became enraged?'

The older man avoids Harkin's cold stare.

'Was Driscoll a parishioner at St Ann's?' Harkin says.

'I wouldn't know.'

Harkin finds that his hands have balled into fists, and when he hears Charlie's footsteps approaching, he is grateful for the distraction.

'I should come down as well,' Sir John says. 'To see the body.'

Harkin shakes his head.

'I would advise you not to. We don't want anyone in authority looking too closely into you and your activities.'

It is almost as though he can hear the cogs of Sir John's mind turning. He nods.

'Perhaps not.'

Charlie joins them, glancing quickly between them.

'Is everything all right?'

'Quite all right,' Sir John says. 'I shall go and see if Billy needs anything.'

Perhaps it is a trick of the light but as Sir John turns away, Harkin catches the echo of another face. It is a momentary image, more of a suggestion than anything, but it gives Harkin pause for thought.

# CHAPTER 38

The rain is in their faces on the walk down to the long strand, and Harkin and Charlie barely exchange a word. Harkin is surprised to find he carries sadness at another death on his shoulders like a weight. First Maud, Teevan and Cartwright, then Matt Breen, then the two Auxiliaries shot the day before, Father Dillon this morning, and now Driscoll. It's hard not to regret another life taken, even if Driscoll may still turn out to be responsible for at least some of those deaths. It's hard also not to question the necessity of the war they are waging, except that the alternative is almost inconceivable. If Irishmen like him fought a war to protect the independence of smaller European nations, it would be strange indeed if, after their victory, that independence did not extend to their own country.

'A penny for your thoughts.'

He turns to find Charlie looking across at him, her face wet with rain and the same curiosity in her expression he noticed earlier.

'I'm not sure they're worth that much.'

'How did you know about Hugo?' The question is almost tentative. 'Or should I say "Mr Tomkins"? He was a little surprised when he found out it was me on the telephone.'

'Did you tell him it was me that told you?'

She hesitates before answering.

'He knew. That was perhaps the most surprising part. As though you two have some shared secret.'

Which is not far from the truth. The question is, of course, why Vane is keeping that secret, if indeed he is.

'How did you know about Hugo?' she asks once again.

Harkin stops and turns to face her.

'Does it make any difference? In the greater scheme of things? I'll be gone from here this evening.'

'Because you think Sean Driscoll was responsible for my sister's death?'

'I think it's likely.'

She shakes her head, as though bewildered by his folly.

'What reason do you think Sean could possibly have had to want Maud dead?'

He takes a deep breath.

'He was having an affair with her. It must have been something to do with that.'

'Maud? With Sean?' Her astonishment is clear. Then she begins to laugh. It's not a happy laugh. 'He wasn't having an affair with Maud, you fool. You have the wrong Prendeville.'

It is his turn to be surprised. It must show, because she laughs again.

'Not me. Do you really not know? After all your years of friendship?'

He looks at her in confusion for a moment, and then realises that he does know. He has always known, but somehow has chosen not to know. The knowledge that there has always been a private version of Billy which his friend has kept from him has never affected their friendship. He has always known that there has been a place apart to which only Billy has held the key, and Harkin has been happy to let him have that place to himself. But now, in this matter, Harkin sees that his unthinking ignorance has been more like stupidity. He has been so busy ignoring Billy's secret that he's missed Driscoll's secret. Charlie watches him and it's clear she is following his train of thought.

'So now you see why my father would not allow Billy to come down to see Sean?'

'I do,' he says, and he does. In his state of distress, Billy might well have betrayed himself. A question is nagging at him, however. In fact, a lot of questions are nagging at him.

'Does your Uncle John know about this?'

She considers the question, her brow furrowing into a frown.

'It's possible John might not, I suppose. It isn't something that has ever been discussed, as you might expect. But we knew. Maud, and I, and Father . . .' She pauses, brushing a slick of wet hair away from her face. 'I've often wondered if it wasn't one of the reasons why Father took Arthur's death as hard as he did. The end of the Prendevilles and all that – which is quite a lot of nonsense, really. John could still have a child. He is not old, by any means, and he is both handsome and rich. I often wonder why he has not married again.'

They turn once again towards the beach.

'If she wasn't seeing Driscoll, who was she seeing?'

Charlie glances across at him, surprised, but Maud's pregnancy remains an undeniable fact. Harkin frowns as he thinks through the possibilities.

'The school friend she went to Paris with?' he asks. 'Do you know her?'

'I've never met her. Her name was Emily, I think.'

'When did they go to France?'

251

'In May. Towards the end of the month.'

Which, if Harkin remembers correctly, is around the time the first payment was made for the weapons. Although he had been under the impression that Sir John had been responsible for taking the money to Paris. Whether Emily ever existed, he has no way of knowing at present but Sir John may be able to provide more information about the mysterious school friend.

'What about Hugo Vane?'

'If you're looking for a possible murderer, shouldn't he have been within a hundred miles of here on the night in question?'

There is, of course, another possibility – and it is one which makes Harkin question almost everything he has uncovered over the last few days. They are passing the gate lodge and Harkin can see that the boarded-up window has been repaired and a column of smoke is snaking up from the chimney. Even the marks left by the bullets seem to have faded into the stonework. In a few weeks there will be no visible sign of Maud's passing.

'He's coming down,' Charlie says, as though remembering an important piece of information. 'He'll be here tonight.'

'Vane?'

'Yes.'

They walk on, out through the gates, and Harkin considers Vane's imminent arrival and what it might mean for him. Then another thought occurs to him.

'What is the White Lady supposed to look like?'

The question must have been in his mind all along, but it is only now that they are nearly at the beach that it comes out. Charlie considers the question.

'I've never seen her. I only know she is supposed to signify a death in the family. I suppose she must be white and . . . she is supposed to carry a bouquet of flowers.'

'What kind?'

'Roses, I think. White roses. Why do you ask?'

'No reason,' he says, his thoughts thick as treacle. 'Only because Billy said he thought he saw her the night Maud died.'

She nods, then appears to remember something.

'They say you can smell the flowers.'

Harkin swallows, knowing that if the story is true, then another Prendeville is soon to die.

# CHAPTER 39

Fat, intermittent raindrops crater the smooth sand beach as they walk towards where several policemen stand, their oilskin capes and helmets slick with rain. In the middle of the group, Harkin sees Dr Hegarty and, beside him, Moira Wilson. She holds an open umbrella so that her father can make notes and Harkin can see, even from this distance, the glimmer of her monocle. On the ground, Sean lies twisted, a darker patch of sand around his body. Inland, above the beach where the coast road runs, men and women have come to watch – a straggling line of featureless black silhouettes in the grey gloom of the rain.

Sergeant Kelly detaches himself from his colleagues and walks towards them.

'I shouldn't go any closer, Miss Prendeville. Perhaps Mr Harkin might take you back up to the house? The body will need to come with us into town anyway, for the post mortem.'

Charlie listens to him politely, then shakes her head.

'Sean was a friend.' She walks past him.

Harkin sees Moira turn towards her as she approaches and stretch out her free arm to gather her in. Kelly watches her, before turning back to Harkin. There is something close to desperation in the big policeman's eyes, out of keeping with his forbidding exterior.

'I told him to be careful. You yourself heard me tell him so only the other morning.'

'I did.'

'I knew what he was up to. I told him it would end badly. I wanted him to get out of here. Go to America or anywhere. There was nothing for him here, but he wouldn't leave his mother, even with her begging him to get out of it as well.' His voice cracks. 'I never had a son of my own. Only daughters.'

'His father would be grateful you watched over him.'

Kelly looks up at him sharply and Harkin wonders what it is that he has said, but the sergeant relaxes and nods.

'No doubt.'

'Do you know what happened to him?'

'Major Abercrombie is what happened to him. He hasn't a tooth left in his head, nor a finger or a toe that isn't broken.'

'You're sure it was Abercrombie?'

'I know his men's handiwork when I see it.'

They stand for a while, the rain falling around them. Harkin glances over to see that two of the policemen have brought down a stretcher.

'I served with him in France,' Harkin says, deciding he should say something. 'I was in the same battalion as himself and Billy Prendeville, all through the worst of it. He was a good man.'

'The finest.'

There is enough resentment in the sergeant's expression, Harkin decides, to allow him to take a risk.

'That was you last night, wasn't it?' he asks. 'When Abercrombie came to Mrs Wilson's? Holding him back?'

256

The sergeant nods.

'He wants you gone from here – he thinks you are interfering in the investigation of Miss Prendeville's murder. Inspector Teevan tried to keep him under some kind of control, to explain the reality of the situation to him, but Abercrombie thought Teevan was weak and that the only way to defeat the rebels was with force. He doesn't understand the country at all. Teevan told me he had written a complaint to the Commissioner. But now he's gone there's nothing to stop Abercrombie doing what he wants. He listened to me last night – he might as easily not have.'

'What was he trying to achieve?'

'A warning, I think.'

'Just because I'm looking into Maud Prendeville's death? Nothing more than that?'

Kelly nods. Harkin looks once again at Sean Driscoll's body, now covered with a blanket, and feels a shiver run through him. If Abercrombie had known he was a Volunteer the night before, there is little doubt that he'd be lying in the sand beside Driscoll.

'How did you know I was at Mrs Wilson's?'

'Abercrombie said we were acting on information received. I know nothing more than that. He didn't even tell us where we were going until we arrived.'

Harkin turns this over for a moment. If Driscoll was tortured, that might explain the major's knowledge of his whereabouts. But if Driscoll told Abercrombie about his being at Wilson's, then why not tell him he was an IRA intelligence officer down from GHQ? Giving up that kind of information might have saved Driscoll's life. And ended Harkin's.

'I understand a Father Dillon was found dead in the town this morning.'

'What do you know about that?' the sergeant says, a wary note in his voice. Harkin decides to take another, greater risk.

'I know Sean was meant to meet him last night and probably did. I know Dillon was passing information to Matt Breen and the IRA from an anonymous police informer and after Breen's death, Driscoll was trying to re-establish contact with the informer.'

The sergeant says nothing for a long while and Harkin is wondering whether he has gone too far, when the sergeant turns to him. He speaks slowly, and every word seems to be weighted with significance.

'According to Major Abercrombie, Father Dillon committed suicide.'

'But you don't believe that?'

'Did your friend?'

'I'm sorry?'

'The big man? He was around there yesterday and there was a report of a car outside the church this morning. It matches the description of his vehicle. I thought he might have been responsible at first.'

'Why?'

'Because Father Dillon was working for Major Abercrombie. I thought your friend might have killed him as an informer.'

Harkin takes a moment to consider all the ramifications of the sergeant's words, not least of which is the likelihood that the source for the information that led to the ambush was controlled by Abercrombie. He forces himself to stay calm. 'But you don't now?' he says, more to say something aloud than anything else.

'I think someone killed him. It wasn't suicide. I know a suicide when I see it. Did your friend kill him?'

'No,' Harkin agrees, speaking slowly, deducing that if Kelly has identified Bourke as an IRA man, then he must have identified him as well. 'Not least because he didn't know about Dillon and Abercrombie.'

'I thought not.' Kelly's expression is grim. 'In which case I think the man who killed Sean also killed Father Dillon,' Kelly continues. 'So that's where we are. Murdering priests, whatever their faults, and men like Sean Driscoll.'

'Why was Dillon helping Abercrombie?'

'He had a hold over him.'

'What kind of hold?'

'An altar boy. Inspector Teevan would have handled it quietly. Dillon would have been disciplined by the church. Only Abercrombie had a better idea.'

'How do you know this?'

'Father Dillon told me. He wanted my help. He was too late.'

Which would explain the K.R. in the appointment book. If Abercrombie was behind Dillon's messages, then he must also have known about his meeting with Driscoll. When he speaks, he is talking to himself as much as to Kelly.

'According to Sean, the details of the ambush came through Father Dillon.'

The two men meet each other's gaze. If it is possible, Kelly looks grimmer still.

'Did they now?'

'Did District Inspector Teevan tell you anything about the nature of the report he submitted? To the Commissioner? About Abercrombie?'

The sergeant's lips tighten. Harkin can see a muscle in his jaw throbbing.

'I don't know that it was submitted. He thought it was only right to talk to the major first before he did that. To give him an opportunity to explain himself.'

'And when would he have given him that opportunity?'

Kelly looks away and Harkin sees a reluctance to speak. A reluctance, maybe, to face the implications of Abercrombie arranging an ambush on himself, which was then redirected, somehow, towards District Inspector James Teevan.

'I believe they were to discuss it on the evening of the ambush. At Sir John's card evening. But whether they did or not, and what happened to the report, I couldn't tell you. Only that man coming down the beach could tell you.'

Harkin turns to see Abercrombie walking across the sand, a trench coat belted tight around his waist, a sodden tam-o'-shanter cap angled towards his right shoulder and a cluster of Auxiliaries following him, faces pale above their dark trench coats. The major seems in a good mood, a cigarette dangling from his lip.

'Well, Kelly? Anything to tell me?'

Kelly might as well be a statue, so immobile are his features.

'The dead man is Sean Driscoll, a staff member at Kilcolgan House. He's been tortured, then shot several times.'

Abercrombie glances towards Harkin, as though assessing his reaction.

'Any indication as to why he might have been killed?'

Kelly walks over towards the uniformed policeman and returns with a wooden board on which has been painted the words: MURDERER, AMBUSHER, TERRORIST.

Abercrombie takes the sign from Kelly, looks at it for a long moment and then shows it to his men. One or two of them look uncomfortable, but others smile as though at a joke only they are privy to.

'It would seem the murderer of Miss Prendeville was under your nose the whole time, Harkin, and some loyal citizens have taken matters into their own hands. I take it you will be returning to Dublin directly. I'm sure you have some files need filing, or whatever it is one does in an insurance office.' Abercrombie leans forwards and presses his forefinger slowly into Harkin's chest. 'Do you know, I once shot a German right there. He was quite indignant, as though I wasn't playing by the rules, but it didn't change things for him. He was dead and I wasn't. Do you take my point?'

Harkin holds Abercrombie's gaze until, eventually, the major smiles and looks to Kelly.

'Why so glum, Sergeant? I thought the Irish were supposed to be a happy-go-lucky race but here you are, yet again, looking like a dog ate your dinner. A treacherous rebel is dead. So why don't you smile, Kelly? Aren't you pleased?'

Kelly says nothing, but there is the glitter of steel in the sergeant's unnaturally calm gaze. Perhaps the major sees it, too, because he gives an uneasy laugh.

'Oh well, be a spoilsport, then.' The major turns to his men. 'Come on, chaps, nothing for us here. We can leave this matter in the capable hands of Sergeant Kelly.'

Harkin watches the major make his way to the two Crossley Tenders that brought him and his men. There is a kind of swagger in the way Abercrombie walks, as though the whole business is some kind of entertainment. He has shown no interest in the man who lies dead behind him – a man he most probably killed – nor engaged with Dr Hegarty or Charlie Prendeville. Harkin turns to exchange a look with Kelly.

'At least he showed up, I suppose,' the sergeant says.

Harkin's curiosity must be apparent because the sergeant nods towards the gate lodge.

'He never even made an appearance when Teevan and the others were killed.'

'But he must have come out when it was reported?'

'He was off on some business of his own that night. The Auxiliaries operate independently from the rest of us, as often as not.'

'It must have been something urgent, surely?' Harkin knows he is treading a fine line. 'For him to be called away from the card game?'

'You would think so, but I've never heard what it was. The next morning he was off organising a sweep of the countryside and raids and what have you, but not once did he visit the site of the ambush or look in on Inspector Teevan's widow, or even visit the Prendevilles. Nothing.' He looks around as Moira approaches. 'Mrs Wilson. If you'll excuse me.'

Kelly raises his fingers to his helmet in salute, and makes his way over to Dr Hegarty.

'What did Abercrombie say to you?' Moira asks, standing beside him and following his gaze up the beach.

'Nothing to speak of.' Harkin shakes his head, keeping his attention on the major, who is now standing with his men beside the Tenders. 'The curious thing was he didn't even mention last night. It was as though it never happened.'

'He is a murderer.'

'He is. You have to be careful of him, Moira.'

'I'll be fine, Tom Harkin. It's you we should be worried about.'

Perhaps Harkin would be worried, were he not a little distracted. He watches Abercrombie until the major pauses momentarily, just before he climbs into the cab of the Crossley, and Harkin finally sees what he has been waiting for.

'Will you excuse me a moment?' he says, not waiting for Moira's response.

He walks quickly up the beach until he reaches the spot where Abercrombie's recently departed Tender's tyre tracks are still visible.

It doesn't take him long to find what he is looking for.

# CHAPTER 40

By the time Harkin turns back towards the beach, Driscoll's covered body has been placed on a stretcher and Sergeant Kelly is escorting the two policemen who are carrying it up to the waiting lorry. Kelly nods to him as they pass each other and Harkin returns the acknowledgement. Moira waits for him, her arms crossed, her monocled eye glittering.

'What was that about?' she asks, in a sharp tone, nodding towards where Abercrombie climbed into the Tender.

Harkin isn't quite sure how to respond, so he holds out his hand and shows her the object it contains.

'Something very interesting.'

She raises a sceptical eyebrow – curiously, it is the one above the monocle.

'I will half forgive you, in anticipation of your imminent explanation. I take it you've heard about Father Dillon? Did you visit him this morning?'

'We did,' he says. 'But he wasn't very communicative.'

He tells her quickly about what they found at the priest's house and their subsequent meeting with Egan.

'So where does that leave your investigation?' she asks.

'This morning it left it with Sean Driscoll as the man who set up the ambush, and who took advantage of it to kill Maud, and then killed Dillon to cover his tracks. But since then I've discovered Billy was with Driscoll at the time of her murder and that, in any event, Driscoll wasn't the one who set up the ambush. So, now I'm not sure where I am.'

She looks at him, her expression grave.

'One other thing, of course,' he adds, 'is I now know for certain he wasn't having an affair with Maud, as I suspected. How did you put it, now that I recall? "It seems unlikely there was an attraction between them"? And now the poor fellow is murdered and I feel a bit of a dunce.'

She looks a little guilty.

'He was entitled to his privacy.'

'It is no criticism of you, believe me. If I was in any way suited to this role, I'd have noticed things that now seem obvious. Instead I feel like I've blundered about for the few days I've been down here, generally making a fool of myself.'

'I thought I told you to avoid stressful situations,' Dr Hegarty says, approaching them and looking from one to the other with an assessing eye. Behind him, on the road, the police lorry has been loaded with Sean Driscoll's corpse and Harkin can hear its engine turning over.

'Sergeant Kelly said Driscoll was in pretty bad shape.'

'Indeed. If they have an open coffin there will be trouble in the town. Would you tell his mother that, Miss Prendeville? There's already been enough in the last few days to last us a while.'

Charlie, joining them, nods. Harkin notices that the bystanders who lined the road are beginning to drift away now that the lorry is leaving with Driscoll's body. The waves are also coming higher up the beach, and in half an hour the sea will have cleansed the sand of Driscoll's blood.

'There *should* be trouble,' Moira says, but when her father looks at her sharply, she holds up her hands in surrender.

'It's been a busy day for you, Doctor,' Harkin says, changing the subject.

'You're referring to Father Dillon, I take it.'

'Yes. A suicide, I'm told.'

'So I'm informed.'

'You're not convinced?'

Dr Hegarty says nothing. His daughter speaks for him.

'He hasn't examined him. Major Abercrombie has decreed that since martial law is in effect, and with the situation so troubled, only police-determined homicides will require post mortems.'

Harkin feels a hard frown tighten his forehead.

'Is that legal?'

'Whether it is or it isn't, there's not much I can do about it.' Hegarty's anger is apparent. 'I could write a letter to someone, I suppose, but the first person the recipient would contact about its contents would likely be Abercrombie. I'm not sure that would end well.'

'Father, I'm sure Mr Harkin didn't mean to cause you irritation.'

'My irritation isn't with Mr Harkin, even if he will ignore my medical advice. I am, however, annoyed with that jumped-up rat of a man, Abercrombie, given he is responsible for half the homicides around here.'

'Where is Father Dillon's body now?' Harkin asks.

'Already with the undertaker.'

'Could you examine it there, quietly?'

Hegarty looks at him, an eyebrow raised.

'Is there a pressing reason why I should?'

'There might be,' Harkin says carefully.

It seems that Dr Hegarty understands his drift when he nods slowly.

'But you can't tell me why?'

'It would probably be better if I didn't.'

Hegarty thinks about this for a little while, before he seems to come to some sort of a decision.

'Is this to do with Maud Prendeville's death?'

'It might even be to do with Sean Driscoll's.'

'I see. Kevin Cunningham, the undertaker, is a friend of mine. I often look in on him on my way home. It would be a purely social call, of course. If I do happen to see the body, it will of necessity only be the briefest of examinations, you understand? But a brief examination is often all that is needed.'

'I would be interested to know what you think.'

'Very good. Moira, will I give you a lift back to the lodge?'

'I think I'll walk up to Kilcolgan. I should go and see Mrs Driscoll.'

Hegarty seems to take a moment before he sighs, appearing older as his shoulders seem to lose their shape.

'I should come myself, but I must do the post mortem on him first. Tell her I will take good care of him.'

The rain seems to have slackened slightly as they pass under the grim gaze of the ivy-wreathed eagles that top the pillars either side of the gates to Kilcolgan. The evening is drawing in and it is dark beneath the trees that line the avenue. They do not speak much as they walk. If Moira and Charlie are in the same state as Harkin, they are wet through and cold. On top of which, there is Driscoll's

268

death and the finality of it. The house, ahead of them, is dark. Not a single light shows, despite the hour, nor even the hint of one.

When they reach the front door, Harkin and Moira stand in the hallway for a moment, listening for any noise within, puddles spreading around their feet, while Charlie finds some candles. The hall fire is not lit and there is no sign of either Murphy or Bridget.

'I'm afraid we cannot expect the servants to be in a state to perform even the most minimal tasks this evening,' Charlie says. 'Tom, once you have got out of those wet clothes, do you think you could light a fire in the drawing room and in the dining room?'

'Of course.'

'In the meantime, I'll see what can be arranged in the way of a meal. Moira, will you stay for supper?'

Moira seems to look his way in the gloom, but Harkin can't be certain.

'I would like to, of course. But the memsahibs will need looking after, as will Mr Bourke, my other guest. Once I have seen Mrs Driscoll, I will make my way home.'

'Can I at least find you something dry to wear?'

Moira holds up the hem of her waxed cloak, to examine the sodden dress underneath.

'If you were able to, that would be very kind.'

'Could I use your telephone?' Harkin asks Charlie. 'I would like to call Mr Bourke, now that Mrs Wilson mentions him.'

'Of course. There's one in father's study but it is probably better if you use the one in the telephone room at the end of the long hall.'

'In which case,' Moira says, 'I might also talk quickly to Mary and make sure everything is in hand. I'll show Mr Harkin where the telephone is.'

She leads him to a room beside the staircase at the far end of the hall, which seems to be a cross between a bathroom and a wardrobe, with a long sink along one wall and a rack of empty hooks and a boxed telephone on another. Their flickering candles show them pale and wet in the wide, gilt-framed mirror, spotted with age, that hangs above the sink. Their reflections seem to belong to strangers. Harkin turns towards her, but Moira holds a finger to her lips and they listen to Charlie climb the staircase and then walk along the landing. Moira, in the meantime, removes her monocle and when they can no longer hear Charlie, she steps into his arms. They do not kiss, but hold each other tight. He is surprised to find they are both shivering.

'I need your warmth, Mr Harkin,' she breathes into his ear.

'It is all yours, Mrs Wilson.'

'I worried, when I heard Sean Driscoll had been murdered, that you might have been killed as well.'

Harkin can think of nothing to say in response.

'You must make your telephone call,' she continues.

'Indeed I must, and you must to talk to Mary.'

'Mary?' she says. 'She's well capable of looking after things until I get back. I only wanted to feel your arms around me.'

And so he holds her for a little longer while their reflections seem to merge into one.

# CHAPTER 41

The conversation with Bourke is short and to the point.

'Did you hear about Driscoll?'

'I did. Are we leaving?'

'No.'

There is a brief silence on the line.

'There's no reason to stay.' There is a slight edge to Bourke's tone. 'He's dealt with. The investigation is over.'

'Except it isn't. Listen, can you come over in an hour or so. I'll explain things.'

'Will I meet you at the back gate?'

'No, the front gate. There's a man we need to speak to there.'

'In an hour, so.'

Bourke hangs up and Harkin listens to the crackle on the line before he replaces the earpiece on its hook. He stands there for a moment, wondering if maybe Bourke is right and they should leave. But then he remembers Vane's swagger on the beach and Maud sitting in her armchair.

He steps out into the hallway and stands still for a moment. The only light in the large expanse of the long hall is his solitary candle. There is an unnatural quiet within the house itself, while the external sounds, of the wind and the sea and the rain, although present, seem to come from a different world. Somewhere at the far end of the hall he hears a small creature's claws scuttling across the marble floor. He presumes Billy is somewhere upstairs, as well as Charlie and Moira. If they are, they have been swallowed by darkness and silence.

Harkin's footsteps echo as he walks towards the staircase, and strange shapes loom down at him from the walls. Sometimes when a flicker of candlelight catches a snarl of teeth or the glint of glass eyes, he feels his breath quicken. He climbs the staircase slowly, the old wood creaking under his weight. His eyes can barely detect the faintest outlines of the gallery windows high above, and he thinks of the White Lady, and Maud – of Arthur at the dining table and the dead soldiers by the graveside – and there is a part of him that wants to run.

But where can he run to? To Dublin? He will have his ghosts there as well.

He stands outside the door to Maud's bedroom and reminds himself to breathe, concentrating on the lift and fall of his chest. He turns the handle and the mechanism gives a low, grinding squeal. He tells himself that there is nothing inside the room – only his clothes and the bed he will sleep in this night – and that even if there is something in there, it is better he faces his fear. He holds close the memory of Moira's warmth and pushes the door open, and when he steps inside there is nothing out of the ordinary, only the same sense of loss that pervades the rest of the house.

After placing the candle on the dressing table, he takes comfort in the routine of laying out his clothes on the bed. He removes his wet garments and rubs himself down with a towel, feeling the

272

chill of the room against his damp skin. He wonders whether anyone will light a fire in it this evening and then remembers that if anyone does, it will have to be him. He dresses quickly, savouring the crispness of the dry shirt against his skin. When he has finished, he examines himself in the clouded mirror. His cheekbones seem hollow, while his eyes appear to have sunk into his skull. He wonders if the distortion is reality or only in his mind. Tomorrow will be the end of it, one way or another. Or perhaps tonight. He retrieves Moira's little pistol and places it in his jacket pocket, thinking back to the beach and Sean Driscoll lying there, his blood soaking the dark sand. It could have been him lying there, either instead of Driscoll or alongside him, and it might still be.

His eye falls on the davenport writing desk. If the letters were not written by Sean Driscoll, then who did write them?

Harkin walks to the dressing table and retrieves the key to the writing desk. He is less worried this time about offending. It seems to him that the situation has progressed past the need for politeness when it comes to the Prendevilles. He goes straight to the bottom drawer, unlocks it and pulls it out.

The first sense he has that something is not quite right is that the small plank which concealed the void where the letters were kept is now missing. He reaches into the secret compartment and finds it lying on the bottom of the void.

The letters, however, are nowhere to be found.

# CHAPTER 42

Billy does not answer when Harkin knocks on the door, but Harkin knows Billy of old and enters. He is sitting in an armchair beside the bed, in the dark. He does not look up.

'How are you feeling?'

'Middling,' Billy says, in a hollowed-out voice that tells Harkin he is on the edge of a precipice they both know well.

'I'm sorry about Sean.'

Billy looks up and Harkin knows instantly that his intonation has revealed his knowledge of their relationship. But then, he thinks, it's better this way.

'You'll always be my friend, Billy. I am not able to say that to many people. I do not change my mind about these things. I want you to be aware of that.'

Billy says nothing for a moment, then sighs.

'I loved him, of course. He loved me. He followed me to France, for God's sake. If that isn't love I don't know what is. It was only a friendship, at first. A very close friendship and a long one, since when we were children. But when we came back here, after all we had been through, it didn't seem there was much point not being true to ourselves. I don't expect you to understand that.'

'I do understand it. He was a fine man. Brave, and loyal and principled.'

'All of that.'

Harkin lets the silence between them linger, while he sits on the bed and makes himself comfortable. All the same, he has come here to ask questions.

'You were with him the night of Maud's murder,' he says.

'Yes. I was with him when I saw the damned ghost as well.'

Harkin leans forwards. His friend's face is gaunt in the candlelight and he does not meet Harkin's gaze.

'I'm sorry I suspected him,' Harkin says. 'I will do what I can to bring Abercrombie to account.'

'Will you kill him?' Billy says, his voice barely audible.

'I don't know. But if it comes to it, perhaps. Sometimes killing is necessary.'

There is another silence.

'How was he?'

'Who?'

'Sean, on the beach. How was he?'

Harkin takes a deep breath, reminding himself that this is a conversation they have had before, many times. About different men, in different places.

'They knew he was a Volunteer, and almost certainly that he was an intelligence officer for the local brigade. They tortured him. They must have done everything they could to make him talk. But he didn't or I wouldn't be talking to you now. I'm not sure I could have withstood what he went through.'

'Thank you,' Billy says, eventually. 'I thought you might be involved. I suppose we both kept secrets from each other.'

'Will you be coming down for dinner?'

'Yes. I need to talk to Father, and it's as good a time as any.'

Harkin walks over and puts his hand on Billy's shoulder.

'I have a spare room in Dublin. The house may be small but it does have working electricity.'

Billy manages a half-laugh.

'And there's a tram fifty yards up the road that takes you straight into town pretty much whenever you like. You could come and stay for as long as you needed.'

'I may well do that.'

'One question before I go.'

'Of course.'

'Did your uncle come and see you this afternoon, after we went down to the beach?'

'No. Thank God.'

Harkin nods, surprised once again at his capacity for missing the obvious.

'I'll see you later on, then. If I'm a few minutes late for dinner, will you ask them to start without me and make my apologies? I will be there, but I might be delayed.'

When he has lit the fires that Charlie requested, and made sure that the flames have taken hold, Harkin walks down the drive to the gate lodge. The rain has stopped but the wind coming in from the sea is damp and the cold it brings with it works its way through his clothing in no time at all. He knows his guilt is probably misplaced – that Abercrombie likely knew about Driscoll weeks, if not months, before Harkin came down from Dublin. He knows he is more directly responsible for the death of Father Dillon, but given the priest was an informer and the indirect participant in the deaths of at least three people, Harkin thinks he can live with his portion of that responsibility.

Somewhere in the woods an owl gives its mournful cry and he hears his own apprehension reflected in the sound. He has a sense of foreboding about what is to come.

There is the crack of a twig and then a voice with a Dublin accent comes from the bushes beside the road.

'Very careless. I could as easily shoot you down as scratch my arse.'

'Just as well you're here to protect me, then.'

'If you'd only allow me to protect you,' Bourke continues, emerging on to the drive. 'I'm telling you, if I get an order tomorrow to take you up to Dublin with me, that's an order I will take some pleasure in obeying.'

'I promise we will be leaving tomorrow, if not before. Orders or no orders. But we need to deal with a few loose ends first.'

'Loose ends? So you're telling me Sean Driscoll wasn't the killer.'

'No, he was not.'

He tells Bourke all that he has uncovered since they last met, omitting only the nature of Billy's relationship with Driscoll. When he finishes there is a long silence.

'Fuck.'

'That about sums it up.'

'Fuck. Fuck. Fuck.'

Harkin decides there isn't much point he can add to that.

'You know what I think?' Bourke says eventually.

'We should go back to Dublin?'

'That is exactly what I think.'

'Let's go and see the gatekeeper first.'

Bourke's silence is the silence of a storm about to break, but he follows Harkin to the gate lodge's side porch and waits while Harkin knocks on the door. After a short interval, there is the sound of an inner door opening and candlelight in the side window.

'Who's there?' an understandably nervous voice asks.

'It's Thomas Harkin, I'm a friend of the Prendevilles, staying up at the house. I'm investigating Miss Prendeville's death on behalf of the insurance company I work for.'

The door opens a crack and an older man with wispy grey hair looks out. He looks from Harkin to Bourke and back again.

'Who is he?'

'Mr Bourke. My associate.'

Patrick Walsh considers this for a moment and then nods.

'Come in, then.'

The small living room is lit by an oil lamp that hangs from a cross beam, giving out a soft yellow light. Harkin looks around him, at the coal glowing in the fireplace and the threadbare furniture, albeit of good quality. He wonders if it may once have belonged in the big house.

'We won't stay long,' Harkin begins. 'I just have a few questions for you about the night of the ambush. Nothing you tell us will be passed on to the police or anyone else, you have my word.'

'Will you sit down?'

Harkin sits down in an old leather armchair, the arms cracked through to the stuffing. He looks up at Bourke, who is still standing.

'Mr Bourke? You'll be more comfortable sitting down.'

Bourke looks as though he's about to disagree, but then he sits down on an ancient hall chair that seems to bend under his weight.

'Is Mrs Walsh at home?'

'She's with her sister in the town,' Walsh says. 'She'll be back tomorrow. The killings upset her, as you can imagine.'

'Can you tell us about the events of the evening? I understand the column took over the house beforehand?'

279

'Yes. They said things could go badly for us with the police if they didn't.'

'And were things difficult? Did the police interrogate you?'

Walsh looks thoughtful for a moment, as though the question has taken him aback.

'Not at all. Sergeant Kelly asked us how we did when His Lordship told them how we'd been tied up,' he says, his tone uncertain.

'They didn't ask you about the ambush?'

'They wanted to know which direction the column had left in, but we didn't know. The car was there, all shot up, and Miss Prendeville and the others were dead. I suppose they knew what had happened all right.'

Harkin nods. 'We've been told there was a single shot, about five minutes after the ambush itself. Can you tell me about that?'

The old man sits back in his chair, his eyes damp.

'I don't like to remember it. You see, we'd have known Miss Prendeville since she was a baby. So would some of the men in the column.' He looks at Harkin quickly, as though he has given something away.

'Anything you tell me is between us alone, I guarantee that.'

'Well,' the old man says, seemingly reassured, 'when they realised she was in the car, they were upset. Her reputation would have been very high in the locality. But they saw she was only unconscious, so the commander said to put a blanket over her, as the people from the house would be down and they would look after her. And then he told them to search the boot and the car for weapons and then, when they'd done that, he ordered them to leave it as they needed to be on the move.'

'And then they left?'

'I wouldn't say it was more than a minute or two after the shooting before they were gone.'

280

'What happened then?'

'Well, then Mrs Walsh and myself, we tried to undo the cords they had tied us up with so we could go outside and look after Miss Prendeville.'

'But you didn't manage?'

'No, we managed.' Walsh seems to look back into the past and not much like what he sees. 'I got my hands loose but then we heard the man coming.'

Walsh stops, and Harkin leans forwards and Walsh looks up to meet his gaze.

'Tell me about the man, Mr Walsh. Anything you can remember.'

'He came from the other side – not the direction the Volunteers left in. From behind us. He took his time and when he reached the car, he had a light.'

'A torch?'

'It could have been. At the time, I didn't know what it was. Only I had a fear of him.'

'What did he do?'

'There wasn't any wind, so it felt like we could hear every noise he made. He was in no rush. He opened the boot, I remember that, and the car doors, and it sounded as though he was moving the bodies around, with him sighing. I wasn't even sure he was human.'

The old man seems to have become older still in the telling of the story. He stops, momentarily overcome, and Harkin takes the opportunity to look over his shoulder at Bourke to gauge his response. To his surprise, the big man seems to have taken on Walsh's fear, his eyes round and shining in the yellow light, his face pale. Harkin turns back to the gatekeeper.

'Would you like us to fetch you something, Mr Walsh?'

'No, I'm all right. Just the memory of it.'

'Do you think the man was searching the car?'

'I would say so. After a while, there was a small click and the light was gone and I thought he might have heard us and be about to come in. I swear to God we didn't breathe until the light came back on. Then there was a scratch and a flame and I think he lit a cigarette and that's when I knew he was a man after all.' There is a long pause and then Walsh wipes something from his eye. 'Then he shot her.'

There is silence for a moment and, once again, Harkin is surprised to see that Bourke's eyes are also moist.

'Do you remember anything about the sound of the man? Anything distinctive?'

Walsh seems to look back into the memory and then he nods.

'I'd swear he was wearing riding boots. I could hear them creak as he moved. I used to be a footman up at the house. I'd know the noise anywhere.'

'Another question, if you don't mind. Was there anything unusual about his gait? A limp or a dragged foot or a steel heel plate? Anything like that?'

'Nothing, only that he was wearing riding boots.'

Harkin thinks over what he's told them.

'Did any cars pass earlier in the evening? From the direction of Ballynan House?'

Walsh considers the question.

'None. I'm sure of it. The first car that came from that direction was Inspector Teevan's.'

# CHAPTER 43

Harkin and Bourke walk down to the beach. It is dark, but there is enough light to make out the white of the waves on the shore, and across the bay there is a solitary light against the low hills. Harkin wonders what it can be, so bright that it can be seen from so far away.

'Why did you ask him about how the killer walked?'

'Driscoll had a limp,' Harkin says.

'I thought we'd ruled him out.'

'It didn't hurt to check. If Walsh could hear the creak of a boot, he would have noticed a limp.'

'So, what do you make of it?'

'I have a theory.'

'Go on.'

'It's tenuous.'

'Tenuous, is it?'

'I'm not certain of it.'

'I know what fucking tenuous means.'

Harkin takes a moment to order his thoughts.

'If Kelly is right about Dillon being in the major's pocket, then we have Abercrombie setting up an ambush on himself. Which would be strange if we didn't know, also from Kelly, that Teevan

283

wrote a report about Abercrombie's activities shortly before his death – and that the report has gone missing. It could be that the report would have finished Abercrombie's career, maybe even landed him in prison. Abercrombie knew Teevan would be at Sir John's card evening. Perhaps he suggested they should talk about the report and that Sir John's house might be the place to do this. Moira Wilson says they went off together earlier in the evening and they were both angry afterwards. Perhaps Abercrombie decided that if the meeting didn't go well, he could be called away, knowing it would mean Teevan would drive Cartwright home. If it went better than expected, he could be waiting for Egan and his men with all the Auxies and peelers and soldiers the town could muster. He could have ambushed the ambush.'

'But it didn't go well, and so he sent Teevan and Cartwright into a trap knowing our lads would be waiting for them?'

'It would have been a neat way to get rid of Teevan. There wouldn't have been any investigation if it hadn't been for Maud, and there wasn't much then. Even if men from the column had been arrested, none of them knew the source of the information that led to the ambush. The only link was Matt Breen, and he was killed a couple of days afterwards. When Father Dillon was murdered, the link was severed completely.'

'But Kelly knows.'

'I don't think Abercrombie is aware that Dillon told Kelly what was going on. Given the sergeant is still alive.'

'And what about Cartwright? Weren't Abercrombie and him supposed to be pals?'

'They served in the same battalion but Cartwright didn't come here to see Abercrombie, he came here to see Billy Prendeville. Maybe it was just a coincidence that Abercrombie turned out to be here.'

'So Abercrombie left Ballynan House in his motor, called away by a telephone call, but Walsh says the car never passed the gate lodge. You think he parked it somewhere and walked over to watch the fun?'

Harkin considers the possibility.

'It could be. When I walked in from the back gate this afternoon it was deserted. The chances of anyone noticing a motor car there would be slim if he coasted it in, or he may have left it somewhere else altogether. If I'm right, he wanted to be there when the ambush took place, firstly to check Teevan was killed and also to get the report. I'm guessing the searching Walsh heard was Abercrombie looking for it.'

'So why did he kill Maud Prendeville?'

'I don't know. I don't even know why she was in the car. There are a lot of things I don't know. But if Maud was involved in the shipment, and the shipment is known about by the authorities, then perhaps that's the reason she was killed. Or it could be something else altogether.'

'So what do you want to do?'

'I want to have a conversation with Sir John Prendeville. But first I want to talk to Mrs Driscoll. Will you drive me over to Ballynan House a little later?'

There is a moment's silence, then a grunt.

'Is something wrong?' Harkin asks.

'It's only Sir John drives a blue Daimler.'

'So?'

'I saw a blue Daimler in town the night Sean Driscoll went missing. The night Abercrombie came to shoot up Mrs Wilson's lodge. He knew you were staying there, because I told him when I dropped over your letter to him.'

285

# CHAPTER 44

Harkin leaves Bourke waiting with his car by the gate and walks back to Kilcolgan, skirting the house, now with light colouring at least some of its windows. He makes his way along the small cobbled lane that runs beside the walled garden and leads to Mrs Driscoll's house. Somewhere out in the darkness, the same owl hoots once again. There is a sense of expectation about the place. Harkin remembers the quiet along the line in the half-light before the dawn of an attack, the tension in men's faces and the absence of birdsong or any noise except, off in the distance, the whirr of an aeroplane's engine. The knowledge, as he looked around at his men's faces, that many of them would be dead before the hour was out. There is the same anticipation here.

The two storey red-brick house in which Mrs Driscoll lives has a small garden around it, bounded by a low wall and chest-high hedges, and even in the dark, he can tell that it is well maintained enough to be a rebuke to the tumbling-down untidiness of the big house not much more than a hundred yards away. The curtains are pulled tight in the windows, but they are edged by light. Harkin stands outside the door and listens once again. Even the breeze has died away to nothing here. There is only the sound of his own breathing and the murmur of conversation from inside. He lifts his knuckles, rests them against the cold wood for a moment and then knocks twice, each knock like a pistol shot.

The person who opens the door is Moira Wilson, wearing her hat and coat. She reaches up a hand to his face, her palm against his cheek. She searches his face for an instant. He wonders what he must look like, standing here . . . death stalking him.

'I'm on my way out. She is expecting you.'

'Is she?' he asks, surprised.

'She said you would have questions and she says she has answers for you. Will I see you tomorrow?'

'Yes.' He hopes he is telling the truth.

'Take care of yourself, Mr Harkin,' she says, smiling, and touches his face again.

'And you too, Mrs Wilson.'

Inside, Mrs Driscoll sits beside the small range, with Bridget alongside her. She is wearing a black dress that runs from a high collar down to black polished shoes. Her face is pale against her clothing. Seeing him, Mrs Driscoll leans forwards and places her hand on Bridget's knee.

'Go up the house and see if there is anything needs doing, Bridget. Mr Harkin will sit with me for a little while.'

When Bridget has left, it occurs to Harkin that he has cleared the house of everyone except himself and its owner in a matter of moments. It is warm, so he takes off his hat and trench coat and places them on a hook beside the door.

'Mrs Driscoll, I wanted to apologise again for earlier.'

She examines him. Her eyes are red-rimmed, but her face is composed and she seems, despite the news of her only son's death, to be calm. She points to the chair from which Bridget recently rose.

'Mr Harkin, please sit down.'

When he is seated, they examine each other for a few moments.

'Mrs Wilson told me you were expecting me,' he says, an opening that allows her to decide how the conversation will progress. She inhales deeply, as though summoning all her energy.

'I'm guessing, by now, you know my son had nothing to do with the death of Miss Prendeville. I presume you also know some other things about him as well.'

'I do.' He is careful to keep his voice as neutral as he can.

Mrs Driscoll looks into the fire that glows in the range's grate. After the persistent cold both outside and in the big house, Harkin finds the heat coming from it to be a welcome novelty.

'He was with Master Billy. That night. He wasn't with me.'

'So I understand.'

'Of course, I couldn't tell you that at the time and I didn't think it would make any difference to your enquiries. But it seems it did.'

'You weren't the only one who misled me about that evening. Everyone did, in different ways. Some more so than others.'

'I suppose we all thought it was obvious no one from Kilcolgan could have been responsible for Maud's death but, then, you aren't from Kilcolgan so how were you to know?'

'That's probably right.'

She sighs.

'I never wanted him to go to the war. It changed him.'

Harkin isn't sure what to say to that. He opens his mouth to mumble some platitude, perhaps something along the lines of it having changed all of them, but she speaks before he can gather the words.

'He should never have come back,' she says, in a low voice. 'He should have gone to London or America. Anywhere but here. Billy Prendeville as well.'

'I'm sorry it came to this.' Harkin is conscious of the complete inadequacy of his words.

Mrs Driscoll shakes her head, her mouth opening once or twice to speak, but seemingly unable to do so. She does not meet his gaze. After a while, he shifts in his seat.

'One of the reasons I thought Sean might have been responsible was because I found some letters – intimate letters – in Maud's room. They were from someone called Sean. I thought it must be your son.'

She nods slowly.

'Would you have any of Sean's handwriting, by any chance? I know the letters aren't from him but I may need to prove it at some stage.'

She stands and walks over to a small dresser, opening one of its drawers. She takes papers out and looks through them before selecting a letter and bringing it to Harkin. He knows immediately that the handwriting is different from that of the letters to Maud.

'May I keep this until tomorrow?'

She nods. Her wariness is not hard to detect.

'As I understand it, your marriage to Mr Driscoll was a very short one.'

He thinks back to the way Kelly behaved when Harkin had mentioned Driscoll's father and wonders if he is on the right track. It takes her a short moment to react, but when she looks away to avoid his gaze, he knows his half-suspicion is correct.

'I noticed earlier today, a passing similarity between Sir John and Sean. I didn't think anything of it at the time.'

She looks up at him now, and her composure seems to return to her.

'It occurs to me,' he says, choosing his words carefully, 'that Sean might have been named for someone. That the other Sean – or John, to give the name its English form – might be the man who wrote the letters to Maud. Strange as that might seem. I wondered if "Sean" might be a name this man uses privately.'

She nods once more, unsurprised by his suggestion, or so it seems. She draws herself up a little straighter in her chair, still looking at her knees.

'He was named for Sir John Prendeville and, yes, I gave him the Irish version of his name, because it is one he uses privately. I did it because Sir John is his father.' She regards him calmly. There's no shame in her expression or, indeed, any emotion that he can detect. 'It was my big secret. My parents helped me to go away to a cousin in Dublin when I knew I was pregnant. I hid the date of Sean's birth so no one would suspect. Sean mainly took after my family in looks so most of the Prendevilles did not know he was their own kin, although I think his Lordship had a suspicion.'

'Billy didn't know.'

She looks away from him.

'That was my big mistake. I closed my eyes to it until it was too late. Even if I'd realised in time, I don't know would I have told Sean. The lie was so old by then it was almost more real than the truth.'

'There was no Mr Driscoll.'

'No.'

'And Sir John, of course, has no idea.'

She laughs a bitter laugh.

'No. He can't see anything past himself. He's always been that way. I doubt he even remembers ruining me.'

'What about Maud? The letters appear to be love letters, although I only saw one side of the correspondence and have only read one letter. Sir John seems to have retrieved them now, so I don't know anything for certain.'

Her forehead develops the furrows of a deep frown.

'They had some secret between them.'

Harkin considers this, remembering that there is also the matter of the arms shipment.

'What makes you think there was a secret?'

'I would see them talking from time to time – very serious and careful not to be overheard. I thought it must be something to do with politics, so I didn't think too much of it.'

'Perhaps it was. But perhaps Sir John wanted it to be something more?'

She considers this, her mouth slowly twisting into an expression of distaste.

'It's possible. I wouldn't put anything past him. And Miss Maud, the last few years, was a little vulnerable, which I think he would have seen as an opportunity, even with her being his niece. He is no stranger to hypocrisy. I blame him for Sean joining up. He was always in the paper, giving speeches. How Ireland would win Home Rule on the battlefields of France. Not him, of course. He had to stay at home to mind the home fires.'

This so chimes with Harkin's view of his former employer that he has to take a moment to let the rage it sparks subside.

'I am sorry for bringing up old memories,' he says, when he is calmer.

She says nothing, only shrugs.

'What will you do now?' Harkin asks, looking around the small room. Empty now, he suspects, without the anticipated presence of her son.

'Moira Wilson says I can go and work for her if I want. I think I'll take her up on it. The Prendevilles can look after themselves.'

'I'm sorry,' Harkin says, and he means it with all of his being.

# CHAPTER 45

Ballynan House is a blaze of light against the black ocean behind it. All of the lower windows are lit, as well as several of those on the upper storey. Light spills out on to the gravel semicircle in front of the building where Bourke has stopped the car. It seems almost profligate.

'The wonders of electricity,' Bourke says, rolling down his window to spit out onto the ground. Harkin takes a deep breath, preparing himself.

'I'll need taking back to Kilcolgan afterwards. But I won't be long.'

Bourke nods with a scowl.

'I'm like a taxi driver. I should be charging you for waiting time. Charging someone, anyway.'

'Vincent?' Harkin says in a quiet voice.

Bourke casts a suspicious glance in his direction.

'What?'

'I'm glad you're here. I'm glad it's you who is watching my back. Sincerely.'

Bourke looks momentarily confused, then smiles with something very much like pleasure.

'Go on, go and hold that fecker's feet to the coals.'

Harkin does as he's told. He is, to his surprise, calm. Almost unnaturally calm. He has decided on his course of action and while he is not certain how the evening will end for him, at least the decision is made. Now it is only a matter of executing his intentions as well as possible.

He doubts this state of calm will persist till morning, however.

Harkin pushes the brass button beside the door, listens to the electric buzz and waits, feeling for Maud's small automatic in his pocket. To his surprise, it is Sir John Prendeville himself who opens the door. The older man stands there, momentarily confused. It does not look as though Harkin's arrival is a pleasant surprise.

'Tom,' he says, warily. 'Is there something I can do for you?'

'We need to have a word,' Harkin says, putting a little bit of menace into it.

Sir John nods and leads him to the library, telling him as they walk that the servants have the evening off to attend the rearranged dance in the town. The room is unchanged since Harkin's last visit, except that there are some sealed envelopes and a half-written letter on the partner's desk which fills one end of the room. Harkin walks over and examines them. They are not the letters from Maud's writing desk but the handwriting is identical. He doesn't bother taking off his trench coat. He doubts he'll be staying long.

'What news do you have for me?'

Sir John's voice is almost querulous. Harkin turns to face him and it is clear that Sir John is not his usual confident self. These last few days have worn away some of his sheen. Harkin can even detect something akin to alarm in the older man's expression and it pleases him. Shaking Sir John's sense of well-being is entirely the point of this visit.

'Why don't you take a seat?' Harkin says, leaning back on the desk and folding his arms across his chest.

Sir John seems to gather himself for a moment, no doubt surprised to be ordered around in his own house. Then he walks to the chair nearest Harkin and sits down with the air of a man who had intended to do that very thing all along.

'You'll be pleased to hear my investigation is largely concluded. I will be leaving Kilcolgan tomorrow morning.'

Sir John nods gravely and if he is relieved, he conceals it well.

'I see. Thank you for letting me know. I will tell your superior I am satisfied the matter is now resolved.'

Harkin allows the silence to extend, all the time holding Sir John's gaze with a deliberate intensity. Eventually the older man looks away.

'I'm not sure the matter is resolved, though, is it?' Harkin says, lowering his voice to a growl.

Sir John makes a good attempt at appearing nonplussed.

'I don't understand. You have established Sean Driscoll killed Maud and he is now dead. What else is there to be resolved?'

'Quite a lot,' Harkin says, drawing out the words. 'In fact, one of the few things I am certain of is that Sean Driscoll did not kill Maud. Nor, as it happens, was he responsible for the arranging of the ambush.'

Sir John's mouth opens and then closes.

'But the letters . . .' he says, after a moment. 'Maud's pregnancy. The timings of the evening. His murder of Father Dillon. It certainly seems conclusive to me.'

Harkin allows the contempt he feels for the man to seep into his smile.

'No,' he says, once again drawing out the word. 'Shall we start with the letters? Letters which you – also a Sean when it suits you to be a little more Irish than usual – claim were written by Driscoll.

Except that they weren't. I presume that's why you removed them from their hiding place in Maud's bedroom earlier today. When you said you were going to comfort Billy. Only you never did comfort Billy.'

Harkin can see how Sir John hesitates, no doubt wondering whether to lie about taking them, before eventually deciding to acknowledge the act.

'I took them to protect Maud's reputation. I would have thought that was obvious.'

'Maud's reputation? Or yours? If the letters came from you rather than Sean Driscoll, then I can see how their becoming public knowledge wouldn't exactly enhance your reputation. I know the disgust I feel for you, a man I once respected, taking advantage of his vulnerable niece in the way you seem to have attempted and most likely succeeded, is profound.'

There is something plaintive in Sir John's attempt at outrage.

'Don't be ridiculous. I was her uncle. I've known her since she was a child. I would never have sent her letters of that nature.'

Harkin leans forwards, catching Sir John's gaze once again and holding it. Then he turns to pick up the half-written letter from the desk and holds it out to him.

'Is this your handwriting?'

Sir John nods as he takes it, his face almost white. Harkin takes the letter Mrs Driscoll gave him from his inside pocket and holds it out so that Sir John can examine it.

'This is Sean Driscoll's handwriting. It bears no resemblance to the handwriting in the letters Maud received. Your handwriting, on the other hand, is identical.'

'Your memory is defective. The letters are in his handwriting.'

Harkin smiles. There is a thin sheen of sweat on Sir John's forehead and his mouth is slightly open, revealing clenched yellow teeth. It looks more like a dog's snarl than the perplexed smile he presumes Sir John intends.

'Shall we do a comparison?'

Sir John opens his mouth to answer but Harkin interrupts.

'Ah, but no, you'll have burned them, won't you? As soon as you scuttled back here from Kilcolgan. Or at least, that's what you'd say in a court of law, isn't it?' He imitates Sir John. '*Mr Harkin, a decorated war veteran and a man I hold in the highest regard, has been subject to the psychological strains of prolonged war service. I can only suspect this has led to his memory being at fault in this matter.*'

'Tom,' Sir John says, gravely, 'I didn't write those letters. Whatever you may think, Sean Driscoll wrote them. I promise you this. Naturally I deny having written them because I didn't write them.'

'Which brings me to the next item of evidence.'

Harkin produces Maud's automatic pistol. He watches Sir John's eyes grow wide as he finds himself staring down the barrel of the little weapon before Harkin shifts his hold so that the gun sits flat in the palm of his hand.

'You recognise this little beauty, do you? It's a four-bullet French pocket automatic, an unusual weapon that fires a .25 calibre bullet. Identical, as it happens, to the one that was taken from Maud's skull.'

'I'm not sure what your point is, but I have never seen this gun before.'

'That's strange, because I found it in Maud's desk alongside the letters you wrote. I wondered if she associated the gun with the letters, because they came from the same person, which is why she kept them together. I mentioned it's French, didn't I? And that it was manufactured last year? You couldn't buy this in Ireland, that's for certain – not these days. But you were in Paris last May for the early negotiations of the shipment. Of course, by complete coincidence, so was Maud. Am I wrong?'

Harkin's assertion about Sir John having been in Paris at the same time as Maud was as much a guess as anything but Sir John's slight hesitation is all the confirmation he needs. By the time Sir John gathers himself sufficiently to deny the accusation, it is too late.

'I don't know what you're trying to suggest but this is all nonsense.'

Harkin doesn't even bother answering.

'So we have your love letters and your joint trip to Paris. And then we have Maud's pregnancy, which you are so keen to suppress any public knowledge of. You would have me believe the child must have been Driscoll's, but there are some practical reasons why that is very unlikely. The most important of which is that Sean Driscoll was homosexual.'

Harkin allows himself another cold smile. Indeed, there is a pleasure to be had in watching Sir John squirm.

'You'll remember that the identification of Driscoll as the father of Maud's unborn child was entirely based on him being the author of the missing letters. Of course, if the letters were written by you, that puts a very different perspective on the business.'

If possible, Sir John becomes even paler, but he seems to gather his strength, perhaps believing that if this is all Harkin has to offer, then he is safe.

'If you persist with this insane series of allegations, I will have to contact your superior.'

'Yes, I suppose you're thinking about the shipment and how important you are to us strategically.' Harkin sounds almost bored, as if he has been reminded of a not very good joke. 'However, our people strongly suspect the arms shipment is known about by the authorities. Where does that leave you, Sir John? I would say it leaves you in a very difficult position. What with you being such good friends with Major Abercrombie. The same Major Abercrombie who, lest we forget, is running around the countryside murdering anyone he feels like, including one Sean Driscoll. A murder, some might think, that suited you very well.'

When Sir John speaks, he speaks quietly, a shard of ice in each word, and Harkin has to admit he is very nearly convincing.

'Your superior is aware of my contact with Abercrombie. It has always been considered essential that I maintain the public persona of a committed loyalist. As for your suggestions about the authorities being aware of the shipment, I suspect this is another figment of your imagination. Finally, the idea I had anything to do with the murder of Sean Driscoll is preposterous and deeply offensive. I demand you withdraw it.'

Harkin regards Sir John calmly, then shrugs.

'Perhaps the boss did suggest you keep in contact with Abercrombie . . .' Harkin pauses, conscious that his next piece of information must be let slip with complete precision. 'Although, having read Teevan's report on the man, you would think anyone in their right mind would stay well clear of him.'

Sir John can't help himself.

'What report is this?'

'Teevan wrote a report for the Commissioner of the RIC concerning Abercrombie's many criminal acts. There was a copy in Maud's desk. Teevan must have given it to her for safekeeping.'

Perhaps Sir John has forgotten he is playing the part of affronted innocent, because there is no hint of his earlier outrage.

'And you have this report in your possession?'

'Back at Kilcolgan. I'll take it with me to Dublin in the morning. I'm sure the boss will have use for it.'

Sir John considers this possibility for a moment and Harkin sees the first hint of suspicion.

'You've never mentioned this report before. Nor indeed that ridiculous pistol.'

'Why would I? I was only ordered to engage with you on the matter of Maud's death.'

Sir John looks momentarily bewildered but he seems to shake himself out of it. He remembers his role and Harkin is pleased to see it.

'All of this is mere supposition and coincidence. It is absolute nonsense and deeply offensive. As for the report, it is none of my affair.'

Harkin nods, as though agreeing with Sir John.

'What about this for another coincidence?' he says, almost as an afterthought. 'Your car was seen in town last night at the same time Sean Driscoll went missing and Father Dillon was murdered. Obviously, if I'd questioned Driscoll about the letters, he would likely have been able to establish his innocence and to indicate their real author, so it's curious he was murdered so soon after their discovery. Likewise, Father Dillon might well have revealed, under the pressure I would have been forced to apply, the identity of the source whose information led to the ambush. The fact that both of them were put beyond my reach, shortly after you were informed we would be questioning them, is suspicious. In any event, it will be up to the boss to decide what to do next.'

Sir John makes as though to speak but Harkin stands, buttoning his coat.

'Good evening to you, Sir John. No need to see me out, I know the way.'

At the door Harkin turns back. He feels a momentary regret, but suppresses it.

'There is something else you should know,' he says. 'Sean Driscoll was your son. There never was a Mr Driscoll. His mother, another vulnerable young woman you took advantage of, hid the date of his birth so you wouldn't suspect. I wonder what people will think if that information becomes common knowledge. Given the circumstances.'

Sir John's expression is one of blank amazement, but Harkin takes no pleasure from it – rather, a sense of guilt. He turns on his heel and makes his way quickly through the empty house, leaving behind him only the echo of his footsteps.

Bourke is waiting in the car.

'Well?' he says, starting the engine.

'We'll see,' Harkin says, allowing himself to relax at last. 'But I think so.'

About half a mile along the road towards Kilcolgan, Bourke reverses the car into a narrow boreen from where it can't be seen from the road but they, on the other hand, can see who comes and goes with ease.

'We could be waiting here all night.'

'Not that long, I shouldn't think.'

They sit in companionable silence, smoking. Sure enough, ten minutes later the sound of a motor car is heard from the direction of Ballynan, being driven at speed. A short time afterwards there is the flash of its lights as it drives past their hiding spot.

'I couldn't make it out,' Bourke says. 'Are you sure it was him?'

'Certain of it.'

They finish their cigarettes and then Bourke drives Harkin to Kilcolgan.

# CHAPTER 46

Harkin is on time for dinner, as it turns out, although he no sooner sets foot inside the house than Charlie, who seems to have been waiting for him, ushers him towards the dining room.

'I need someone to open the wine. You do know how, don't you?' she says, taking his trench coat and hanging it on a hook beside the hall door.

'I think I remember.'

Seeing that Harkin is still wearing his hat, she takes it and places it on a side table. She nods down the long, dark hall in the direction of the dining room.

'Come on, then,' she says, gesturing with the oil lamp she is carrying, and marches him briskly along to their destination. Their progress is interrupted by the jangle of the telephone. Charlie turns to look at Harkin.

'Could you answer?'

'Of course,' Harkin says and finds his way, in the dark, to the small telephone room. He lifts the ear piece and wonders, for a moment, what to say.

'Kilcolgan House?' he says, after a moment's indecision.

'Harkin?' Dr Hegarty's voice is gruff.

'Yes.'

'It is as you thought. If you need to know more, you'll have to come to see me. I can't talk about the matter over the telephone.'

'Of course, I understand.' He would say goodbye, but there is a click as the doctor disconnects.

Harkin makes his way to the dining room, with only the glow of light from under its door to guide him. The long table has been laid, at one end, for five, leaving the rest of the table empty. Ten minutes later, with the wine opened and the fire tended to, there are only four seated at their places: Harkin, Charlie, Billy and Lord Kilcolgan.

The room is lit by a scattering of candles, predominately clustered at the end of the table where they are sitting, and two oil lamps on the side table on which is arranged a buffet of sorts. Despite Harkin's fire, the room retains its customary chill and Harkin regrets not having worn an extra vest. He finds that he is shivering intermittently but it occurs to him that this might not be due solely to the temperature. The day, after all, has been a bewildering series of events and emotions, with death and fear in plentiful supply, not to mention the numerous revelations and his own confusion. Now, for a moment or two, he is standing aside from the momentum of it all. Perhaps this is why he feels a wave of exhaustion sweep through him. He places his knife and fork back on the table when they rattle briefly on his plate. He breathes deeply for a while, until he regains some sort of composure. He looks up to find that the others are watching him. He smiles.

'Just a chill. I'm sure it will pass.'

The meal is made up of whatever Charlie has been able to throw together. Harkin looks at his plate of cold ham, boiled potatoes still in their skins, and boiled eggs still in their shells. He has eaten far, far worse and the wine, as it happens, is superlative. A 1900 Château Latour that is as good as anything Harkin has ever drunk.

'I found it in the cellar, an entire case of it,' Charlie is saying, before adding, with some sympathy, 'Murphy can't have known it was there.'

'Where is Murphy?' Lord Kilcolgan asks, looking towards the kitchen staircase. He has had to help himself from the side table and appears to be still affected by the novel experience.

'He is . . .' Charlie pauses while she considers how to continue. Eventually she decides on a suitable word. 'Incapacitated.'

'A shame,' Kilcolgan says, his brooding air of discontent broken for an instant by the briefest of smiles. 'And Bridget?'

'Also incapacitated,' she says, before adding, after a moment's thought, 'Although in her case, solely by grief.'

'I see.'

Kilcolgan's voice is low, his eyes momentarily pained. He looks around the table, as though searching for a change of subject.

'Well, Harkin? Is your investigation concluded?' he says, before seeming to remember who Harkin's investigation concerned. Even in the half-light, it is clear that he wishes he could withdraw the words.

Harkin, however, is barely listening. The room, lit as it is solely by candles and oil lamps, appears distorted. The faces of the living Prendevilles, sitting around him, and the dead Prendevilles, looking down from the paintings that line the walls, seem to crowd in on him. Something about the sensation of being surrounded in this way triggers a vivid recollection of a dugout in France he entered after a shell exploded outside its entrance. He remembers how his torch played around the underground space, over the cluster of men sitting around on empty ammunition boxes, hunched forwards so that their heads are almost touching the mess tins they had placed on the empty wooden wire reel they used as a table. Everything in the dugout had been covered by a thin layer of chalk dust so that the soldiers, frozen in place, seemed like pale sculptures. The torch beam moved around, as though of its own accord, to other soldiers looking down at the diners from the bunks that lined the wall. One of them was still smiling, a broken tooth black in his open mouth. The soldiers were all dead, killed by the concussion wave from the explosion. Yet they had seemed so alive, even though Harkin could smell the rot already.

The image is so clear that his head jerks back, his nostrils inhaling sharply, and for a moment Harkin is almost overwhelmed.

'Are you all right?' a voice asks. He cannot tell who it belongs to.

'Quite all right,' Harkin says, feeling as though he is coming up for air. He looks around and sees the faces of the living Prendevilles once again – orange half-moons in the candlelight, their features indicated by deep shadows. 'I'm sorry. I was thinking about something else. What was it you asked?'

Kilcolgan looks at him, his mouth turned down.

'I was asking whether your inquiry was concluded, but it really isn't important.'

Harkin looks at Lord Kilcolgan, his brain slowly catching up.

'No,' he says, still finding it hard to breathe. 'Not quite. I think it will conclude tomorrow. Or perhaps tonight.'

Perhaps the Prendevilles are too polite to ask what he means, or perhaps they are worried about what he might say.

'Very good,' Lord Kilcolgan says, eventually, and makes it sound like a full stop.

'Father,' Billy says, when the silence continues, 'I think I should go to Dublin for a while. Tom says I can stay with him until I find my feet. The change would do me good.'

Harkin watches as Charlie's eyes turn first to her father and then to Harkin. There is a half-suppressed desperation in her expression, perhaps at the thought of being left in the house on her own. Kilcolgan looks from his son to his daughter, and then back again. He sniffs.

'We will all be leaving,' Kilcolgan says, matter-of-factly. 'At least for a while.'

His children's expressions are hard to read in the candlelight. Lord Kilcolgan addresses some cold ham on his plate, ignoring them.

'The government have made another offer to rent the house from us. Greater than before. More money for a year than we'd get if we sold the place, lock, stock and barrel. That's if anyone would even buy it, the way things are. What's more, they'll insure it against damage and loss and put it back in proper order afterwards.'

There is no outrage at the suggestion from his children. In fact, there is barely any reaction at all.

'Uncle John might buy it,' Charlie muses. 'He's always thought he would have done so much better with it.'

'I doubt if he would now,' Lord Kilcolgan says. 'What with Maud's death and the IRA burning houses like this up and down the county. He would be mad to. If he has any sense, he'll shut up Ballynan as well. Wouldn't you say so, Harkin?'

Harkin tries to think of a sensible response.

'I wouldn't know,' he manages.

Lord Kilcolgan looks surprised that Harkin doesn't have a firm opinion.

'The fact is, even all John's money wouldn't be enough to bring it back to what it was and keep it that way. And even if it did, it could never be the same with the Troubles as they are. There'll be a new government in Dublin one way or another soon enough, and we'll see then what can be done. I am not certain, however, that houses like this will serve any purpose in the future, if they ever did. I doubt the new government will make much effort to preserve them – or us. Quite the contrary.'

It is as though, by saying it out loud, a weight has been taken off Lord Kilcolgan's shoulders. He manages a smile.

'Anyway, I signed the lease yesterday. We have a month's forbearance, but the house and its problems now belong to someone else for the next three years and I, for one, am relieved it's so.'

There is silence around the table for almost a minute. Harkin wonders who will be the first to break it and what will they say. Eventually Billy taps his plate with his fork.

'You didn't boil the egg for long enough, Charlie,' he says, indicating the yellow yolk that has spread across his plate. Charlie looks across at her brother and gives him a half-smile.

'I did my best,' she says. 'And that's all anyone can do.'

The silence that follows is broken by the rattle of a motor car's engine coming up the drive. They listen in silence as the car approaches, then comes to a halt. There is a pause and then the noise of the car's door being closed. Another long pause, during which no one speaks, and then someone rings the doorbell, which gives a rusty jangle. None of them move to answer it. Meanwhile, the motor car starts up again and drives away.

'He'll find his own way in,' Lord Kilcolgan says, almost to himself. 'People generally do. It is a shame, though. I always think it looks better if Murphy answers the door, ideally sober. But often as not he misses his chance these days. Too slow.'

'We can't leave Murphy to the Auxiliaries,' Charlie says, as an aside. 'Nor Mrs Driscoll.'

'Nor Bridget,' Billy says.

'Particularly not Bridget,' Charlie agrees.

They hear the sound of the hall door being opened and then firmly closed, followed by the march of footsteps along the long gallery. A man's footsteps. Confident. Sure of their place in the world. No one mentions the imminent arrival but Harkin notices that all eyes are fixed on the door through which he must enter. The arrival is what Harkin has been hoping for, but now that the man is about to enter, he experiences a shiver of concern.

The door opens with the squeal of an unoiled hinge and Hugo Vane enters, barely visible in the gloom that pervades the far end of the room, although his eyes catch what little light there is, and it seems that he is almost amused.

'I'm sorry I'm late. The train was delayed. I do hope there's some supper left – I could eat a horse.'

# CHAPTER 47

It is no surprise to Harkin that he finds himself, half an hour later, alone with Vane in a small sitting room, with an oil lamp on the low table in front of the armchairs in which they sit. The fire has not been lit and the temperature would be good preparation for an Antarctic expedition; when he exhales he can see his breath hanging there in front of his face like a small cloud. Vane arranged this encounter so smoothly that he is not sure the Prendevilles have even noticed they have left them. Then Harkin corrects himself. The Prendevilles know who Vane is, and if they don't know who Harkin is, they probably suspect. They will therefore be intensely aware of every interaction between them. Fortunately there is probably a rule of etiquette that applies in this situation; Harkin suspects it's frowned on if guests shoot one another within the demesne walls. The beach might well be acceptable, however.

Vane and he regard each other across the low table, and Harkin wonders if the major is similarly uncertain how to begin. Eventually Harkin takes a deep breath, but it is the major who speaks first.

'Well, Harkin.' Vane seems more relaxed than he should be. 'You know who I am and I know who you are.'

'I wondered if you might show up with a squad of police.'

Vane smiles.

'I did consider it, but I think we have a common interest in bringing Maud's murderer to justice. I take it you have uncovered evidence she was not killed by your comrades?'

Harkin feels a moment of relief. It seems his gamble that Vane's attachment to Maud might lead to cooperation will pay off. 'Why do you think that?'

'Otherwise you wouldn't be here.'

It's a fair point.

'She was not.'

'I suspected as much. It does seem as though there has been quite a lot going on down here. Have you been stirring up trouble?'

'I might have been,' Harkin agrees.

'Good man.'

'I've also been very stupid from time to time.'

'I always think awareness of one's own faults is a sign of wisdom.'

Thanks to the oil lamp, Harkin can see Vane clearly, even if the walls of the room are barely visible. There is, underneath the charm, an angry grief that bodes well for their conversation.

'Would you like me to tell you who I think murdered Maud?'

Vane leads forwards and, while it is as if his face is made of stone, his pupils remind Harkin of the blackest opal.

'That,' Vane says, 'is something I should like above all things.'

Harkin could swear that the very walls of the room come closer in anticipation, as though the ghosts of the house have gathered around them, listening in. He shivers.

Vane's gaze does not waver from Harkin's while he tells his story. He tells him where Sean Driscoll was on the night of the killing, and that Driscoll was not the one who told the IRA about Abercrombie's movements. He explains how, instead, it was a priest whom Abercrombie had under his control who was used to set up an ambush on the major – and how Abercrombie then sent Teevan and Cartwright into it instead, along with Maud. He tells Vane about the report that Teevan wrote about Abercrombie's activities, and how the men argued at Sir John Prendeville's card evening. He confirms that the flying column left Maud alive and how the gatekeeper heard a man in stiff riding boots search the car.

Vane shows no surprise when Harkin hands him the two cigarette butts he has gathered: one from the ambush site that Abercrombie had apparently not visited, and the other dropped by Abercrombie on the long strand. He listens while Harkin tells him how the cigarettes are a Turkish blend sold under the name Péra by a tobacconist on Bond Street, an establishment Harkin, by coincidence, knows from a leave he spent in London five years previously. It is a brand almost certainly unique to the major in this part of the country. Harkin tells Vane about the letters to Maud, and the brand new French automatic pistol, and how Maud, and possibly Sir John, had recently visited Paris. Harkin tells him about Abercrombie's visit to Moira Wilson's lodge the night before – when Sir John was one of only a handful who'd known he would spend the night there – and how Sir John's car had been seen in the town earlier that evening. Finally, he tells him about the the subsequent disappearance and murder of Sean Driscoll and the purported suicide of Father Dillon.

Through every word, Vane's gaze remains unemotional and completely focused.

'To sum up,' Vane says, when Harkin stops speaking, 'you think Abercrombie murdered Maud.'

'There is another possibility, of course.'

'Sir John?'

'I think he had some involvement anyway – there is a connection between them.'

Harkin tells Vane about his visit to Sir John earlier in the evening, and Sir John's departure immediately afterwards in the direction of the town.

'Sir John is right, of course,' Vane says. 'It could all be explained away. Why would he kill Maud, though? Or want her killed?'

'She was pregnant. If it had come out, his reputation would have been destroyed.'

'It's not that. I knew Maud was pregnant,' Vane says. 'I would have been the father. We were to marry, although we hadn't announced anything. It seemed more sensible, given her condition, to do things quietly. However, Sir John had been her lover and those letters almost certainly came from him. I can't say I was happy when she told me, but I loved her and found I couldn't blame her. She was not quite well when it began and she had ended it by the time we met. It was in the past for Maud, if not for Sir John.'

Vane takes a deep breath and produces a cigarette case from his pocket. He hands one over and Harkin sees a slight shake in his fingers.

'Player's Navy Cut. Not some Bond Street tobacconist's attempt at a Turkish blend.'

'Thank you.'

'Jealousy is, therefore, one possibility,' Vane says, through a cloud of smoke. 'Although I'm curious about these papers Moira Wilson said she and John argued about.' Harkin detects a precision in Vane's choice of words that implies some knowledge of the papers in question. 'Do you have any idea what they might have been?'

This is the point where Harkin has to risk betraying his cause, even if he thinks it has been betrayed already.

'Am I right in thinking you are aware of some political business Maud was involved in with Sir John.'

Vane takes a moment to reply.

'What we say here must be between us, as friends of Maud. What I tell you must not be repeated to your colleagues – although it seems some details are already known to them. In the same way, I will not pass on the information you give me. Both of us would suffer if it were thought we had conspired together on intelligence matters. It is bad enough we have shared information about Maud's murder.'

Harkin nods slowly.

'I think we are in agreement.'

'Good.' Vane allows a trail of cigarette smoke to sneak out of the corner of his mouth. 'If you are talking about the arms ship- ment Sir John claims to be arranging for your organisation . . . then, yes, it is known about.'

'Did you tell Maud?'

'Yes. She was in great danger, from both sides.'

'Might she have been confronting Sir John?'

There is something like pain in the major's expression for a moment, then he nods.

'I think it is very possible. You were right to suspect Sir John accompanied Maud to Paris in May of last year.' He hesitates, then continues. 'Some of this I have only become aware of quite recently. It was, for reasons you will understand, restricted to only those who had to know. They were not alone on their journey. We make it a practice to keep an eye on known rebels, even if they do not appear to be active. As a result, it was discovered that Sir John and Maud met with an American arms dealer – a matter of interest to us, as you can imagine. It was also noticed that Sir John and Maud were . . . how shall I put it . . . intimate. Once confronted with the evidence, Sir John was in our pocket and the arms shipment became a means for us to inflict damage on the IRA. Once I became aware of Sir John's situation, I told Maud most of this and the intention was to extricate her from the mess. However, perhaps she lost patience.'

Some of this is information Harkin had guessed at, but much is new. He takes his time considering it before answering.

'One thing bothers me . . . If Sir John was at risk of exposure, why did he ask for someone like me to be sent down to dig into Maud's murder? How does that make sense?'

'An excellent question. It is possible he intended to cause some dissension in your ranks, but I wonder if he genuinely believed the column killed Maud.'

'If Abercrombie arranged the ambush, then he could as easily have been searching for whatever papers Maud argued with Sir John about as for Teevan's report.'

'Except that he seems not to have known she would be in the car.'

Harkin considers this, trying to unravel the threads of possibility and probability.

'Maud's being present may have been a surprise, but if he thought Maud might warn the IRA about the shipment, then the killing may have been opportunistic. I doubt Sir John would have wanted her dead, however, so perhaps Abercrombie didn't tell him he was the one responsible.'

'It's possible. Only Abercrombie can tell us for certain. Which brings us back to this evening. What will Abercrombie do, do we think?'

Harkin shrugs.

'I think he'll come here tonight to retrieve the report and kill me. Or he'll try to, at least.'

'Given you are an IRA intelligence officer, I suppose I should let him.'

'That would be your choice to make.' Harkin wonders whether he should reach for the small pistol he still carries in his jacket pocket.

'Does Abercrombie know you are a rebel?'

Harkin feels his frown as a tightness on his forehead.

'That's the strange thing. I don't think he does. Or, at least, I don't think he knew this afternoon, and certainly not last night, given I am still breathing.'

'Why do you think Sir John didn't tell him?'

'I don't know. Perhaps because I used to be his secretary when he was an MP? It's a question I've asked myself as well.'

Vane exhales another stream of smoke.

'I can clear up one matter. The small pistol you found is not connected with the murder. I gave it to Maud. If she was killed with a similar pistol, it's a coincidence, nothing more.'

In the silence that follows, the sound of the telephone's bell can be heard from the long gallery. They exchange a glance.

'I am not sure,' Vane says, 'that Abercrombie will be a predictable opponent. You should go and see what he has to say.'

Harkin leaves Vane sitting in his armchair and exits the room, telling Charlie Prendeville, when he sees her coming out of the drawing room, that it is for him. The conversation, when he picks up the apparatus, is brief and brutal, although because of the shared exchange, the brutality is masked.

'Harkin?'

He recognises Abercrombie's clipped tones.

'Yes?'

'I'm with Sir John Prendeville at Ballynan House. Will you join us for a nightcap? Mrs Wilson is here with us. I'm sure we would all enjoy your company. It seems she has grown quite attached to you in recent days.'

Harkin finds that he is unable to speak at first. But when he does, his voice sounds far calmer than he feels.

'Of course, I shall walk over.'

'Excellent. No later than an hour, please, or we shall be most offended. And you can bring that document you were discussing with Sir John. I should be grateful for that.'

# CHAPTER 48

Harkin's concern must show when he comes out into the hall, because Vane holds up the oil lamp he is carrying to examine him.

'I take it that was not good news,' Vane murmurs.

'He is over at Ballynan with Sir John. Moira Wilson is with him.'

Vane considers this information, frowning.

'Do you think Sir John would allow harm to come to her?'

'Do you think Sir John has any control over Abercrombie?'

Vane's frown deepens still further. They are keeping their voices low so as not to be overheard, and it is as though the house is holding its breath so as to better listen.

'No, but what can he do? Kill her? She's an officer's widow, a family friend of the Prendevilles.'

'He could leave her at the side of the road with a sign around her neck saying she was a British informer. Or she could just disappear. The RIC might investigate but, down here, Abercrombie is the RIC, at least until a new district inspector arrives. By then there will be ten more reprisals and ambushes that need investigating and she'll have been forgotten.'

'And if I call out the police or army, the chances are one of his men will warn him.'

They regard each other glumly for a moment, but the beginnings of a plan are forming in Harkin's mind.

'He probably doesn't know that you are here.'

He examines Vane in the glow of the oil lamp. The major is as inscrutable as ever, but Harkin would be surprised if he is not coming to the same conclusion about the necessity for immediate action.

'Well, Major Vane. I intend to make my way over to Ballynan House and address the matter directly. The question is, what will you be doing?'

Vane considers the question, the curve of a smile shaping his thin lips.

'I always enjoy a walk after dinner, when the opportunity arises.'

While Vane goes up to his room to fetch a coat, Harkin walks slowly towards the entrance hall. Charlie Prendeville is waiting, a candlelit face in the gloom, her eyes dark shadows. He wonders if she can have heard any of their conversation. The house is so quiet that noise can travel surprising distances.

'Who was it on the telephone?' she asks, her question low and urgent. She holds herself like a runner at the start of a race, all angles and tension.

She might say the same about him, he thinks, aware of the suppressed adrenaline that is coursing through his body.

'No one in particular,' he says. 'But Vane and I intend to walk down to the beach before bed.'

He can hear Vane coming down one of the smaller staircases and Charlie's questioning eyes move in that direction.

'Is something going on?' Her voice seems to rise in volume. 'Is something wrong?'

'Nothing,' Harkin replies. 'We'll be back soon.'

Lord Kilcolgan appears at the door of the drawing room, a silhouette against the faint light that comes from within. When he speaks his voice is calm, but firm.

'Come in to us, Charlie. Leave our guests to their walk.'

Harkin can see Billy standing behind his father, his hands in his pockets, a cigarette in his mouth. Even in the darkness, Harkin is aware that his friend is observing the scene with a focused intensity.

'Leave them to their business, Charlie,' Billy says, when his sister turns towards them.

The warning is clear. For a moment Harkin finds Billy's detachment more than a little surprising, although he is glad to not involve him. After all, all of this business is Prendeville business. Charlie stands aside, her dark eyes coming into focus as he passes her. There is fear there, but not for herself.

For him, he thinks.

'We'll be fine,' he says in an attempt to reassure her. But the words sound false.

Outside the sky is clear, a crescent of moon visible to the west. The broad swathe of the Milky Way snakes across the sky, illuminating the home meadow which shines silver with the remnants of the earlier rain. There is a strange silence that is broken only by the sound of the gravel underfoot.

'Are you armed?' he asks Vane.

'As it happens, I am.' Vane opens his coat to show Harkin an automatic pistol in a shoulder holster.

Harkin holds up his arm and waves towards the trees and a familiar figure comes out from under the overhanging branches, walking towards them across the home meadow.

'Would that be your colleague, Mr Bourke?'

'The very same. If we travel some of the way in his motor car, we can be there more quickly than Abercrombie might expect. Which may give us an advantage.'

They go out to meet Bourke, and Vincent looks quizzically at them when he approaches.

'Should I be worried?' he says, indicating Vane.

'Any other evening,' Harkin says. 'But not tonight. Have you your picks with you, Vincent?'

'Always.'

'There's been a change of plan,' Harkin says.

They drive without lights, coasting the last part of the journey and parking the car on the Kilcolgan side of the rise in the road, on the other side of which Ballynan is located. The plan, such as it is, has been agreed on the short drive. As soon as the car is parked, Vane and Bourke set off through the fields to approach the house along the coast, leaving Harkin to come at the house from the road, where he will be expected. Bourke hangs back for a moment before he leaves.

'Take as much time as you can,' he says in a whisper. 'It may take us a while to get there along the coast. We'll be as quick as we're able.'

'I'm hoping he won't shoot me straight away. There will be some chat first. He's going to want to know where his report is, for a start. Then he'll shoot me.'

Bourke raises his eyebrows.

'So don't dawdle,' Harkin says. 'And keep an eye on him.'

Bourke looks after the major, and spits on the ground.

'I'll be keeping two eyes on him.'

'I'll see you in a while, then.'

Harkin watches as the two men make their way briskly towards the line of gorse bushes that mark the edge of the low cliffs. They soon disappear out of sight. Harkin checks his watch. He is to give them ten minutes to get into position and then begin his own approach. He stands there, looking up at the stars, so numerous in the clear, rain-washed night that the whole sky seems to shine. His insignificance in the vastness of the universe seems strangely reassuring, given he is waiting to walk over the hill to his possible death. It occurs to him that in a normal life – the life that had been mapped out for him before the war – he might never have experienced this heightened awareness of his own physical presence, nor the awareness of its fragility. It is as though, at times like this, his senses attempt to cram as much as possible in to his last moments, if that is what they are to be.

If, God willing, he survives until the morning, he promises himself a life of only mild excitement.

Harkin's train of thought is broken by a noise from the direction of Kilcolgan. He turns to face in that direction, listening, but whatever it is he has heard, it is not repeated. He tries to recreate the noise in his mind; it sounded like the low, irregular beat of a drum, even though it only lasted a few seconds. He is almost convinced it is his imagination, heightened by the situation he is in. He looks down at Moira Wilson's lodge and wonders if the memsahibs are awake, waiting for her return. Then he remembers the warmth of Moira's body against his and finds that he is blinking a stray tear from his eye. Without another thought, he turns and begins to walk slowly across the crest of the small hill.

*

The lights are still blazing at Ballynan, and the house reminds him of an ocean liner, placed as it is against the backdrop of the bay. Harkin is surprised he is so calm. His fingers, for a change, barely shake when he decides to have a last cigarette to keep him company on the short distance that is left to his destination. He takes the cigarette case that Maud gave him in a happier time from his breast pocket, removing two cigarettes. He takes a moment to look at the inscription on the inside, the one he never looks at these days.

*I will always be with you. M.P.*

He thinks back to the events of the last few days and wonders if it might be true – that Maud is walking with him towards the house in which a man waits to kill him. He hopes so.

He replaces the case where he found it and lights one of the cigarettes. Soon he is inhaling smoke. He stands for a moment, wondering if the servants might come back from the town and interrupt them, but decides it is too early for them yet. He sighs. If Harkin has one regret, it's that he didn't anticipate that the major would think to use Moira.

He can see Sir John's blue Daimler, but no other cars – which is, he thinks, a good sign. If there had been another car, it might have meant Abercrombie had brought some of his own men, presumably just as implicated as he is by Teevan's report. Harkin walks slowly towards the entrance portico, without rushing, becoming aware that the silhouette of a man is watching his progress from one of the ground-floor windows. For a moment, he thinks he hears that strange drumming noise from the direction of Kilcolgan, only closer now, but he doesn't stop to listen. He recognises the silhouette as belonging to Abercrombie, and feels a surge that is almost electric course through his body. He checks himself, conscious that he should appear calm and relaxed when they meet; his breathing is short but in control. His feet have not faltered in their rhythm and are still moving forwards – the left one, then the right one. He feels an ill-defined nausea, but nothing that he can't manage. Then he is at the door and he uses the butt of his first cigarette to light the second, takes a deep breath and presses the bell.

Abercrombie opens the door carefully, using it as a shield and covering Harkin with what looks like a Colt automatic pistol.

'Mr Harkin. Good of you to come.' The major scans the surroundings behind Harkin. 'And apparently alone. Very satisfactory. We don't want the whole world knowing our business, do we?'

'That's not very patriotic,' Harkin says, nodding towards the Colt. 'I would have thought you would be the type of man to buy Empire goods only.'

Abercrombie smiles and opens the door a little further, waving Harkin in.

'Gallows humour. Anyway, the Colt is an excellent weapon and excellence is always to be admired and sought after. Most importantly, it does an awful lot of damage at close range. As you may well find out should we not come to a satisfactory arrangement. Come in and turn to face the wall.'

Harkin does as he's told and stands there, his hands above him while Abercrombie frisks him quickly and thoroughly, pocketing Maud's small automatic without comment.

'Please,' Abercrombie says, standing back and gesturing towards the library. 'The others are waiting for you.'

It is the third time in the last few days that Harkin finds himself in Sir John's library and he hopes it will be the last, before it occurs to him there is a good chance it will be his last time in any room. The room is unchanged, except that a pale Sir John

Prendeville, carrying a chrome-plated revolver as though it is infected, is standing beside the desk where Harkin stood before, while Moira sits in a hard-backed, wooden chair in front of him. Sir John looks up at Harkin as he enters and he shakes his head slowly, as though in disbelief that it should have come to this.

'Are you all right?' Harkin asks Moira, and is rewarded with a quick smile.

'I'm fine. The chair is not the most comfortable, I have to say. I am sure other kidnappers are more considerate to their victims.' She turns to examine Sir John with contempt. 'Sir John feels dreadful about everything, however, and that is making me feel much better.'

'Sir John Prendeville,' Harkin says. 'The champion of Home Rule, one of the original founders of the Irish Volunteers . . . and a British spy.'

Sir John says nothing, although it seems to Harkin that he becomes paler still.

'He is a very good spy,' Abercrombie says, his tone amused. 'Malleable, which is always a useful quality from an intelligence point of view.'

Harkin's attention is on Moira, however, who has turned to look at him intently, as though searching for a sign from him. He notices she is not wearing her monocle and, for some strange reason, it is that more than anything which causes him alarm. Harkin reminds himself he has to keep this conversation going for as long as possible if the others are to reach them in time.

'He must have been very malleable to murder his own niece.'

'I didn't kill Maud,' Sir John says, his voice hoarse. 'I had nothing to do with her death.'

Harkin turns back to Abercrombie, who seems amused by the turn in the conversation.

'Not directly, perhaps,' the major says, shrugging. 'Direct responsibility lay with me. Although when he told me she knew he was working for us, he should have known I would have to deal with the matter, one way or another.'

Harkin raises an eyebrow.

'You were the one who set up the ambush, through Father Dillon?'

Abercrombie smiles, as though impressed. 'Bravo. You have been busy, haven't you? The original intention was to be waiting with my men for the rebels, but then I changed my mind.'

'Why?' Harkin still finds it hard to believe that the major could have arranged the execution of not only Teevan, but his old comrade Cartwright.

'Why not? Teevan was weak, and a constant hindrance in our battle with the local rebels. Removing him has removed that hindrance. It was unfortunate about Cartwright, but you'll know that leadership in war requires making decisions that cost men their lives. Maud Prendeville was an unexpected addition to the mix. I didn't know she would be in the motor car.'

'So it wasn't to do with the report he wrote?' Harkin is more than a little sceptical.

'There was that, too,' Abercrombie admits, with a smile that seems almost abashed. 'You've read it, I take it, so you'll understand why I needed to prevent it being passed on. My methods may not be . . . how shall I put it? . . . palatable – but they are effective. You fight fire with fire, bullets with bullets, terror with terror. A war is not the time to be talking about legalities, even if I doubt the Commissioner would agree with me entirely on this point.'

'You think you're winning this war?'

Abercrombie considers the question before shrugging.

'I have no intention of losing it, that's for certain. However, as you suspect, my primary intention was to recover Teevan's report from the car. To my surprise, I couldn't find it on his person, even though he had shown it to me earlier in the evening. Then I found it in Miss Prendeville's evening bag. I was confused by that, but now I realise, thanks to your revealing the existence of another copy, that he must have been working with her to make it public.'

'And you felt you had to kill her?'

Harkin's anger causes a vein in his forehead to pulse. He sees Moira give him a warning look.

'I hadn't expected her to be in the car. My understanding was that she would be staying the night here. On the other hand, I knew this fool –' Abercrombie indicates Sir John with a dismissive inclination of his head – 'had given her an opportunity to unravel all the time and effort we had put into the arms shipment deception, when we were on the point of pulling off a great coup. I was considering what to do when she woke up while I was retrieving the report. She recognised me and so I shot her.' Abercrombie shrugs, a slight hint of regret apparent in the gesture. 'It was unfortunate, but I think I can live with the guilt.'

Harkin turns his gaze to Sir John.

'Was that what you were arguing about, earlier in the evening?'

Sir John looks at Moira, as though deducing who Harkin's source must have been. Harkin, meanwhile, is straining to listen to any sounds of approach from outside the room, hoping against hope that Vane and Bourke will arrive in time.

'I overheard you,' she says, with a hint of defiance. 'If I'd known what you were about, I'd have come in and spat in your face.'

Sir John looks as though he would like to be sick. It takes him a moment to gather himself. Time enough for Harkin to realise

328

that Sir John and Abercrombie won't allow Moira to live and that her death will be his responsibility.

'She confronted me about my relationship with Abercrombie. She had found some notes from the major in my desk. I shouldn't have kept them. I never intended for her to be caught up in the whole mess. It was one of my conditions for agreeing to co-operate. I was being blackmailed. I had no choice.'

'Because your reputation needed to be protected? Did you think about Maud's reputation when you seduced her?'

Moira looks at Harkin, her shock readily apparent. When he nods his confirmation, she turns to Sir John.

'It wasn't like that,' Sir John says, almost desperate. 'We grew close when Arthur was dying. One thing led to another. It was her reputation I was hoping to preserve, not mine.'

Moira shakes her head in angry disbelief and gives a low moan somewhere between pain and anger.

'You seduced her when she was at her lowest ebb and now she's dead and you're alive,' Harkin says. 'And then you involved me.'

His contempt is real enough but he also wants to ensure he has their full attention. He is almost certain he's heard the slightest sound of a door being opened at the rear of the house. Sir John returns his gaze and it is as though the man is in physical pain.

'I didn't know he was responsible,' he says, gesturing towards Abercrombie with his pistol. 'I thought Egan's column had killed her and I wanted them punished. I didn't even know you would be sent down, and I didn't tell him anything about you. Not until now, at least.'

'When you chose your reputation over my life.'

Abercrombie smiles, although there isn't much humour in it.

329

'It was only when you found his letters to Miss Prendeville that he came looking for my assistance. Of course, I wasn't averse to dealing with Driscoll in the way he suggested and I thought, since the priest was showing some backbone after Miss Prendeville's death, that I could deal with him as well. Just in case. My intention was to make it look as though Driscoll had killed him and made a clumsy effort to make it appear like a suicide but you, rather unhelpfully, took the appointment book which meant there was nothing to link him to the death. So I allowed the fabricated suicide to stand.'

'And when did he tell you about me?'

'That you are an IRA intelligence officer? Only this evening. It does seem ironic the IRA were asked to investigate a killing carried out by a policeman. Quite amusing. For me, at least.'

Sir John's glum expression tells Harkin all he needs to know. Harkin is listening carefully now. He is almost certain the others are in the house. He can feel a chill draught coming under the door. He has the sense that Abercrombie is growing weary of the conversation and knows he must give the others as much time as possible.

'I'll let you have Teevan's report if you let Mrs Wilson go. She'll undertake to say nothing about all of this.'

'And what about you?' Moira asks.

'I'm sure I can reach a satisfactory arrangement with the major.'

Abercrombie smiles at this. 'Of course,' he continues, 'if Sir John had told me about you earlier, we could have saved ourselves this tedious conversation, and Mrs Wilson's involvement. I may have killed Driscoll and Dillon and Miss Prendeville, but in each case it has been his weakness that has resulted in my taking the actions I have. Sir John doesn't want to admit it, but it's true. His actions and inactions have caused all of this. It must be a great consolation to you to see how upset he is.'

'You'll promise to say nothing, won't you, Moira? After all, Abercrombie, no one would believe her even if she did say anything.' Harkin says, conscious that the time for talking is almost done. He braces himself to rush Abercrombie. He has little chance of success but, if nothing else, it will distract the major for a moment or two.

Abercrombie points his gun at Harkin's chest.

'Where is the report?'

'In Kilcolgan. I didn't bring it with me for obvious reasons.'

'I can't help wondering if there never was another copy of the report. What if you just caught the tail end of a rumour and decided to use it to draw me out?' Perhaps he sees the truth in Harkin's expression because his smile hardens. 'That was a mistake, Harkin.'

'You promised not to hurt them,' Sir John says, his desperation clear. 'Tom is a family friend. As is Mrs Wilson.'

Abercrombie laughs, and as he does so Harkin is conscious that the handle of the door is turning very slowly.

'The report exists all right. I left it in a sealed envelope with Lord Kilcolgan to be opened in the event of my not returning.' Harkin notices that Moira has leant forward slightly, bringing her legs under her.

'I don't believe you.'

Sir John takes a step forward. 'This isn't what we agreed.'

Sir John lifts his pistol towards Abercrombie, who responds by taking a small black automatic from his pocket, a little larger than the one he took from Harkin earlier, and pointing it at the older man.

'I warn you . . .' Sir John says, but the old authority has gone.

331

Abercrombie, with a shark's smile that doesn't reach his eyes, turns to examine him.

'Shall I tell you what the story will be, Sir John?'

'What story?'

'Harkin came here with Mrs Wilson to confront you about your betrayal of Sean Driscoll, amongst others. Unfortunately they shot you. But then I arrived on the scene and killed them after a desperate battle. This is the pistol I used to kill Maud Prendeville. The same type of bullet as will be found in your body. The gun will be found in Mrs Wilson's dead hand, linking her to the murder of Maud Prendeville. I feel strangely certain I will uncover papers that will show Mrs Wilson to have been a long standing rebel, determined to punish Maud Prendeville's treachery. There are a few loose ends need tidying up but, all in all, I think it will be enough to stand scrutiny.'

There is a loud report, deafening in the enclosed space, and Sir John looks at Abercrombie in stunned surprise, then down at the small hole that has appeared in his chest, soon joined by another. Abercrombie quickly turns his attention to Harkin firing with the Colt. Harkin is already moving, however, aware from the corner of his eye that the door to the library has now opened wide to reveal a figure standing there, gun outstretched. Harkin feels the bullet whip past his ear, so close he feels the heat of its passing, and he moves in closer, intending to rush Abercrombie, conscious that Moira is out of her chair and seems to have the same intention. Abercrombie fires again, this time with the pocket pistol he'd shot Sir John with. Harkin feels an explosion of pain in his chest, and, as he falls backwards, finds himself looking up at the moulded ceiling.

And then there is nothing.

# CHAPTER 49

'He's coming round.'

'He'll be all right, I think.'

The voices seem to come from a great distance, but Harkin thinks the speakers must be closer than that. There is a great weight on his chest, a pressure mixed with pain. Someone is holding his hand, squeezing it, and he thinks he recognises the strong, slender fingers. He opens his eyes to find Vincent Bourke's face looking down at him, large and concerned, alongside Moira. He decides the fingers are more likely to belong to her.

'I don't think I am all right,' Harkin whispers.

'I don't doubt it. Someone just shot you in the chest.'

'That might account for it.'

'Do you want the good news or the bad news.'

'What's the good news?'

'You're going to be fine. Just a bruise.'

Harkin tries to understand what Bourke is saying. He remembers Abercrombie's small pistol pointing at him.

'But I was shot in the chest.'

Harkin searches out Moira's gaze. He can see echoes of fear in her eyes, but also something like happiness. She squeezes his hand.

'That's where the bad news comes in,' Bourke says. 'You need a new cigarette case.'

'That's a shame,' Harkin manages to whisper. 'I was very attached to it.'

'Well, now there's a bullet attached to it instead.'

Bourke holds up Maud's cigarette case, with a flattened grey lump embedded in its centre. He thinks back to the inscription. Perhaps Maud was with him, after all.

'I don't suppose the cigarettes are smokable,' Harkin asks, to mask an almost overwhelming surge of emotion. Bourke rewards him with a smile.

'Thank you,' Harkin says.

'For what?'

'Coming in time.'

'About that,' Bourke says. 'We weren't here in time.'

Harkin changes his focus to the man standing behind Moira. Billy Prendeville looks down at him, his face pale.

'I listened into the call from Father's study. I thought it best to ride after you. Lucky I did. Lucky also that Moira knocked him off balance before he finished the job.'

'One cannot always be ladylike,' Moira says, with an attempt at a smile. 'Fortunately Billy shot him before I descended to fisticuffs.'

Harkin looks from one to the other. Both of them look shaken by the violence. As well they might be. 'Thank you,' he says, and is not sure the simple words are quite enough, but can't think of anything else to add.

'You can't see it from the road but there's no easy way through along the cliffs,' Bourke says. 'We had to climb down to the beach and then back up. We were just coming in the back of the house when the shooting started.'

334

'And Abercrombie?'

'Dead,' Billy says in a dull tone, but he has walked out of Harkin's view.

'We need to get out of the house.' Harkin hears Vane's voice, although he can't see him. 'Mr Bourke, if you could go and fetch your motor car. I doubt Mr Harkin can walk that far.'

Harkin doubts he can walk any distance at all. He sees Bourke nod and then the big man is gone, clearing his view.

'I thought you were dead,' Moira says.

'I would have been if he'd shot me with the Colt. How is Sir John?'

Moira looks behind her as if to check and Harkin, realising the older man must still be clinging to life, tries to roll on to his side, feeling the pain instantly.

'Can you help me up?'

Vane leans down beside him and with Moira's assistance, along with Harkin's best efforts, they manage to get him to his feet. He looks around the room. Abercrombie is lying in a pool of blood beside an overstuffed armchair, his arm still outstretched, clutching the small pistol in his hand. Harkin leans down to take it from his dead fingers but Vane takes his elbow.

'Leave it. It all makes sense. They argued, there was shooting, they both died.'

Harkin turns to see Sir John lying on the ground beside the desk, blood bubbling in his mouth. He may not be dead, but it will not be long. Billy kneels beside him, holding the older man's left hand in both of his. As Harkin approaches, Sir John looks up at him, his eyes already losing their colour. His face is yellowing, the skin tightening across his skull.

'I'm sorry for all the trouble,' the older man manages to say.

The transition from life to death is quick. One moment Sir John Prendeville is there; the next he is not, and all that is left is his body. After a few moments, Billy places his uncle's hand back over his chest and stands to his feet.

Harkin wants to say something, but what is there to say?

They wait for Bourke outside the house, Harkin being supported by Moira. When the car comes over the hill, Harkin notices that the horizon to the east is tinged with orange. He finds himself pondering what it could be, as it's another nine hours till the dawn. The answer comes when Vincent Bourke leans out of the car's window and addresses Billy.

'I'm sorry, Mr Prendeville,' he says, his face grave, 'but Kilcolgan is on fire.'

# CHAPTER 50

By the time they reach the burning building, the fire is well established and there is nothing to be done but get out what can be got out. Harkin, his ribs grating against one another within his chest, assists as best he can. Lord Kilcolgan strides the long hall, pointing the helpers towards what should be saved and what can be left. His decisions are practical. Furniture, when it can be moved, is taken. Books are scooped up, entire shelves at a time, and run out to be left with everything else. Portraits of more recent Prendevilles are taken; the more ancient are left. The fire is spreading quickly from the kitchen where it has been set, streaking up the rear of the building so that parts of the upper storey are already alight, but the front of the house is still relatively untouched. Sir John's servants, returning from the town, join Murphy and the others in their efforts. As the fire spreads, the long central hall is once again lit as it must have been in the old days, and stuffed animals and the fans of pikes and swords are no longer strange shadows in the dark.

The rescued belongings are collected into a growing pile about fifty yards from the house, lit by the spreading flames. Harkin sees Billy help Pat Walsh carry out a full-length portrait of Maud, and she is left leaning against a long table to watch Kilcolgan burn.

Through snatched conversations, Harkin hears of how the column had arrived not long after Billy left for Ballynan. How Egan had told Lord Kilcolgan, with some pretence of regret, that the house could not be tolerated as an Auxiliary barracks – Maud Prendeville or no Maud Prendeville. How the Volunteers meanwhile, by now well practised in the art of arson, had poured petrol from jerry cans around the kitchen and the lower level and wished them luck with rescuing what they could.

The Prendevilles seem stunned in the orange light, even as they run again and again into the building to bring out photographs and silver and whatever else that holds some worth to them, of whatever kind. He sees Mrs Driscoll, running out with an armful of tablecloths and linen. When the police arrive there is some talk of attempting to bring the conflagration under control, but the talk is brought to an end by a shower of glass from a window on the upper storey that is blown out by a torrent of fire. Soon, the heat and the swirling embers make entering the building impossible, and the crowd stands back to watch in silence. By the end, every window spews up fire until, with a great groan and a volcano of flame, the roof collapses inwards.

Harkin finds himself standing beside Bourke at the back of the ring of onlookers. Bourke's hair is singed and his face black with smoke. He coughs into his sleeve as Vane approaches.

'Gentlemen,' he says.

'Is this where you tell us to be on our way?'

'I think it's for the best. The bodies will be found soon, if they haven't been already. The sooner you are well clear of here, the better. If there is a closer examination of the circumstances then questions may be asked.'

Harkin sees Billy watching them from a distance. He nods when Harkin catches his gaze, then turns away.

'I'll meet you at the car, Vincent.'

The big man nods and turns to walk away. Harkin turns back to Vane.

'Thank you for this evening. Perhaps we'll meet again some time. In happier circumstances.'

'Perhaps.'

It takes Harkin a little while to find Moira. She bears, like many of the others, the marks of the battle with the fire.

'We have to leave.' He sees how her mouth sets into a stubborn downward curve.

'And so you've come to say goodbye?'

'I've come to ask you to come with me, if you're willing.'

# EPILOGUE

The ship's whistle blows loud and long and Vincent Bourke looks at his watch.

'I've only a few minutes.' He reaches inside his pocket to produce a large envelope. He hands it to Harkin. 'The boss wanted to be sure you had something to get you on your feet.'

Harkin lifts a corner of the envelope's flap and looks inside. He raises his eyebrows. It contains a thick wad of American currency as well as a sheaf of smaller envelopes.

'I thought we were short of cash.'

'Well, maybe he found some down the back of the sofa.'

'Give him my thanks.'

Bourke nods at the envelope that Harkin is placing inside his pocket.

'There are some letters of introduction, as well. People who can help you. Most in New York and Boston, but other places too. You'll be looked after. When things quieten down . . .'

'I'll come back.'

'Or not. You've done more than most.'

Bourke grips Harkin's hand and squeezes it.

'Maybe I'll see you over there myself at some time.'

'You'll be welcome.'

341

'In the meantime, I'll keep an eye on your place – make sure Billy Prendeville doesn't wreck it.'

'Thanks, Vincent. I'm grateful for everything.'

They lean against the rail of the ship, watching as the gap widens between the hull and the quay. Above them, the ship's whistle sounds three long notes and, in response, the crowd that is gathered to bid the ship farewell waves and cheers. Harkin can't hear them over the churning roar of the ship's engines, but he can see their open mouths, the happiness and the sadness and all the other emotions that go with parting. He can even make out Vincent Bourke, standing to one side, and watches as he raises a hand in final farewell and turns to walk back to the car in which he came. A hand slips in carefully between Harkin's elbow and his still-bandaged chest, taking a hold of his bicep.

'Well, Mr Smith?' Moira asks, leaning in to him.

'Well, Mrs Smith?'

Moira gives a small curtsey.

'Smith,' she says, smiling, 'is a blank page of a name. I think it suits us. We can write our own story on it.'

He nods, then frowns, looking across the dockyards towards Belfast and the mist-shrouded hills beyond it. Black columns of smoke rise from the terraced streets in places. There has been rioting during the night.

'Will we miss the place?' he asks, thinking he will not. Not like this in any event. Perhaps when things have changed.

'I don't think so.' She raises a hand to his cheek. 'You might miss it if you were unhappy in our new life, but I don't think that will happen. Come down when you're ready and I'll show you how I intend we should go on.'

Then there is a flash of teeth and she is gone, swaying her way along the crowded deck, knowing he will be watching her.

When she has disappeared down the companionway, Harkin turns back to look down once again at the crowd of onlookers and well-wishers that line the quay. He doesn't know what or who he is looking for, but he has a feeling that he is missing something. He scans the faces, even as they are becoming less distinct – even as some of them turn away. Then in the shadow of the long shed he sees her, little more than a shadow herself. He knows she is not there – cannot be there – and yet there she is. Maud Prendeville. And she is smiling. He watches her until she merges into the gloom of the grey morning and is no longer visible – if she ever was.

Then Harkin turns away from the city and the land and makes his way down to the cabin.

# AUTHOR'S NOTE

This novel is a work of fiction, intended to entertain and, perhaps, inform along the way. It may well be that students of the Irish War of Independence will note similarities between this novel's characters and well-known historical figures but, while those similarities are not completely coincidental, the characters remain entirely fictional creations. Similarly, the events you'll find within these pages never took place in the way I have represented them and the locations are also largely invented.

This novel, as with all of my novels, owes a great deal to the support, enthusiasm and incisive direction of my editor, Sophie Orme, for which I'm very grateful. I would also like to thank Ciara Corrigan, Jenna Petts, Nick Stearn, Bill Massey, Steve O'Gorman, Jon Appleton and the rest of the team at Bonnier Books. Finally, I would like to thank my agent, Oli Munson and his assistant, Florence Rees, for all their efforts on my behalf.